# The Abandoned Girl

Diane Winger

THE ABANDONED GIRL
Copyright © 2017 Diane Winger. All rights reserved.

ISBN: 978-1542598583

# Books by
# Charlie and Diane Winger

## Fiction
### by Diane Winger

Faces – book 1 of the FACES series

Duplicity – book 2 of the FACES series

Rockfall

Memories & Secrets

The Daughters' Baggage

The Abandoned Girl

## Non-Fiction (Memoir)
### by Charlie Winger

Two Shadows – a true story of triumph over adversity

## Guidebooks / Adventure Photography
### by Charlie & Diane Winger

Highpoint Adventures – The Complete Guide to the 50 State
  Highpoints

The Essential Guide to Great Sand Dunes National Park & Preserve

The Trad Guide to Joshua Tree – 60 Favorite Climbs from 5.5 to 5.9

Because It's There - A Photographic Journey

Visit **The Winger Bookstore** on the web at:

**WingerBookstore.com**

## Dedication

To all the children left behind.


To Charlie,
for his love, support, and inspiration.

# Contents

# PART ONE
## LEFT BEHIND

# CHAPTER 1 - ROBIN

Trying the door to our apartment, I slip into my protective big sister mode, hoping to ward off Annie's tears because nobody is home. "Remember, I told you Mom said she'd be out late," I say as I fish my key from its warm spot dangling on a string tucked inside my blouse. "We'll show her your new finger puppets in the morning."

She makes a beeline for our bedroom to retrieve her ragged stuffed rabbit – a sure sign that she's distressed. I head for the refrigerator, already wondering what I can come up with for our dinner. I stand in front of the open door, relishing the cold air spilling into the hot room, and contemplate its contents with a frown. Mom promised she'd buy groceries today, but it looks like we're out of luck. Again.

I'll worry about dinner later. Annie ate most of her giant slice of pizza plus a cookie, so she'll probably be fine for another hour or so.

I plop onto our sagging couch, replaying the scene from this afternoon in my mind one more time.

"Robin," my mother said as she pressed a bill into my hand, "take your sister to the mall. This should cover the bus ride and lunch at the food court."

A million questions popped into my head, but I was

speechless at this unprecedented gift. I forced myself to close my gaping mouth.

"I'll be out late, kiddo. Take care of supper."

Placated by her familiar words, I nodded. When she says she'll be out late, that can mean she'll arrive home shortly after the bars close, or sneak in just in time for breakfast. When I was younger, she used to claim that she'd gotten up before us and already gone out to run some errands. Once I pointed out that she was wearing exactly the same clothes as she had when she left the previous night and that her hair was messy and makeup faded, she stopped pretending. "Don't bother making up stories to try to fool Robin," she'd tell her *gentleman friend* of the month. "She may only be ten years old, but she has a built-in lie detector."

Which is why I'm replaying that scene from this afternoon. My built-in lie detector is telling me that something's not right. I examine my new mood ring to see if its colors reveal anything, but it still looks exactly like it did when I put it on at the novelty store. Determined to bury my anxiety, I pick up the book I've been reading and attempt to lose myself in its fictional world. Three chapters later, Annie's voice jolts me back to our small, dingy apartment.

"I'm hungry." She stares at me, looking as forlorn as a starving orphan.

With a sigh, I perform an inventory of our food choices. In the refrigerator, there's a dried-up onion, half a head of wilted lettuce, and something that once may have been part of a tomato. I toss that in the garbage. I sniff at the carton of milk and decide it's marginally drinkable. I'm pleased when I peer into a package of bologna and find two slices remaining.

Examining the loaf of bread, I flip though slices until I find four near the middle that don't exhibit spots of green. I discard some of the loaf, deeming it too moldy to salvage, and scavenge through a kitchen drawer, discovering a single packet of catsup. Triumphant, I prepare two sandwiches with the ingredients I've located and hand one over to my little sister. She knows better than to complain, but I can see the disappointment in her eyes.

"Mom will probably buy some food in the morning. Don't worry," I tell her as I begin fretting again about what set off my internal alarms. I'm able to distract her for the rest of the evening by playing boundless rounds of Go Fish and Old Maid before sending her to bed. She whines, still asking for Mommy, but nods off once I crawl into my own bed and promise I'll stay close by. Hours later, after the movies in my head play through all the times Mom has stayed out longer than expected, I finally fall asleep.

I arise early the next morning, frustrated but not surprised that my mother's room looks untouched. Since she started dating "Uncle" Roger, she's often not returned home until late morning on weekends. During the week, she'll sometimes just call when she gets to work around 8:30. Today's Saturday, so I figure she'll show up in time for lunch. Hopefully, with some groceries.

Sniffing at the milk again, I have my doubts about pouring it on cereal. I sample a sip and spit it into the sink, quickly rinsing my mouth with tap water. We'll have to eat the last of the corn flakes dry. Fortunately, Annie accepts this development silently.

I'm running out of options for begging food from our neighbors. Mrs. Nelson flat-out refused to give me anything else last time I hit her up. "Young lady," she said, "go tell your mother that it's her responsibility to feed her children, not mine." Old Mrs. Thornsby is my only possibility, but I'll bet she's almost as poor as we are. I feel bad about asking her for food, even though she usually manages to give me *something.*

Noon passes without any contact from our mother. Annie has been whiny all morning, clinging to me and asking me repeatedly about Mom. With a hollow pit in my stomach, I put on my best act of pretending everything is fine.

I perform surgery on two more slices of bread, relieving them of green mold, and toast them, slathering them with margarine. Lunch is served. We eat in silence, other than my sister's sniffling between bites. My stomach feels like I've swallowed a rock, but I force myself to eat my toast.

By mid-afternoon, I'm pacing to the window every few minutes, scanning the street below for any sign of my mother. I even pick up the phone a few times, listening for a dial tone that hasn't been there for weeks. I've sent Annie up to the Barolo's apartment to play with her friend, unwilling to leave the apartment myself in case our mother swings by. I cautioned Annie not to say anything about Mom's tardiness, echoing the message she's hammered into us ever since the divorce.

When my sister returns for dinner and discovers me still alone in our apartment, she falls apart. "Why isn't she back? I'm hungry! I don't like it when she doesn't come home." Annie collapses in a heap in the middle of the kitchen floor, sobbing loudly. "I want Mommy!" I feel tears beginning to burn my eyes as I try to be the "big sister" who takes care of her. I snatch a dish towel and sink down beside her, trying to dry her tears and wipe her dripping nose as my own face grows wet from the tears I can no longer hold back. We grasp each other in a tight hug, rocking and weeping.

I take deep breaths and force myself to be calm. "Shh," I whisper as I dab her face and mine, then stroke her hair. She begins to settle down. "I'm sure she'll be home soon. Meanwhile, I'll get us something to eat."

After washing my face and running my fingers through my hair, I exit down the hall to borrow two eggs from Mrs. Thornsby. "Mom forgot to put eggs on the shopping list, but she'll pick some up tomorrow," I tell her. Mrs. Thornsby plasters a pained smile on her face and has me wait as she hobbles to her kitchen. When she returns, she presents me with a bag containing four eggs in a carton and a chunk of cheese. "I don't know what I was thinking when I bought cheese this time. I got way too much and it's just going to go to waste. I hope your mother can use some..."

With shame, I accept her generous offering. She must realize I come around begging because my mother forgot to go shopping or couldn't afford enough food.

Having a bit of food in her stomach seems to help Annie cope. She has stopped crying for the moment, but she's exceptionally quiet. She retreats to our room and I can hear her talking softly, probably to her favorite toy, Bunny, a scruffy, holes-in-its-seams, barely-stuffed rabbit. My sister isn't terribly imaginative when it comes to naming her toys. I'm feeling more and more restless and uneasy as I resume pacing and watching out the window for a familiar walk as people pass under the streetlights. I put my sister to bed at 9:00, but stay perched at the window for hours, jerking awake again and again during my vigil. My stomach aches and my nose is raw from blowing it so much. I curl up on the couch, determined to hear Mom if she returns in the middle of the night. When the brightening sky wakes me before 6:00 the next morning, I double check that she's still not home. I close myself in the bathroom and cry into a towel, hoping that Annie doesn't hear me.

Trembling, I step into her bedroom and begin a careful survey of her belongings. I try to remember what she was wearing on Thursday when she sent us to the mall, but I'm uncertain. She doesn't own a lot of clothes, but I've never paid that close attention to her wardrobe. On the other hand, as often as we're left alone, I've had plenty of opportunities to explore her closet and dresser drawers, so I focus on those.

I'm surprised to realize that her favorite "fancy" earrings are missing. They're made of some sort of fake stone that sparkles like diamonds. She only wears them on special dates with her boyfriends. Continuing to explore, I gasp when I realize that her small suitcase is gone. The big, beat-up one is still shoved to the back of the closet, but the little one is nowhere to be found.

It's hard to swallow. Did she pack a suitcase after sending us out? Where was she going? Why didn't she say anything?

"I'll be out late, kiddo. Take care of supper."

I replay her words, trying to remember exactly how she spoke, the expression on her face. I was so startled by her generosity of giving me money for the mall that I didn't think about what else seemed off two days ago. But didn't she sound just a bit odd? I can't remember for sure.

Her nightgown! I pull open the dresser drawer again and feel a rush of relief as I confirm that her familiar nightgown is still there. I lift it out and hug it to my body, snuggling my face into the fabric, but drop it as I remember that she had another nightie, a sexy one that I'm sure she didn't want me to see, tucked beneath her sweaters. I fling open another drawer, shoving sweaters aside and find... nothing. I yank all the drawers out of the dresser and dump their contents on the floor. It's not here. I fling an empty drawer across the room, glad for the loud smashing sound as it strikes the wall and cracks.

She packed a bag and left us.

Some kids – even Annie – might think she'll be back

tonight. Or tomorrow for sure, since she has to go to work in the morning. Not me. I know that she isn't coming back. Ever.

I sink down in the middle of the room and start to wail, no longer caring if I'm acting my role as the strong big sister. "Mom," I cry, "why did you leave us?" I barely realize it when my little sister joins me, our sobs filling the apartment with anguish and heartache.

\*\*\*

The airplane lady is back again, asking me if I'll eat something. I shake my head, turning toward the window, looking over Annie's head and watching the clouds below us. I always thought it would be really fun to fly in an airplane, but my stomach is so knotted up that I can't imagine eating anything. My sister is curled up in her seat, clutching Bunny. Her lips are moving, but the noise from the engine is so loud that I'm not sure she's actually speaking out loud to her mangy stuffed toy. The lady offers me a book – her niece's favorite, she says. I read it when I was in 3rd grade, but I accept her offer and pretend to start reading, just so she'll go away and leave me alone. They wouldn't let me bring along my stack of library books.

It's been just three weeks since I last saw my mother, but it feels much longer. Annie must have said something to Mrs. Barolo when she went to play with Alice, because she was there at our door with the police Monday morning. They took us up to the Barolo's apartment and fixed up a place for us to sleep there. There was a lady named Dorothy from "Family Services" who took me back to our apartment where she asked me a lot of questions while a policewoman hung close by.

"Did your Mom stay out overnight very often?"

I felt wary. What if I was wrong, and my mother really was coming back? If I got her in trouble, would they take her away from us? How did Dorothy already know that Mom didn't come home every night? I shrugged. "Maybe a couple of times," I lied.

I wasn't lying when I couldn't supply a last name for "Uncle" Roger. Or tell her where he lived. He was just another of a string of "special friends" my mother sometimes brought home. The men were usually gone by morning, but I knew they stayed in her bedroom for most of the night.

"What about her suitcase?"

In the first hours when police were looking through her room and asking about the broken dresser drawer and the mess I'd made, they asked what had happened. Usually, I'm pretty good at coming up with a story right off the top of my head, like that time Mr. Howards at the grocery store wanted to know where I'd come up with all those empty bottles I was bringing in to get the deposit back. I said I'd gone around our apartment building and collected them. He believed me for a while, until he caught me out back of the store collecting the empties that he'd set out there to go back to the soda pop company.

Anyway, when they asked me about the disaster area of my mother's bedroom, all I managed to say was, "I was looking for her other suitcase. I couldn't find it anywhere."

Stupid answer.

"So, you emptied all the drawers out on the floor, looking for her suitcase? It wasn't like this when you came in?" She didn't ask about the broken drawer and the dent in the wall, but she glanced in that direction.

I nodded.

Over the next few days, Dorothy's questions revolved

around what we ate and when, what we did while our mother was at work, even about the times I'd been held after school last year and why I sometimes broke things. I figure they asked Annie some of the same questions, and she's the world's worst liar. I find it best to say as little as possible.

Dad finally called us last night. It was clear that the police or maybe Dorothy had been talking to him all along, even though nobody let us in on that.

"Hey, sweetie, I know this has been a tough time for you and your sister, but I'm counting on you to be strong. Your mother isn't coming back."

"I know." I bit my lip, determined to be the strong daughter he wanted me to be. "Are we gonna come live with you now?" I felt proud that my voice didn't waiver.

"I really wish we could do that, but it's just not possible. You know how much I travel for work, and with a baby on the way, Glenda just won't have the energy to take care of the two of you plus the little one. And then there's the money. I mean, I'll still be sending checks like I was doing before for child support, but having you here – well, we just can't afford it. Glenda's not working any more, with the baby and all, and our house is too small."

I blinked rapidly, trying not to cry. "Will we still stay here with Mr. and Mrs. Barolo?" I choked out.

He cleared his voice. "Oh, no, sweetie. We couldn't ask them to do that any longer than they've helped already. No, no – you'll be with family. We're going to put you on a plane tomorrow and fly you out to live with my folks. You'll be with your Grandma and Grandpa."

The tears I had been fighting to hold back won the battle. "But we don't even know them. You said we went to see them once when I was really little, but I don't remember. Anyway, you told me your father was mean and used to hit you all the time!" I clutched the phone tight in my fist, horrified at this news.

My father let out a long sigh. "Well, he was mean to me sometimes, but I was a boy. He would never hit you. He never laid a hand on your Aunt Sophie or on my mother. In fact, he used to lecture me about what a horrible thing it would be to ever strike a woman – or a girl. You'll be fine. He's mellowed over the years." He didn't mention the part about his father beating him when drunk, or that he and his father weren't speaking to each other, but I remembered his stories.

"But..."

"It's not like we have a lot of options, here. You should feel thankful that you have family to take you in. The only other option would be foster care, and you and your sister would be separated. You don't want that, do you?"

I didn't want *any* of it, but nobody was giving me any choice.

My thoughts are interrupted by the airplane lady again. "We'll be landing soon, girls. I'll stay with you as we get off the plane and we'll meet up with your grandparents. It won't be long now! I'll bet you're excited to tell them all about your first plane ride."

I wrap an arm around Annie, who is staring at the woman with a look of horror in her eyes. "It's okay," I whisper. "We're together and I'll take care of you."

I wonder who's going to take care of *me*.

# CHAPTER 2 - KATHARINE

"Good night, Mother. Good night, Father." Mother glances up from her book and offers me a nod. Father doesn't react at all.

I retreat to my bedroom, play-acting my normal routine of retrieving my nightgown from the dresser, opening and closing the closet door as if I were putting away my clothes, then crawling into bed, still fully dressed and pulling the covers up to my chin in the off chance that Mother might look in on me. A warm breeze billows the curtains and I'm tempted to throw off my covers for some relief from the warm night, but I hold off.

At last, I hear my parents retreat to their room and shut the door. Only after Father's snoring has been marking time for at least twenty minutes do I move in slow motion to roll out of bed, arrange clothing under the covers, and silently remove the screen from my window. Smoothly and soundlessly, I slip out and lower myself to the ground, reaching high above my head to replace the screen. I crouch and skim across the lawn to the street, moving quickly from tree shadow to tree shadow until I reach his car, the passenger door already open and waiting.

"Ready?" Steve asks as we synchronize the closing of the

door with the starting of the engine. Within moments, we're on our way to our favorite spot.

"You're awfully quiet tonight, baby." He parks the car and we both peer out at the lights of the town displayed below us. "Your father get after you again?"

It's a peculiar way to word it, but even my father won't use words like *beat* or *hit* to describe his actions. He'll use a quote like, "Spare the rod, spoil the child." Or declare that he is saving my soul. But my silence tonight isn't about my father's form of discipline, nor my mother's sharp tongue. I take a long, slow breath before speaking the words that I've rehearsed for over a month.

"I'm pregnant." My voice comes out soft and raspy. He's silent and sitting totally still and I'm worried that he might not have been able to understand me. I don't think I can manage to repeat it.

Finally he reaches for my hand. "Are you sure?" His voice doesn't sound any stronger than mine was.

I nod. "I'm usually regular as clockwork. I've missed my period twice now. I took one of those home tests, and it was positive." I raise my eyes to look directly at him. "Yes, I'm sure." I watch his face, waiting. It's hard to breathe. "My father will kill me."

"Yeah. He's not exactly open-minded."

I clasp his forearm with a vise-like grip and he winces slightly. "I don't mean it like kids say all the time. I mean he might *literally* kill me. You don't know how he can get when he's really, really angry. I need you to help me!"

He covers my hand with his free one, coaxing it to release his arm. "Baby, you know I love you. We'll go away. Elope. It'll be all right."

Tears spill down my face. "But I'm only sixteen. I need

their permission to get married, don't I? Where can we go?"

Steve considers this for a moment. "We'll go to Las Vegas. Laws are different there. Plus, I'm over eighteen and you're pregnant, so that makes it legal without their permission." He reaches for my face, softly wiping away my tears with a thumb. "It'll be all right," he says again.

I use the handkerchief he offers. "Really?" I whisper. "We'll elope?"

He nods, smiling.

"So we're...engaged?" A quivering smile begins to emerge on my face.

"If you don't mind if you don't get a ring until later. I'll buy you one when we get to Vegas, okay?"

Flinging my arms around his neck, I nod vigorously. "We're engaged!" I whisper in his ear.

We make love to celebrate our engagement. Later, after we've cleaned up and dressed, I ask, "When? When do we leave for Las Vegas?"

"Friday night. Meet me like we normally do, but bring along a change of clothes. Something...modern. So you don't stand out so much. Can you manage that?"

Fingering my skirt, I nod. My parents insist that I never leave the house wearing slacks, that my skirts fall well below my knees, my blouses button up to my throat. But I've borrowed outfits from Sheila before – normal clothes that normal teenage girls wear. Before Steve and I started coming to this make-out spot, my late-night forays were to parties and I sure as hell (Father would strike me for using that word) didn't go out wearing this prudish outfit. I just need to figure out how to ask her to borrow some clothes for a few weeks – until I can buy some new clothes in Nevada and ship hers back. This can work.

"It's late – I'd better get you back home. I'll see you Friday night, baby." He laughs as he starts up the engine. "I'll need to call you something different than *baby*," he says, patting my belly. I snuggle close to him as we head toward my neighborhood, my smile wider than it's been in a long time.

\*\*\*

I'm mesmerized by the little mileage signs along the highway, counting down minute by minute to the state line. I've never been outside of my home state before – didn't even understand the significance of the signs until Steve explained them to me about thirty miles ago. In another twenty-three miles, we'll cross from Arkansas into Oklahoma and the numbers will be large again.

Steve turns off the radio in the middle of a song about someone's heart being broken like breaking a young colt. "We'll take a breather up ahead at the truck stop," he says. "Get something to eat. Take a piss. Fill 'er up."

My momentary disappointment in slowing our progress to the next state is placated by my curiosity about visiting an actual truck stop. The sky has brightened in anticipation of the sunrise and I realize I'm starving, even though I normally wouldn't eat breakfast for another few hours back at home. It must be all the excitement of running off with my fiancé in the middle of the night, heading across the country to a new life. Steve pulls off at exit number twenty-one.

After filling the tank, we park outside the truck stop's diner. Rows of semis sit on the far end of the lot, a few adorned with lights and rumbling even louder than my stomach, others sitting dark and silent. A brightly-colored neon sign blinks beside the entrance – *Open 24 Hours,* it declares again and again. "I'm taking in your bag," Steve says as he grabs my knitting bag from the back seat. I stashed my skeins of yarn under my bed and used the bag to carry a couple changes of clothes, my toothbrush, and a few other necessities. "You should change clothes before we leave here. Maybe fix your hair different, too."

"Why?" I hurry after him, clutching my purse close to my chest, my eyes darting around, trying to pick up on some unobserved threat. "Do you think someone's recognized us? I wouldn't think my parents will even realize I'm gone for another hour, at least."

"Just being careful," he says as he holds the door for me.

We step inside and a large, round woman wearing a pink apron calls out to us to sit wherever we like. Making our way past mostly empty tables, Steve leads us to a booth at the far end of the room. Men who I guess belong with some of the tractor-trailers out front glance up from their meals as we pass, some digging into steak and potatoes and other opting for eggs and hashbrowns. I suppose if you're a truck driver, this could be your suppertime or the beginning of your work day.

"Order me the Number Three and coffee. I gotta take a whiz." Steve tucks his menu back into the holder on our table and slips out of the booth.

"What'll it be, hon?" the waitress asks a minute later. She has long hair tucked neatly in a net, a warm smile, and a twangy accent. I order for both of us, opting for scrambled eggs and bacon for myself.

Steve returns and tosses something onto the seat beside him. He takes a loud slurp of his hot coffee. "Just what the doctor ordered," he says as I realize he's removed his red and black flannel and is now wearing a blue t-shirt.

"Should I go change?" I ask, pulling my bag into my lap.

"Nah, not yet. Wait till we've eaten," he says with a warm smile that makes my heart pound. I return the smile.

Our food arrives quickly, steaming hot and served on enormous plates. We both chuckle as the waitress heads back to another table.

"Well, you *are* eating for two, now," he says. "This'll probably hold us until suppertime."

We dig in, but the massive helping of eggs and bacon is far more than I can manage. "I'll go change clothes while you keep after that platter," I say, scooting across the bench.

"Wait. I've got something for you." He pulls a pretty tortoiseshell barrette from his back pocket and hands it to me. "Put your hair up like you sometimes do. You look like a movie star when you have your hair up."

I gasp in delight as I take the gift. "Steve, this is beautiful. Thank you!" I reach for my purse, but he holds up a hand to stop me.

"Leave your purse. I put another little something for you in there, but you don't get to see it until you come back out."

"But I need my brush."

He takes my purse from me. "Okay, I'll get it out for you," he says as he peers inside. "Anything else?" he asks after handing me the brush.

I smile and shrug. "I guess not." I'm trying to imagine what he's tucked into my purse without my knowing. It's got to be something quite small, since all that's still in there is my wallet which is so thin it barely counts, a small pack of tissues, and a compact I found and kept because of the mirror. I prance off to the restrooms, sure that he's watching my hips sway the whole way. When I realize that the truckers in the diner might be watching as well, I tame my movements, flushed with embarrassment as I escape into the ladies room.

Delighted that Steve wants me to look glamorous, I choose the outfit I borrowed from Sheila. The skirt feels scandalously short, although I know that many girls wear skirts far shorter. The snug blouse accentuates the shape of my breasts. I try several variations of up-sweeps with my hair, finally settling on a style I think will please Steve. I should have asked Sheila if I could borrow some makeup, too, but it's too late for that. Examining myself in the restroom mirrors, I decide I've achieved a look that fits my new image of myself. Mrs. Steven Gwinn, movie star.

Ready to knock Steve's socks off, I exit the ladies room and head toward our booth. I'm disappointed to discover that he's not there. I look around for him as I settle back in my seat, wondering if he's headed back to the car or might be picking up something for us in the convenience store that fills the other half of this building. In the middle of our table sits a neat pile of money topped by our tab and held in place with a salt shaker. I finger my purse sitting beside me, slightly irked that Steve would leave it sitting here unattended, but realizing there's so little cash in it that it wouldn't really matter if it were stolen.

I wonder what his other little present might be.

After several minutes of alternating between sitting quietly and twisting around to check out the store, I decide Steve must be outside doing something with the car. I gather my purse and bag and step outside.

My mind can't quite grasp what I'm seeing – or, rather, what I'm *not* seeing. Didn't we park right there, in front of the newspaper stands? I walk to the end of the building and back again, looking at each of the cars parked in front of the diner. Steve's car isn't here. I cross the lot for a better look at the gas pumps, then break into a near run to head over to where the big rigs are parked. Nothing.

My heart pounding and my thoughts spinning out of control, I dash back into the eatery and rush through the convenience store, checking every aisle. I scurry back toward the front door and find our waitress.

"Did my fiancé say where he was going? I can't find him!"

She reaches out and places a hand on my shoulder, probably thinking I'm having some sort of fit. Some of my hair has slipped from the barrette and is hanging in my face.

"Oh, dear. C'mon, let's sit you down before you fall down, hon." She leads me to a chair at the nearest empty table and I plop down. She lowers herself into another chair and looks me in the eye.

"That good-looking young man with the dark hair and the blue shirt?" she asks, although it sounds more like a statement than a question.

I nod. "Do you know where he went?"

She licks her lips and lets out a long breath. "Hon, I think he's gone and left you here. When you were in the little girl's room, he headed out the door and right after I heard a car go squealing out of here. I'm sorry."

I stare at her like she's grown a second head. "Gone?" I choke out. I let my bag and purse drop to the floor with a thump as I turn to stare out at the parking lot.

"Hon, how old are you? You look like you're just a child. Is there someone you can call?"

My mind races, but there's no one. I had a few girlfriends back home in Markerton, but what could any of them do that would keep my parents from knowing where I've gone? Or that I'm pregnant and was ditched by my boyfriend? There is no one. And if I tell this stranger the truth, what if she calls the authorities and they force me to go back home?

No. I've got to deal with this on my own. This isn't the new life I imagined, but it's all up to me now. Like the times the school counselor asked me about bruises on my arms or legs, or when Ginger's mother wondered why I was walking stiffly after Father beat me so badly I could hardly sit down. I just have to pull myself together and convince my questioner that everything's fine and under control.

I straighten my back and look her straight in the eyes. "I'm sorry about acting so upset, Sally," I say, only now noticing her name tag. "I should have seen that coming. Good thing I found out what a jerk he is now instead of later, right?" I reach down and pick up my things. "And I know I look young, I get that all the time. Actually, I'm eighteen."

She nods tentatively.

"I'm keeping you from your customers. Don't worry about me. I'll figure out who to call for a ride and everything will be fine. Thanks for checking on me, Sally."

With that, I rise and walk purposefully toward the far end of the convenience store. I don't look back to see her reaction. Planting myself in front of a display case filled with cold drinks, I pretend to be considering my purchase options while in fact my mind is swirling with possibilities of what I might do next. Where I might go.

Somehow, getting across the state line seems imperative – as if crossing that border might prevent my parents from tracking me down. Perhaps I should hitchhike, despite the fact that I've never tried it before. My mind races with stories Steve used to tell me about his vagabond days of hitching across the country, seeking adventure but sometimes encountering more adventure than he wished for. "I always look for a car with a couple, or maybe just an older woman. Not with a single guy. There's some sick characters out there," he said, shaking his head. I'm not entirely sure what he meant, but the thought of climbing into a strange man's car and heading down the road with no one else around makes my hands begin to perspire. I wipe them on my skirt, wondering about my other options.

Bus? Train? I think about the pathetic amount of sewing money I was able to hide away from Mother and bring with me. I shake my head in frustration. How far can I get with $4.75? Maybe I can earn more doing some minor sewing jobs, but without Mother's sewing machine, I certainly can't offer much.

With a sigh, I open my purse, wanting to feel my life's savings in my hands. For an instant, I'm baffled at the sight of a white envelope beside my billfold, but then I remember Steve's comment about a surprise he tucked into my purse. Extracting the envelope delicately, as if it might also disappear if not handled properly, I stare at it for a minute. My name is written on the outside in his distinctive scrawl. I slide my finger slowly along the flap, unsealing it carefully, as though I'm trying not to leave any signs that it's been opened.

Inside, I discover cash and a hand-written note that reads "Bus station" plus an address here in this town. Probably not far from this truck stop just twenty-one miles from the border with Oklahoma. I flip over the piece of paper, searching for some personal note. There's nothing else. Money for the bus. He must have decided to ditch me before we even left Markerton in the middle of the night. The creep didn't so much as wish me good luck.

So, he thought I should go buy me a bus ticket and head...where? Home? Someplace else?

Anywhere, so long as Steve isn't there.

I pull the tortoiseshell barrette from my hair and finger-comb it so it hangs loose to my shoulders. Dropping his cheap gift on the floor, I stomp on it as hard as I can manage, hearing a satisfying crunch. I actually consider cleaning up after myself until I notice how much trash and spilled food is strewn on the floors of the store. There's nobody here to beat me for leaving a broken bit of plastic on the floor. I walk away, heading back to look for Sally.

She's just finished handing change back to a trucker who's paid his tab. When she notices me, she scoots from behind the cash register and comes over to me, immediately reaching out to give my shoulder a squeeze.

"Did you get through to someone for a ride, hon?"

I manage a stiff smile, but shake my head. "I think I'll just catch a bus, instead. That's simpler. Do you know how far it is to the bus depot?" I ask, showing her the address.

Without more than a glance at the paper, Sally says, "It's only about three miles, hon, but if you're thinking of walking, I don't recommend that. It's across the train tracks and along a narrow, busy road. Tell you what," she says, glancing up at the clock above the café door, "I get off in less than an hour. I'll give you a lift to the bus station. That'll be a lot safer and I'll bet I can get you there quicker than if you try to hoof it."

My smile feels genuine. "Thanks, Sally. Really. That's so kind of you."

She waves off my gratitude. "Hon, it's nothing. Right on my way. Now, why don't you sit yourself down and I'll bring you a nice cup of coffee – on the house."

I don't tell her I've only once tried a sip of coffee and found it dreadful. I figure I can load it up with cream and sugar and manage to drink enough so I don't hurt her feelings.

She takes a few steps toward the kitchen, but turns back. "Hon, I never asked your name."

I almost tell her but catch myself. "Katharine," I say. The image of a dark-haired actress I admire popped into my mind. Sometimes I fantasize that I might be mistaken for her, even though she's far prettier and sexier than I'll ever be. I rehearse the name in my head, preparing to be taking on a new identity and discard another aspect of my old life.

I have no idea where to go once I reach the bus depot other than head west and get away from Arkansas. As far away from Father and Mother as I can.

# CHAPTER 3 - ROBIN

"Is that yours?" my grandfather asks when I gasp at the sight of a familiar suitcase sliding down a conveyer belt and crashing into other peoples' baggage. For an instant I forgot that Mrs. Barolo and that lady who worked with the police, Dorothy, had helped us pack our "essential" clothes and favorite belongings into our mother's large suitcase. For a teeny, tiny moment I thought Mom had turned up here at this very airport and this was all just a little *misunderstanding* – one of her favorite terms when I'd ask her why she missed a meeting at school with my teacher, or didn't show up for dinner when she'd promised to fix us a hot meal.

I'm not sure what I'm supposed to call these people. My father never called them "Dad" or "Mom" – they were always Clay and Doris. I've heard other kids talk about their "Grammy" and even puzzled over Stephanie's mother gush about a visit with "Grandma and Grandpa," not realizing at first that she was talking about Stephanie's grandparents, not her own. In our house, these people were Clay and Doris, nothing else.

Clay takes the lead, carrying our worldly possessions in

Mom's suitcase, with Doris herding us behind him. He's a big man – about the same height as my father but much stockier, like a barrel. Annie is practically running to keep up, her precious Bunny clutched to her chest, eyes on the heels of Clay's work boots. Doris is nearly as tall as our grandfather, but slim. I've never seen anyone walk like her – it's like she has a broomstick strapped to her back. I manage to look around as we march out the door and into an enormous parking garage.

We're stuffed into the back seat of a bulky sedan and sit silently as Clay mutters and sometimes curses the traffic around us. Doris sits tall, her gray, unmovable hair almost touching the ceiling of the car. I gape out the window, spotting skyscrapers in the distance with a backdrop of deep blue mountains on the horizon that seem unreal, like someone has painted a gigantic mural on the horizon. The car aims in the opposite direction. Doris swivels around now and then to check us out, her face scrunched up like something unpleasant has settled behind her in the car. She rotates back without a word.

Clay keeps driving as we pass large warehouses, then office buildings, then old houses with tiny yards, all flashing past my view as the traffic thins and the car is able to move faster. The vivid sky shines a brighter blue than at home, the few tiny clouds sparkling white.

"How much further?" I ask, my voice slightly hoarse.

They either didn't hear me or don't feel like answering. I try again, this time raising my voice over the road noise.

"Clay, how much further is it?"

Doris spins around in her seat and glares at me while Clay throws me a harsh glare in the rear-view mirror. "What did you call him, girl? We heard you were a troublemaker – disrespectful and *independent*." She sneers as she enunciates the last word. "Well, you aren't with your mother now, and we're not going to put up with that sort of attitude. You hear me?"

Of course I hear you. You're shouting right into my face. "Yes, ma'am," I answer, uncertain what I've done wrong.

"You're to call us Grandpa Clay and Grandma Doris. You got that, young lady?"

I nod and lower my gaze to my lap. From the corner of my eye I can see Annie stick her thumb in her mouth and start sucking. I don't remember her doing that for at least a couple of years.

"Oh, great," Grandma Doris says, turning her attention on Annie. "Five years old and still sucks her thumb."

"What did you expect?" Clay pipes in. "Once the divorce went through and they were left with *that woman*, things went to hell in a handbasket with *her* raising these kids. We always told him she was bad news, but he had to go and find that out for himself. Hopefully this new one's a decent woman who'll make sure their kids aren't left on their own, running around like feral dogs."

Doris nods in agreement and finally twists forward in her seat again. She rummages in her purse, pulls out a pack of cigarettes, and uses the car lighter to set one on fire. I open my window part way, but Clay immediately uses the driver's controls to close it again. "Leave that window alone," he growls.

I dig my nails into my palms, determined not to cry in front of these people. Annie sucks harder on her thumb and buries her face against her rabbit toy, now soggy from her tears.

After what seems like hours, we turn onto a gravel road in the country, walls of tall corn lining the road on each side.

"Gonna show you where our old place was," Clay says, his voice oddly calm and friendly now. He stops by a mailbox and points down a long, dirt drive that seems vaguely familiar. Maybe I've seen a photo of this place, or I could just be remembering something Dad once described to me.

"Your Dad and Sophie grew up in that house. See that?"

I nod obediently.

"Yep. Lived there for more than thirty-five years. Your Grandma and I decided a couple years ago that it was too much for us anymore and sold the farm." He chuckles. "Got ourselves a nice little place in the 'burbs now. A little development right where the Jamesons used to farm. Your Dad would be so surprised to see it – probably wouldn't even know where he was no more!"

I nod again, managing a wobbly smile when he looks into my face. That seems to satisfy him. He squints at Annie, who has at least managed to peek out the window toward the farmhouse, and shakes his head slightly, exchanging a glance with Doris who sighs and actually makes a tut, tut, tut sound under her breath. He turns the car around and we head back the way we came, back to the paved road. I'm grateful that we aren't going to be living way out here in the corn fields.

It isn't long before the farms fade into clusters of houses. Clay zig-zags his way into a neighborhood and pulls into a driveway. I let out my breath in relief. It's a pretty little house with grass and flowers in front and a fence around the back yard. Compared to our apartment building and grounds, it seems like the most beautiful home I can imagine. There's a tall tree in the front yard with branches like curtains of beads dangling all around it, nearly touching the ground. "What's that tree?" I ask, pointing. I can already imagine hiding within its canopy of leaves where no one can see me or bother me.

"Weeping willow," Clay answers. "Well, go ahead. I can see you want to check it out."

"C'mon," I say, grasping my sister's hand and prancing over to the tree. I spread the drooping curtain of branches aside and step through. It's even more magical than I had imagined.

Annie spins slowly around, enchanted. "This is cool," she says – possibly the first words she's uttered in hours. Maybe things aren't going to be so terrible after all.

"Girls, let's go. We need to get you settled."

We follow Clay's order and follow him and the suitcase into the house and down a short hallway into a bedroom with just one bed.

"You girls can share for now. We'll make other arrangements later," Doris says as she pops open our mother's large suitcase and frowns down at the contents. "Unpack your things and put them away in the dresser," she says, indicating the small, three-drawer piece of furniture. "Help your little sister," she adds, directed at me. I nod. It seems like the safest response.

We had two small beds in the apartment, each much narrower than this one. I'm sure we can fit, although I'm not crazy about the idea of having to share a bed. Still, Doris said they'd make "other arrangements," so I guess I can live with it for a while.

Finished with my task of unpacking, I dash outside to visit the willow tree again, Annie close on my heels. I leap off the porch, skipping over the two steps and she loses ground. "Wait!" she wails as she navigates the steps.

I figure the tree's not going anywhere, so there's no reason to wait for her to catch up.

A strident voice stops me. "Where do you two think

you're going?"

I look back over my shoulder as Doris stomps down the stairs, reaches down, and grabs Annie firmly by the upper arm. "You don't leave the house without permission, you hear? And what makes you think all your chores are done, huh?" She shakes my sister while glaring at me. "Get back in here. You have work to do."

With that, she drags Annie into the house and I dart to her side, afraid of what she might do to my little sister. I don't remember Dad saying anything about his mother being the mean one – just his father – but now I wonder if I got it backwards.

"You," she says, a finger almost poking me in the face, "You'll dust on Sundays and Wednesdays. Wash the dishes after meals."

I nod. I've never dusted before, but it doesn't seem like anything I'll need to be taught how to do. I know how to wash out a couple of dishes after I fix lunch for my sister and me, but I sense that Doris has something more involved in mind.

"And you," she says, this time pointing at Annie, "You'll dry the dishes. And you both can set the table. That's it – for now."

Fists at her hips, she stands and shifts her focus from me to Annie and back again. "Well? You planning on just standing here all day with that stupid look on your faces?"

Unsure what she wants from us now, I meet her gaze and wait, trying to read her expression. With a dismissive sigh, she waves us toward the door. "Go on, then. Go play in the yard until I call you."

Annie is out the door before I even turn around.

Inside the sheltering arms of the weeping willow tree, I try to understand this strange woman. Our mother rarely asked where I was going or where I'd been, and never assigned "chores." Sometimes she noticed we were out of clean clothes, and sometimes not. Lugging the laundry down to the washing machine in the basement of our building was more than I was ready to do just for the sake of wearing a clean shirt, but I think eating off a dirty plate is pretty gross, so I worked out how to clean up the two glasses and plates, spoons, and forks that Annie and I use for our meals.

My sister is engrossed in a game of wrapping the dangling branches around her arms. I exit the canopy of leaves and set out to explore the neighborhood. The houses along my grandparents' block are similar to theirs, with grassy front yards and trees (but not a weeping willow!), flower gardens, and identical mailboxes by the street. A dog behind a fence barks as I walk by. A tricycle and large red ball sit near the front sidewalk of another yard and I look around for the child who lives there, but don't spot anyone. A woman with short, dark hair like my mother's kneels by her garden, digging. She glances up as I pass and nods, smiling. I smile back. In the next block, I stop for a minute to watch two teenage boys playing basketball in a driveway, leaping high to try to slam the ball into a hoop mounted above a garage door. One glances at me for an instant, but returns to his game and doesn't look my way again.

Suddenly I hear the blasting of a car horn. I turn to see my grandparents' car on the far side of the road, Doris leaning out the driver's seat, her other hand again pressing the horn. "Get over here right this instant, girl," she hollers, the volume of her voice rivaling that of the horn. I edge toward the car, stepping into the street to approach it.

"Watch where you're going, stupid! Don't you know to look both ways before you cross the street, girl?"

I jump back onto the curb, look to my left and to my

right, and step forward again.

"Hurry up. Get in the car. I don't have all day."

Figuring there's no time to lose by walking around the car and getting in the passenger side, I open the back door behind her and hop in. She scowls at me in the mirror. "Stuck up, too. What do I look like, a taxi driver? Your personal chauffeur? Get up front, girl."

I start to open the door, but she stop me with, "Never mind. I should have known you'd be stupid enough to try to step out into the traffic. Stay put. We're going home."

She drives around the block and gets us back to her house. Exiting the car, she slams the door and stomps around to the front walkway. Remembering how angry she got when I was about to get out on the driver's side, I scoot across the back seat and deposit myself on the sidewalk by the mailbox.

"Don't you ever leave this yard without asking permission first! You got that, young lady?"

"But I only went a little ways away. Back home, I used to—"

"Enough of your back talk, girl! This is your home now, and the rules here are that you ask permission before you go anywhere. Is that clear?"

I lower my head and execute a tiny nod.

"Now get inside and go to your room. I'll let you know when you can come out."

Relieved to be putting some distance between us, I quick-step to my new bedroom, closing the door behind me, and fling myself onto the bed, staring at the ceiling. I have plenty of time to consider what just happened, but I still don't understand it when she raps on the door much later and orders me to come help Annie set the table for supper.

What I do understand is that nothing is going to be the same as before.

# CHAPTER 4 - KATHARINE

Poring over the bus schedule, I quickly eliminate Las Vegas. If I'm not eloping, there's no reason to go there. Truthfully, from everything I've ever heard about the place, it sounds terrifying. I was willing to go there with Steve to protect me, but alone? No way.

Steve must have figured out the cost of a ticket back home, because he left me just enough cash to go there plus buy something to eat. I have no desire to head back east again. Fortunately, I discover that I can make it as far as Oklahoma City and possibly have enough cash to get by for a few days, assuming I can find someone like Sally to let me sleep someplace safe and not have to pay. I've never stayed at a motel, so I have no idea what that might cost, but I'm guessing it's far more than I have. Besides, the thought of going to a motel alone is scary. And wouldn't the front desk clerk call the cops or something, figuring I'm a runaway? Not everyone is going to be as easy to fool as Sally.

I assume an air of confidence as I step up to the ticket window. The man working there never even glances at me as we complete the transaction, so my act works once again. When I board my bus, I find a seat toward the back and spread out my meager belongings, hoping I can ride the entire way without anyone sitting beside me.

Although I managed to doze a little bit last night while Steve drove, I find the rhythmic sway and steady hum of the bus is like a sleeping potion. I don't remember anything after the first few minutes when the bus started rolling down the highway until I open my eyes and realize we're approaching a large city.

Exiting the bus station in Oklahoma City, I stand at the edge of a parking lot, blinking in the bright sunlight. Now what?

I need food and shelter. Therefore, I need a way to earn some money. Clutching my clothing bag in one hand and my purse in the other, I set off along the streets, looking for a simple place to get something to eat with the negligible funds I still have. I pass several motels and keep walking, hoping I'm heading in a direction that'll lead me to businesses, not just to large areas of housing.

After trekking for what feels like at least a mile, I reach a busy intersection where I gaze along each of the three directions I might select. Thinking I see signs in the distance if I turn, I set off for several more blocks before the discomfort in my shoe transforms from unpleasant to painful. Spotting a bench in the next block, I step gingerly until I'm able to sit and remove my shoe. Sure enough, I'm getting a blister. Now what do I do?

I'm still experimenting with creating a cushion using part of a tissue from my purse when a city bus pulls up to the curb in front of my bench. The driver opens the door, but I shake my head, signaling that he should drive on.

As I limp along the sidewalk, I try to distract myself from the pain in my heel by reading every sign along the way. Storage Solutions, No Parking, Gas 4 Less, Right Lane Must

Turn Right. I try hopping several times on my left foot to give myself a brief reprieve from the pain. Three hops and a short step, three hops, short step. I hop over to the curb and sit, carefully removing my shoe. The tissue has turned bloody and is sticking to the wound on the back of my heel. Stuffing both shoes into my tote, I wonder if my decision to go without hose was to blame for my blister. Nothing to be done about it now.

My progress is faster walking barefoot, but I have to keep my eyes lowered to watch for pebbles or broken glass. Each time I step on something sharp, I wince, more from worry about what will happen once my feet can no longer tolerate these small invasions than from the actual pain, which is no big deal compared to what I've known from my father's beatings. Sweat drips into my eyes and I touch the V of my borrowed shirt, feeling the heat radiate from my skin. My face burns in the bright sunshine, and I imagine it is already an angry red. With my parents' insistence on covering up in the sun and my Mediterranean complexion – a term my father used to describe our coloring – I've seldom suffered a sunburn before, but I'm surely working on a doozy out here along this broad road.

When I finally spot the grassy park up ahead, I quicken my pace.

The cool, spongy grass feels exquisite under my aching feet. I stroll beside a paved path into the core of the park, swerving farther from the path when the shade of a tall tree beckons. I walk more swiftly when I spot a building with a drinking fountain in front, and slurp shamelessly from the arc of water, splashing cold water on my face and neck. Inside the women's restroom, I use the privacy of a stall to change back to my own skirt and blouse, wondering how I'll ever manage to return the borrowed clothes – now sweaty and dusty – to Sheila back home in Markerton.

My skirt, which usually fits rather loosely around my waist, is getting harder to fasten. When I get a chance, I'll shift the button over, but soon I'll have to find some different clothes. Or add elastic to the waists of the skirts I have with me. My belly doesn't look any different to me yet, but it's just a matter of time before my pregnancy will begin to show.

I brush my damp hair and tie it back with the plain hair clips I brought along. It feels great to get my hair up off the back of my neck and to feel the cool concrete under my feet in this refuge from the brutal sun. I linger, sometimes cupping my hands under the faucet to drink more cold water, then dabbing my cool, wet fingers on my sunburn. But when a woman enters with her toddler and gives me a strange look, I gather my bags and exit.

No longer thirsty, but now realizing how hungry I've become, I'm at a loss for what to do next. I make my way to the base of an enormous elm tree and sit leaning against its trunk, tucking my full skirt between my legs for modesty, and wriggling my toes in the grass. I watch the people on the paved path. A young couple breeze by on bicycles. An older woman strides purposefully in the opposite direction. Several minutes later, two young women stroll into view dressed like they probably work in a fancy office, except for their identical white sneakers, which seem out of place. They each toss a paper bag adorned with the distinctive McDonalds logo into the trash can beside the restrooms and continue their walk, slurping their drinks through straws.

Seeing no other pedestrians or bicyclists at the moment, I dash over to the garbage can and snatch up both bags which, to my delight, feel too heavy to contain only paper trash. I scurry back to my tree to examine my loot.

Bingo! Between the two, I recover the equivalent of

almost half a hamburger and over a dozen French fries. I eat the cold food slowly, savoring each bite. When I'm finished, I saunter back to the building to discard my trash and drink from the water fountain. I'm startled when I stand up and realize a man is standing close behind me.

"That your bag over there?" he asks, aiming a thumb toward my tree, where I've foolishly left my bag, unattended. My purse is tucked at the bottom of the bag, which seemed like a smart move for carrying my belongings along the road.

"Yes," I answer, already moving swiftly back toward the tree, hoping nothing is missing. Especially not my remaining cash. I glance behind me and realize he's following.

"You should be more careful. Somebody could have taken your stuff."

I'm holding my bag in both hands, trying to gauge if its weight has dropped but unwilling to look through it with this man now right beside me.

"Thanks," I say, turning away from him again. "I'll keep a better eye on it."

His hand grasps my shoulder and forces me to turn toward him. "What's a pretty girl like you doing out here by yourself? You got a boyfriend?"

Thinking quickly, I reply, "Yeah. He's meeting me here. He'll be along any minute now." I pull away from him and walk swiftly to a different tree. This time he doesn't follow. Now I just have to hope he doesn't hang around, waiting to see if my boyfriend will appear. I pretend that I'm ignoring the man, but check on his location out of the corner of my eye. He stares at me for a while, but finally wanders away. As soon as I'm sure he's gone and can't see me, I scurry farther from the path in search of a place where I won't be so easily noticed.

I try working my way beneath the limbs of a large pine, but there's not even enough room to sit comfortably without bumping my head on a branch. I emerge on the side facing away from the walking path and explore other options. Somewhat closer to the path, but offering privacy and shade, I spot an old evergreen with enormous branches drooping nearly to the ground. I part two limbs and step through toward the base of the tree. Perfect! I spend a few minutes clearing an area of fallen needles and soon I'm stretched out within its sheltering greenery, feeling safe and invisible.

It's cool and dark in my den, but my blistered heel is throbbing, my face and neck are burning, and my legs are aching. I know from experience that the pain will eventually fade into the background and I'll be able to sleep, but the thought of spending the night nestled under this tree in a strange park in a strange city is frightening. I'd rather sleep now and stay alert during the night, ready to flee if that man or someone even worse discovers me here.

I close my eyes and try to ignore the signals from my body.

# CHAPTER 5 - ROBIN

Doris marches us into the school building and we follow signs to the office. When she declared that we were heading off to get registered for school, I felt a surge of hope. School starts here in another ten days, which will mean getting out of the house and away from my grandmother five days a week. Our new home feels like a prison. First she tells me I have to ask permission to leave the yard, but then she turns me down every time I ask to go explore the neighborhood. She won't even let me take a bus to go to the library, even after I explained that I took the bus by myself all the time back home. Instead, I had to wait almost two weeks before she finally drove us to the library. I checked out as many books as I could carry. I've been sent to my room so many times these past several weeks, I would have gone crazy without plenty to read. I'm so excited to see my new school that I can't sit.

As she fills out paperwork, I browse a bulletin board with photos of the teachers in this school. Miss Erikson looks like a fun lady with the most natural smile among all the pictures. I'm not so sure about the other 5th grade teacher, Mr. Friend. He seems to be smirking at the camera, plus his name makes me suspicious of what he's really like.

"Robin, come over here. Mrs. Ridgway wants to speak with you. Annie, stop touching everything. Go sit over there until we're finished." Doris directs my sister to a chair outside the principal's office but in view.

Mrs. Ridgway smiles at me. "Welcome to North Elementary, Robin. Since you missed our regular registration last week, I'm going to show you around so you'll know where to go on the first day of school. I understand you've just barely gotten settled, but how do you like Denver so far? Have you been up to the mountains yet?"

I'm a little confused, since Clay and Doris told me our address is in Mills, Colorado, but I also remember Clay talked about living *in the 'burbs*, which I've since translated to *suburbs*. So it must be that Mills is a suburb of Denver.

I realize that I never answered her question when Doris nudges me. "Where are your manners? Mrs. Ridgway asked you a question."

"I like Denver okay," I stammer, even though I haven't left the vicinity of the house except to help Doris with grocery shopping and that one time I explored the block north of ours. "I've never been to the mountains. They look really far away."

She chuckles and places a hand on my upper back, gently directing me out the door and into the hall. I'm happy to realize that Doris has stayed behind to keep an eye on my sister. Another bit of good news – Miss Erikson with the genuine smile will be my teacher.

When we return to the office, Doris rises from her chair. "Thank you, Mrs. Ridgway. Be sure to let me know if Robin gives you any trouble at all." She gives me a sour look.

"I'm sure she'll be fine, Mrs. Milstead," she says, nodding at me. "It was nice to meet you Robin. We'll see you next week."

As she turns to step back into her office, I realize both she and Doris consider our visit to be complete. "But what about Annie? Where's her classroom?"

Mrs. Ridgway stops and looks at my grandmother, her eyebrows knit together. "Did I misunderstand? I thought the younger girl—"

"You understood perfectly, Mrs. Ridgway. Thank you again for your time. Girls, let's get going." Doris's voice turns bright and phony as she practically shoves us out the door, "We have places to go, people to see." She rushes us down the hall and out into the parking lot, snarling "Hush!" in a low voice when I try to protest.

We ride in silence for several minutes before I decide to ignore her orders to keep my mouth shut. "Why didn't we get to see Annie's classroom or talk about her teacher? Isn't she going to be at North, too?"

After a long pause, Doris finally responds. "No, she is not. She'll be starting kindergarten in a different school."

"Why?" I demand, outraged that I won't be able to watch over her.

"I want to go to school with Robin!" Tears begin streaming down her face. "Why can't I go to that school? I don't want to—"

"Enough!" She jerks the wheel and pulls over to the side of the road, turns off the engine with such force that I wonder if she might break the key in the ignition, and spins around to better look at me in the passenger seat and my sister in the back. "You," she spits, her finger inches from my face, "are going to school at North Elementary. And you," now directing her focus on Annie, who is choking back her tears, "are going somewhere else. There's nothing to discuss – this is just how it's going to be. I don't want to hear a word out of either of you the rest of the way home. Stop that crying."

Lacking her toy rabbit to hug, Annie pulls her knees close to her chest and tucks her face out of Doris's sight. I can almost hear her whispering to herself, but it might be my imagination.

With one more angry glare in my direction, Doris resumes her normal rigid position behind the wheel and proceeds to drive us back to the house. Can't she see that my sister needs me more than ever? Why can't we go to the same school?

I leap from the car the moment it stops in the driveway and run. Doris is screaming at me, but I don't care. I gallop faster and faster until her shrieking voice is masked by the sound of a lawnmower, dogs barking, and the slap of my feet against the sidewalk. I slow to a walk, my heart pounding, gulping for air. Reaching into my pocket, I retrieve the permanent ink marker I discovered in the school office and stop, scanning all around to check if anyone is watching me. Satisfied that I won't be stopped – at least not right away – I lope from mail box to mail box, drawing stick figures on one, bold Xs on the next, and random squiggles on the rest as I make my way down the street.

An angry woman screams at me to stop, so I take off running again, this time cutting through yards and behind hedges until I'm sure she's not following me. I spend several hours exploring block after block, locating the main road that leads to all the interesting places like the grocery store, library, and my new school, and strolling along, checking out the businesses. All the places I could have discovered weeks and weeks ago if stupid Doris didn't always have to know everything I do.

This time it's Clay who tracks me down and orders me

into the car. "Grandma Doris is beside herself with worry about you, girl. What got into you?"

I shrug and keep my thoughts to myself.

"We were this close to calling the police," he says, holding his thumb and forefinger an inch apart. "You've got to stop running off." He shakes his head. "You're like some wild thing raised by wolves and your sister is so quiet, you'd think she's half dead. It's all *that woman's* fault."

He never refers to our mother by her name or as "your mother." She's *that woman,* and his lips curl into a sneer every time he speaks of her.

I turn away, hiding the smile that comes to my lips. *Raised by wolves.* I like the sound of that.

Back at the house, I'm sent to my room while the others sit down for dinner. I'm soon engrossed in one of my library books which takes my mind off the growling of my stomach. When the door swings open, I keep reading, anxious to finish the chapter.

"Hey! Put that down." Clay stomps over to my bed and snatches the book from my hands, flinging it to the floor.

Shocked, I open my mouth to protest, but I'm knocked to the floor by a powerful slap across my face. I clutch my jaw, tears filling my eyes.

"Look at me. Look at me!" he roars, so I raise myself on one elbow and lift my eyes to meet his. He's balancing a drink with ice clinking against the glass in one hand as he raises the other as if he might strike me again. "Don't you ever run away like that again. You hear me?" he shouts.

I nod vigorously, still clutching at my throbbing jaw.

He stares at me for a few more moments that drag on forever, then staggers out into the hall. Doris is there, and she jumps back to let him through.

"See what you made him do," she says, her usual scowl mixed with something else – is she frightened? "Don't forget this, young lady. Next time you get it in your mind to run off, don't you forget the consequences."

I spot Annie hovering in the hallway behind her. As Doris steps out of our room, my sister darts in, immediately dropping to the floor beside me and wrapping her arms around me.

My father was wrong when he told me that Clay would never hit a girl and that he'd mellowed since Dad was growing up. I wonder if he lied to me or if he couldn't face the thought that he was sending his daughters to such a terrible place and was lying to himself as well.

The next morning they're back to their usual patterns. Doris snaps at me about not folding the napkins just right when I set the table for breakfast and Clay pretty much ignores everyone, reading his newspaper and drinking coffee. Everyone eats in silence, the clinking of our spoons against our cereal bowls the only sounds in the room.

"Got a lawnmower to fix," Clay announces suddenly as he gets up and steps out the back door to go to his shed, where he maintains a small workshop. The screen door slams behind him.

"Clay..." Doris rises from the table and goes to follow him, then seems to reconsider and returns to the kitchen.

"What are you two waiting for – the maid to come clear the table and do the dishes?"

Annie and I leap up to take care of our chores. She hovers over us, smoke from her cigarette stinging my eyes, and I'm afraid I'll drop a bowl as I rinse it in the sink or my sister won't place it in the dishwasher the way she wants.

"Your Aunt Sophie is coming to visit day after tomorrow.

Robin will ride to the airport with Grandpa Clay to pick her up and Annie, you get to go with them when she leaves to go home."

Annie frowns, squinting up at Doris. "I don't wanna go to the airport."

I'm waiting for her to blow up, but she smiles instead. "But Aunt Sophie will think you're mad at her if you don't see her off."

"I don't even know who she is."

"She's your Daddy's sister."

I try not to roll my eyes. Our parents divorced when Annie was two. He wasn't around all that much when I was younger, and he's only visited us four times since they split up. He's almost as much a stranger to her as this Aunt Sophie, whom we've never met.

"Anyway," Doris adds, her smile beginning to look painful, "Aunt Sophie told me she's going to buy you a toy at the airport. You too, Robin." I've never heard her voice sound so sunny and cheerful.

My sister is pleased with this prospect. I sense there's something important she's not telling us, but I can't work out what it could be. My internal lie detector is jumping all over the place.

"Now, go out in the yard and play. I have a lot to do this morning and I don't need you two underfoot."

Her normal dour expression has returned and I relax. I scurry to our room and retrieve the book I was reading last night, then join Annie and Bunny under the willow tree.

# CHAPTER 6 - KATHARINE

The sky is finally turning bright enough that I can scan the park, on the lookout for anybody around. I've tried to brush the dirt and pine needles off my clothes and from my hair so I don't look like I've been living under a tree, but I won't know how well I've done until I make it to the restroom and check myself out in the mirror. I stride quickly across the damp lawn, leaving bare footprints on the concrete outside the restroom, but I think I've made it inside without being observed. That's a good thing, since my hair looks frazzled and dirty, and plenty of dirt flies off my skirt and blouse as I shake them off in the privacy of a stall.

After doing my best to wash up in the sink, I gather my belongings and head outside. I'm still plodding around barefoot, since the wound on my heel looks and feels even worse this morning than it did when I stopped wearing my shoes. I'll need to find a way to really clean it up and bandage it before it gets infected.

After drinking my fill at the water fountain, I spot two women deep in conversation not far from me along the walkway. One keeps a hand on a shopping cart, like the ones at the supermarkets. She's dressed in layers, pants peeking out beneath a skirt that's much too large for her, a sweatshirt topped by a man's vest, her hair poking out beneath a knit cap. The morning is refreshingly cool, but she must be overheating in all those clothes. The cart is overloaded with what appears to be more clothing, or perhaps blankets, plus a large, folded piece of cardboard. I can imagine Mother labeling her a bum or a freeloader. Still, my parents insist on having me volunteer at our church's soup kitchen once a month, and they even pitch in on Christmas day each year to serve those same bums and freeloaders.

The other woman is neatly dressed in simple slacks and a blouse, a large bag slung over one shoulder. Her hair is done up in a perfect bun tied with a narrow ribbon and she's wearing clean, white tennis shoes. She's black and the disheveled woman is white. They're an odd pair.

The shopping cart lady shakes her head several times in response to the other woman, but finally nods and accepts some sort of papers from her before wheeling her cart away. The other woman shifts her focus directly toward me and smiles warmly as she advances toward me.

I consider taking off, but realize how ridiculous that would be. She doesn't strike me as any sort of threat – not like that man yesterday afternoon. It's not like I'm going to find a job and a place to stay and food for my belly if I run away from every stranger I encounter. I manage a feeble smile back at her as she approaches.

Offering her hand to shake in greeting, she says, "Hi. I'm Joyce. You're new to this area."

It's a statement, not a question. "Katharine," I reply without hesitation, my practicing starting to pay off.

"I help people find services to assist them when they're down on their luck," she says in a matter-of-fact tone. "How are you doing? Did you sleep here in the park last night?"

My eyes go wide and I try to calculate if I can outrun this woman in my bare feet, and if she'll even chase after me.

As if she reads my mind, she smiles and gives my shoulder a friendly squeeze. "Don't worry. I'm not here to tell you where you can sleep or kick you out of the park. I'm just here to let you know what's available if you need a little hand. Food, shelter – I can even help you find work. Get back on your feet." She reaches into her bag and pulls out a business card.

"Social worker?"

"That's my title, but I like to think of myself as being a friend when you need one. Tell me, Katharine, are you hungry? Let's start with that. I'll take you to a place where you can have a hot meal and then we can talk about your situation, see about a real bed for tonight and getting your foot fixed up," she says as she leans her head to one side, checking out my gory heel. "How does that sound?"

My gut tells me she's telling the truth. Then again, my gut is also saying it's famished, so as she put it, let's start with that.

When we arrive, most of the people are already finishing their breakfasts. A smiling girl close to my age passes me a plate filled with two large pancakes plus half a banana. I decide to give coffee another try as I slide my tray to the end of the counter and smell it brewing. Joyce pours herself a cup as well and accompanies me to a dining table where another teenage girl and a woman old enough to be her mother are finishing their meals. At the next table, an old man with the most wrinkled skin I think I've ever seen waves a greeting our way with a wedge of pancake stabbed onto his fork. I wriggle my fingers in a sort of wave back, keeping the gesture very small in case he was gesturing to someone only he can see rather than addressing me.

Joyce introduces me to the girl and lady, who seem to know her already. I dig into my meal, trying not to shove it down so quickly that they'll think I'm crude.

"You staying at the shelter?" the girl – Sylvia, I think – asks just as I stuff another wad of pancake into my mouth.

I shrug and chew quickly, partially covering my mouth with my napkin.

"We haven't talked about that yet," Joyce tells her. "I wanted to get her over here before breakfast closes."

Sylvia nods knowingly. I'm guessing she's a bit older than me – eighteen or nineteen, maybe. Although her hair is combed and her clothes are clean – unlike mine – there's something frazzled about her appearance. I glance at the older woman at our table and she smiles at me, then extracts a small pad of paper and a pencil from her pocket and quickly scribbles a note, which she slides toward me.

*Hope you stay. Empty bunk above me in shelter.*

I'm trying to figure out if I'm supposed to write a response back to her, like passing notes in class, when Joyce explains. "Penelope is deaf. She can talk, but she prefers to write notes to hearing people. She's excellent at reading lips, so remember that she needs a clear view of your mouth when you're speaking."

"Thank you, Penelope," I say, waiting until I've finished chewing my food before I try to speak to her. "I guess Joyce and I will talk about it."

My hunger satisfied, I take a few moments to look around me. This set up is similar to the soup kitchen back in Markerton, although there are more windows letting in natural light, and there's a cheerful mural of fruits and vegetables along one wall. I turn to watch the people working behind the counter as they clear food containers and wipe down the surfaces, already preparing to serve lunch in a few hours.

"I used to volunteer at a place a lot like this," I say, turning back to my table. "I helped serve food and wash dishes."

"Did you enjoy the work?" Joyce asks.

Despite it being something Mother and Father insisted I do, I realize that I liked being there. I felt like what I contributed made a difference to the people who ate there. In fact, it was one of the few times I felt like I mattered to anyone. "Yes, I liked it a lot. Especially being on the serving line, since I got to talk to people."

"That's good to hear. We need to talk about some options for you, now that you've eaten." Joyce turns to Penelope and Sylvia. "Please excuse us. It was nice seeing both of you."

She starts to rise and I follow suit, but Penelope gestures for us to stay and stands, tapping Sylvia on the shoulder and indicating that she should do the same.

"Stay and talk here," Sylvia says. "We'll catch you later – I hope."

With their departure, I notice that only a few people remain toward the other end of the room. Joyce glances at the clock above the kitchen. "We'll need to head out of here in another ten minutes, but let's talk about some options before we leave. First off, are you planning on staying in the area for a while?"

I have no idea what I'm doing next or where I'm going. Questions like those floated through my head all night as I huddled under the tree, waiting for the time to pass and the sun to light up the spooky park again.

Friday night I ran away with my boyfriend, heading to Las Vegas to get married. Saturday morning he abandoned me at a truck stop. Saturday night I slept in a park beneath a tree. And this morning I'm sitting in a soup kitchen. No home, no money, no job, and pregnant. If Joyce can offer some idea on what I can do to fix my life, I'm wide open to suggestions.

"I don't really have any place else to go."

"All right, then. Let's talk about a job. What do you think about working right here at Daily Bread, at least for a few weeks? They have an opening right now for someone to bus tables and wash dishes. It's twenty-five hours a week, plus you get three meals a day, every day, not just the days you work. Minimum wage, so it won't be a lot of money, but we can also talk about a place for you to live. You already have an offer to bunk with Penelope at the shelter, but there are other options for longer term. But before that, let's get that foot fixed up and find you some shoes you can wear while it's healing."

I feel like a great burden has been lifted from my shoulders. Although I can't picture myself washing dishes and living in a shelter forever, it's a start.

It's a start.

# CHAPTER 7 - ROBIN

Aunt Sophie chatters nervously as we stride back to Clay's car and I ignore her, thinking instead of the previous time I followed this path, wondering what my grandparents would be like and where they lived and the questions that always float around in my thoughts – why did Mom leave and where is she and will I ever see her again? In the month since we arrived, I haven't found any answers to my questions.

Dad's sister doesn't mention buying me something at the airport, but I never really expected her to. I figure she's like Dad, who always tells me on the phone that he'll call more often or come visit soon. I know that's just something he thinks he should say. So far, Aunt Sophie is living up to my expectations.

"She's here," Clay announces as we enter the house.

Doris appears from the kitchen, an apron tied around her waist. "How was your trip?" she asks from across the room.

"It was fine," Sophie answers. "Billy is very excited about meeting his cousin, but we told him—"

Clay interrupts her as Doris shakes her head. "That's nice. Come on – we've made space in your mother's sewing room. The sofa folds out into a bed. I'm sure it'll work for just the one night." He picks up her small suitcase in one hand, places his other at the small of her back, and hurries her down the hall. It's the first physical contact he's made with her. Doris doesn't seem to even want to stand in the same room as her.

I have memories of Mom hugging me when I was younger. She hugged me before I went out to play or when I'd bring her one of my drawings. I try to recall a time when Dad hugged me, but nothing comes to mind. He tussled my hair sometimes. I kind of figured that Mom stopped hugging me because I got to be too old to hug, but I can't picture her hugging Annie after she was about three. I guess Dad never grew up with hugs.

"Where's Annie?" I realize my sister hasn't even seen Aunt Sophie yet.

"Out back, playing. Go join her. We'll call you girls when it's time for supper."

I join her in the back yard where we entertain ourselves with a game of hide and go seek. Since we aren't allowed to leave the property, the hiding options are terribly limited, so I try to come up with silly hiding places to make her laugh. I stand behind the trunk of a skinny, young tree, my arms held out alongside its branches. Since my body is much wider than the tree, she finds me the instant she turns in my direction. Another time, I stick an empty plastic flowerpot over my head. Soon, she gets into the spirit of this twist by lying stretched out on the grass with a length of garden hose on top of her. We decide to call our new game *silly* hide and go seek.

As I'm waiting for Annie to finish counting to ten, I look back toward the house and realize Aunt Sophie is standing at the back door watching us. When Annie hollers, "Ten!" and spins around to search for me, Sophie steps onto the back porch.

I'm lying sprawled on the lawn. I've torn up a few handfuls and have strewn grass over my body.

"That's the silliest hiding place ever," Annie declares, giggling.

I pretend to be surprised that she's found me. "No. You're still ahead. Yours was sillier." It's turned into a contest to invent the most ridiculous hiding place, and I want her to win.

"That's a pretty funny game you girls have come up with." Aunt Sophie ambles over, yanks up more grass, and tosses it into the air so it will rain down on all three of us. Annie giggles and imitates her.

I'm about to tear up more grass when I hear Doris shout, "What do you girls think you're doing? Stop messing up the lawn. Robin, get up. You think it's easy getting grass stains out of clothes, young lady? How stupid can you be?"

I leap to my feet and shake like a dog to throw off the torn grass. Sophie leans down and whispers, "Oh, oh. We're all in trouble now," then rolls her eyes dramatically. Annie finds this hilarious, which seems to be what our aunt was hoping for.

"Do you know how to play Simon Says?" she asks.

We answer *yes* in unison and the three of us play until Doris calls us to set the table for supper.

"She's nice," Annie whispers to me after we've cleared the table and loaded the dishwasher. Aunt Sophie helped our grandmother put away leftovers, but Doris shooed her away when she began helping us with our chores.

I agree, but wonder how much we'll see of Aunt Sophie after this visit. Doris snaps at her as much as she does at me and Clay seems indifferent about her being here. I can't imagine wanting to come visit these people if I had a choice. Sophie seems to be here to meet us, but now that she's done that, will she be back anytime soon? It's hard to picture Clay and Doris allowing us out of their sight to go to California to visit Aunt Sophie there, but I suppose it's possible. She says she wants us to meet Uncle Brad and our cousin, Billy.

When Annie's bedtime rolls around, Aunt Sophie insists on reading her a story and tucking her into bed. I mope, meandering in and out of our bedroom as she sits in my usual spot on the edge of the bed, butting in on our usual routine. It's only this one time, I tell myself. I'll read Annie *two* stories tomorrow night to make up for it.

In the morning, I awaken and hear angry voices coming from the kitchen. I can't make out much of what they're saying, but I'm surprised when I hear Aunt Sophie yell, "You're just making this harder than it already is." Someone stomps down the hall and slams a door – the door to the sewing room, where our aunt slept last night. I hold my breath, listening, but the voices of my grandparents are now even more muted.

I wait, not wanting them to know I heard them arguing, then get up and head to the bathroom. "Good morning," Sophie says as I emerge. "Is your sister up yet?"

"Don't know," I mumble, stepping into our room. She follows on my heels.

"Good morning, sleepyhead!" She throws open the curtains and smiles down at Annie. "Rise and shine."

Annie stares at her, disoriented and puzzled. This is like a scene from a TV show – neither of us has ever heard someone talk like this in real life.

"Come on now, Annie. Time to get up."

This she understands.

As we finish breakfast, Clay rises, looking at his watch. "We need to get moving. Don't want to miss your flight."

For the first time since we came here, Annie is excused from helping clean up after a meal. Of course this means it's all on my shoulders, but actually I can probably do it faster without my five-year-old sister trying to help out. Aunt Sophie gives me a hug, much to my surprise, then prompts Annie to hug me as well. Unlike a few days ago, now my sister is excited to accompany our aunt to the airport, and I'm not even sure she remembers the promise of shopping for a new toy.

Doris suggests that we wave goodbye from the porch as Clay backs down the driveway and takes off for the airport. Maybe waving is her version of hugging her daughter goodbye. Once they're out of sight, she's back to her usual commands. "Go play outside. Thank God school starts Monday and you won't be moping around the house all day long, getting in my way."

I snatch up a book and head toward my favorite spot under the weeping willow.

"And don't you leave the yard!" she hollers after me. If she'd let me leave the stupid yard, I wouldn't be getting in her way. I keep this observation to myself.

Engrossed in my reading, it barely registers when Clay pulls up to the house. I hear a car door slam and continue reading, rushing through the words before Annie comes in to interrupt me. When I reach the end of the chapter, I get curious and head inside.

My grandparents are sitting on the couch in the living room doing absolutely nothing, as best I can figure. They both scrutinize me as I enter.

"Where's Annie? Out back?" I ask.

Clay points to the chair facing the sofa. "Come sit down. We need to talk to you about something."

After I'm seated, Clay draws a deep breath while Doris peeks at him out of the corner of her eye. She takes a deep draw on her cigarette. Clay clears his throat and my stomach begins to hurt, just like it did when I realized my mother wasn't coming home.

"We've decided it's best for everyone if Annie goes to live with Aunt Sophie and Uncle Brad."

"What?!" I try to say more, but the words won't come.

"She has different needs than you do. We didn't realize how much your wildness would impact your behavior, but the truth is we can't get *you* straightened out and give her the attention she needs at the same time. We ain't as young as we used to be. We don't have the energy to deal with the both of you."

I'm choking, gasping for air. It seems like all the oxygen has been sucked out of the room.

"This is for the best," Doris adds, "for both of you. Sophie really took a liking to Annie, and I think the feeling was mutual."

"Annie needs a calm, peaceful environment. With all your running away and temper tantrums, she's much better off somewhere else."

"But...you can't! Dad said we'd be together!" My chest heaves as I struggle to speak.

Clay shakes his head. "Your father has no idea what it's like dealing with you. When's the last time he saw you – last November? For a couple hours? Why do you think he asked us to take on you kids instead of moving you into his house? He knew he couldn't handle you. You're like a feral cat."

"But he said it was because of Glenda and the baby

coming and..."

"Right. Well, no matter what he said, bottom line is he ain't takin' you. Sophie ain't takin' you, either. Just your sister."

I jump to my feet. "You can't—"

Doris speaks up, her eyes burning into me with anger. "Enough, girl. It's done and nothing's going to change, except your bad attitude. Now get to your room and stay there until you can be civil. This is your home now, we are your guardians, and that's that. Get!"

I stumble away and fall onto my bed. I feel like I'm dying. What is Annie going through, tricked to get on an airplane and stolen away from me? Will she ever forgive me for letting this happen?

# CHAPTER 8 - KATHARINE

"What the hell?"

I snatch the borrowed travel alarm clock and stuff it under the covers, fumbling for the button to stop its shrill sound. "Sorry," I say. "I've got breakfast shift this morning."

"Fuckin' A!" the woman snipes when I turn on the flashlight so I can see to get dressed. I keep the light pointing toward the wall beside my bunk, trying to disturb her and Penelope in the top bunk as little as possible. Penelope, of course, isn't bothered by the alarm or the loud protests of this new roommate in the other bunk. With luck, she won't return to the shelter tonight.

The fourth woman in our room mumbles something in her sleep and resumes snoring. She's been here all week and I keep thinking I'll get used to her snorts and wheezes, but so far even stuffing cotton in my ears hasn't helped. I hurry to dress, gather up my toothbrush and hair brush, and tiptoe out into the hall.

The work isn't bad. Mother always gave me plenty of housework to do, including clearing and washing the dishes, pots, and pans. While there are certainly a lot more dishes and kitchen supplies to bus and clean, the industrial dishwashing system is fast and simple to use. I only have to scrub out some of the bulkier pots that won't fit inside.

Fridays are my longest shift, since I handle both breakfast and lunch, but by 1:45 I'm done with work until Sunday's dinner. As I leave the building, Joyce – the social worker I met in the park – is waiting to talk with me.

"Katharine, I've been doing this job for a while, and I know you haven't been homeless for long. I want to help you, but I need to understand your situation better in order to do that."

I nod. There's something I learned early on about lying – don't say too much and keep track of what you've told people. Stick to your story. "My situation?" I ask, playing dumb. No reason to answer questions that she doesn't raise.

In my mind, I review my earlier lies. Forced to improvise quickly when they wanted me to fill out a form with my social security number and full name, I used my real number, but entered "Katharine" as my first name. A song by the BeeGees had been going through my head since hearing it playing on the radio earlier, so I carefully printed "Gibb" beside it. Middle initial "S." For...Sue. Hesitate too long and people will catch on to your lies.

"I'm guessing you to be about sixteen, is that right?" Joyce asks.

"I know I look young – I get that a lot," I say, smiling. "Actually, I'm eighteen."

"Eighteen." Her mouth is drawn into a thin line. "Katharine, look. I'm not looking to turn you in or force you to go somewhere you don't want to be. I want to help. Do you have family wondering where you are? Even if you don't feel like you can go back to your previous situation, I can help pass along a message, just so they know you're okay."

Does this woman read minds or what? "I can't go back

and they can't know where I am. They can't!" I didn't mean to say so much but my pulse is racing and it's hard to act calm.

"C'mon," she says, leading me to a bench in front of Daily Bread. "Let's sit and talk."

I sit, my hands clutched tightly.

"Let's start again. How old are you, really?"

I exhale slowly, forcing myself to calm down. "Sixteen."

"Thank you for your trust, Katharine. Now, did you run away from home, or were you kicked out, or something else?"

My eyes focused on my hands, I answer, "Ran away. Eloped – kind of."

"Eloped? What happened?"

It takes me a minute to answer, but she sits quietly, giving me time. "He took off at a truck stop. Left me there without even saying goodbye. But he left me enough money to catch a bus home." I snort and stare off at nothing in particular, not wanting to see her reaction.

"And then you came here."

I nod, still turned away.

"What do you think would happen if you went back home, Katharine?"

My head snaps back to face her. "I can't! You don't know my father. I wouldn't just be in trouble or be grounded or something. No. He would say I've been possessed by the devil. He would...he would..."

"What? What would your father do?"

I shake my head. "It would be bad. You don't know..." I swallow. "Bad. Really bad."

Joyce reaches out and takes hold of my hands, which I realize are trembling. "It's all right. It's all right. Nobody's going to force you to go back there."

We sit like that for some time. Finally, she pats my hands and sits back. "Let's talk about something else. What about school? Were you going to school regularly last term?"

I'm relieved to move onto something different. School was my refuge. I always submerged myself in my homework which seemed to placate my parents while also keeping me separated from them physically. I'd shut myself into my room and study, inventing additional homework for extra credit just so I could stay there as long as possible. Mother would look in on me at random times, probably trying to catch me doing something she didn't approve of, like listening to music other than the recordings of hymns that my parents had given me. But I was clever. When I wanted to escape their unyielding rules, I found ways to meet my friends late at night or to forge a permission slip to skip a class now and then for a fictional dental appointment. With my strong grades and eager participation in class, teachers and administrators never suspected my occasional absences were fake.

"Without a parent or guardian's permission, you won't be able to enroll in a regular high school. However, I can get you into classes to prepare you for your GED – Graduate Equivalency Degree. With grades like you've told me, it would be a shame for you to quit your education."

Only when I'd seen ads for back-to-school supplies recently had it occurred to me that school would be back in session soon. I knew I couldn't go back to my old school to start my junior year. I pictured myself in a cute little house somewhere out west, fixing dinner for my husband while our little girl – or sometimes it was a little boy – played happily at my feet with brightly-colored blocks. Steve would arrive home from work and I'd greet him at the door with a kiss. Sometimes he'd bring me flowers.

It was all a load of crap.

Classes. Finish school. I'll have to let her words sink in for a bit.

After Joyce leaves, as I do many days, I walk the seven blocks to the branch library where I read the previous week's newspapers from several major cities and browse for a few new books to check out when I'm finished with the previous batch. There aren't a lot of options for my free time that don't cost money. There's a cheap matinee at a nearby movie theatre on weekdays, but I'm not going back there alone again. The place was nearly empty and this man who reeked of booze came in and sat right next to me. I wasn't about to wait around to find out what he'd do next, so I took off and ran all the way back to the shelter.

A few days after I arrived in Oklahoma City, Joyce brought me the classified section of the local paper, a dozen or more bright red circles around ads for jobs and a few more circles under *For Rent*. "In case you want to find something other than the Daily Bread," she said.

We've already discussed my dilemma. I'll need to be earning a lot more than I'm getting now if I want to move into an apartment – even subsidized housing. So, first on the list is finding a better-paying job. At sixteen, with no real experience, the options are limited and nothing I read in the circled ads sounds like it'll bring in enough money for me to afford my own place.

Sylvia shows up at dinner and sits with me and Penelope like we did the very first time I ate at the soup kitchen. I've seen her around and we've talked, but her appearances are sporadic. She never sleeps at the shelter and I've never asked where she stays at night.

"San Francisco – now there's a crazy place! You ever been there?" she asks, but as talkative as she's been tonight, I simply shake my head and let her continue with her whirlwind verbal tour of all the places she's been. She sniffs a few times and continues.

"You wouldn't believe how cold it is in the middle of summer. I guess it's on account of the ocean winds, or something like that. And the people are crazy, I tell you. There's this park where people run around dressed in these wild outfits or half naked and it's just crazy! I mean, real, I'm-not-shitting-you *crazy*."

Penelope is trying hard to follow her words, but her rapid speech and habit of stuffing food in her mouth while continuing her stories must make it nearly impossible to lip read. That and Sylvia's constant sniffling – I hope I don't catch her cold. My bunk mate purses her lips and turns away from the show, catching me watching her. With a sideways glance at Sylvia followed by a raised eyebrow and a mischievous grin, she's got me giggling. Sylvia continues her blabbing, oblivious to our reactions. I can't imagine what's gotten into her – she's not usually like this.

"Denver. Yeah. I'd like to move back to Denver again. The mountains and all that sunshine – and the people. I mean, you've got everything. Mellow people and crazy people and hip people and straight people. And mountains. You ever seen mountains?" she asks, directing her focus toward me.

"Um. Sort of. I guess."

"Not puny little mountains like in the east. Real mountains. Huge mountains. We gotta go to Denver, K. You and me."

I decide that "K" must mean me. "I don't know. I'm trying to figure things out. I don't know where I want to be or what I'll be doing."

"Denver. I'm telling you." She blows her nose into her

paper napkin and wads it up on her plate. I'm surprised to see how little of her dinner she's actually eaten. Grabbing her tray, she jumps up and unloads it on the bussing cart, calling back over her shoulder, "We'll talk later. Think about it, K – Denver!" In a flash, she's out the door.

Penelope jots something on her pad of paper and slides it toward me.

"Crazy." She tilts her head and looks toward the door after Sylvia.

"Kind of. But I like her." I wish I could be that animated and free-spirited.

She writes again. "Be careful. Nice but trouble maybe." She underlines *trouble* several times and taps her pencil on the word for emphasis.

"Okay, I'll be careful." I wonder how much Penelope really picks up from the conversations around her and imagine how Sylvia's energetic behavior might come across as wild and odd. I shrug off her note, since I'm not planning on taking Sylvia up on her suggestion that she and I head to Denver or anyplace else.

Yet, my thoughts keep returning to her verbal travelogue and invitation to hit the road. I've always dreamed of traveling and places like San Francisco and Denver sound exciting and fun.

Who am I kidding? I'm pregnant and broke. I'll be doing well if this time next year my baby and I have a roof over our heads and food on the table. Glancing over at a young mother and her toddler eating at the next table, I shudder. I don't want that to be me. What kind of future is that?

Damn you, Steve. And damn you, Mother and Father. I hope I never see any of you again!

# CHAPTER 9 - ROBIN

After passing out textbooks and having each of us tell the class our names, Miss Erikson is walking up and down the rows of desks, checking for the required inventory of pens, pencils, and notebooks laid out in front of each pupil. Doris took me shopping a few days ago, supply list in hand, and we even visited the clothing department where she picked out several blouses, two skirts, and one dress for me to wear to school. I wandered through the racks of clothing, delicately touching the fabrics, my mouth open in wonder. The department store was unlike the thrift shops where my mother used to take us – so many clothes arranged in a rainbow of colors and available in multiple sizes. And all *new*.

It's been a rough week and I'm relieved to get away from the house and into my new school. After much beseeching and plenty of arguing, I finally got to talk to Annie on the phone. She begged me to come to our aunt and uncle's home and I promised to do everything I could to make that happen, knowing what an impossible task that would be.

"They're a lot nicer than Grandma and Grandpa," she whispered over the phone, "but I miss you so much! Come stay here with us."

"I'll try," I repeated. "I miss you, too."

That night, after a second call from California, Doris and Clay made it clear that phone calls were "far too upsetting and disruptive" for my sister. In the future, I could write her letters, but must not speak to her on the phone.

It's difficult to focus on my lessons. At recess, I walk around the perimeter of the playground, the laughs and shouts of the other children barely registering. Annie started school today, too, and I wonder how she's adjusting to yet another new environment. Will she make friends right away, or be like me, just wanting to be left alone to try to take it all in? She cries easily – will her tears label her as a baby to the stronger kids in the school and make her a target of their cruelty? I was her guardian when she started preschool last year, but I won't be there for her now.

"Hey, Gloomy Girl. What's the matter? Got no friends?"

Two girls, smirks on both faces, plant themselves in my path.

"Get lost," I say, plowing straight ahead between them, shouldering them aside.

"Hey!" the shorter, stockier one hollers. She grabs me by the arm. "You pushed me. Your mama ever teach you any manners, Gloomy Girl?"

I spin around, yanking my arm from her grasp. "Screw you," I say as I give her a powerful shove. She crashes to her butt on the playground sand, her face reflecting fear and astonishment.

"You can't do that!" her friend declares as she kneels down to see if the other girl is hurt.

I laugh loudly. "I just did, bitch," I say, then turn and continue on my original path.

Before recess ends, I'm sitting outside Mrs. Ridgway's

office, once again gazing at the display of teachers' photos and names like I did when Doris brought me here to register for school. I inhale deeply and blow out, buzzing my lips noisily and the school secretary looks up from her desk, glowering at me. I've set a new record for myself – sent to the principal's office on the very first day of school.

That seems to work in my favor. Since it's my first offense, I'm sent back to my class after a brief lecture. She'll get to know me better soon enough, like the principal at my old school. I chew my lower lip, wondering what'll happen now when they contact my guardian about my behavior. Mom never cared. She used to toss the notes into the trash with a sigh, turn to me and say something like, "Not again" or "What am I going to do with you?" But she wouldn't *do* anything and that would be the end of that. I picture Doris and Clay going through the roof.

The two girls – Denise and Betty, I've now learned – stare at me and whisper to each other during recess the rest of the week, but they don't approach me. Two of the wimpiest bullies I've ever dealt with. Another girl, Lupe, walks with me sometimes and we comment on the cliques that gather in small groups scattered around the playground like distinct solar systems, kids gravitating toward an obvious leader, clearly seeking the light of their attention.

"Those are the WASPs," Lupe says, indicating a cluster of girls who might as well be clones. Ponytails (mostly blond), outfits straight out of teen style magazines, and all of them white (or, as Lupe puts it, "Anglo"). "And the gangsters," she says. That group is a mixture of boys and girls, but mostly boys. We laugh at the exaggerated swaggers and especially at the guy with what might be a cigarette pack rolled into the sleeve of his shirt. "That boy's been watching old movies, or something!"

Lupe seems to be a loner who doesn't like much of anybody, including the other Hispanic students. I suppose she figures I'm a loner, too – and I guess that's who I've become. When I was Annie's age and maybe even a bit older, I felt like I was one of those suns with other children revolving around me. I remember always having plenty of friends to play with and kids would look to me for ideas of what to do next or where to go. I sat up front in my classes, teacher's pet. The pupil who read the most books and brought the best show-and-tell items to school. Things seemed different after the divorce and our move to the small apartment. Mom had to work more hours, so she tied a long string around my neck to hold a key and I'd let myself in when I got home from school. I'd fetch Annie from the neighbor down the hall and keep an eye on her until our mother got home to fix dinner. After a year or so, she sometimes had me take care of our evening meal, but that was just heating up leftovers. It seemed like I had too much else to do to have much time to hang out with friends.

I don't tell Lupe all this. We walk around in a large circle, watching the others and doing very little talking. It suits me fine.

Every night, after I do my homework, my chores, and after dinner is eaten and the dishes are done, I write Annie a short letter. Doris says I can't be mailing stuff every day, so I bundle them up and turn them over to her to mail once a week. I thought about telling my sister about Doris calling me nasty names after I tore all the petals off the flowers in the garden, but then I'd need to tell her about how Clay slapped me again after the time I took off during recess and didn't go back to class. I don't want her to get too upset when she gets my letters, or they might not even let me write to her. She's too young to be able to read my notes very well, so I'm sure

Aunt Sophie is reading them to her.

I don't get any letters in return, but I remind myself that she's only in kindergarten, so she's just learning to write.

Finally, I hear from her. "Something for you," Doris says, holding out two colorful sheets of paper that were included in a letter she's reading.

I grin, examining her artwork. The first one is a flower which fills the entire page with reds and yellows and purples. The other drawing shows four stick figures of different heights. The shortest must be Annie, with a purple skirt (her favorite color) and short, brown hair. Beside her is a taller boy, who I assume is our cousin Billy. Two adults stand high over the children – Aunt Sophie and Uncle Brad. There's also a mysterious blob next to the group – a very large dog, perhaps?

I blink rapidly, running a finger over the smallest stick figure. Annie's new family. I've never even met two of them. I sniff and swat away a tear, turning away from Doris so she won't see, and retreat to my bedroom to spend time with my sister's drawings in private.

My chest aches as I stare at the family scene. I should be there beside her. I feel like she's already forgotten me. Do they even read her my letters? My tears begin to flow and I jerk the paper away as a drop lands on the picture and the paper begins to warp. It's then I notice the sun she's drawn in the upper corner. It has two brown blobs dangling from each side. Sophie and Brad probably thought they were strange rain clouds or that she'd added drooping rabbit ears to the sun, but I know better.

Annie always draws me with long pigtails, like I used to wear before we came here and Doris decided my hair was too long and scraggly, and cut it much shorter. I'll bet they told her she couldn't draw me as part of her family anymore, but she did anyway. I'm the sun.

I slide the picture to "her" side of the bed and start to sob, my entire body shaking and tears spilling onto the bedspread. I'm crying but I'm smiling at the same time.

I miss her so much. I miss Mom, even though she must not even care where we are. I miss Dad who has never been around much, but always calls me Sweetie, even though he lied about keeping Annie and me together.

Quickly hiding Annie's artwork under my bed in case Doris decides I can't keep them, I race through the living room and out the front door. I hear her shouting after me as I fly down the street and cut through peoples' yards to throw her off so she won't know where to find me. A few blocks farther, I see large trash containers lined up along the street. Screaming in frustration, I shove one onto its side and dash to the next, which I kick over, karate-style. I continue down the block, booting discarded cereal boxes and pop cans, flinging papers and smashing bottles until I'm panting too hard to continue. Hearing angry voices, I scamper away and crawl into a hedge to hide from the neighbors.

It's almost dark when I emerge. Not knowing what else to do, I shuffle back to my grandparents' house, knowing Doris will be livid and hoping Clay hasn't been drinking.

# CHAPTER 10 - KATHARINE

"Ooo, try this one on, K. It goes with the shirt." Sylvia loads another pair of slacks onto the growing pile of clothes in my arms.

"Hold on – I can't carry any more. Will they let me take this many items into the dressing room?" I say, already heading in that direction.

Sylvia caught me as I was leaving Daily Bread after my lunch shift and insisted we visit the thrift store. Since arriving, she's been picking out an entire wardrobe for me – pants and shorts, blouses, a skirt, sandals and dressier shoes, jackets and sweaters.

As I expected, the woman guarding the dressing room insists that I can only try on three items at a time. I transfer the remaining items into Sylvia's arms and move my mouth close to her ear. "I can't afford all this," I whisper.

"Yes, you can," she replies, loudly enough for the woman watching over us as well as anyone else within thirty feet to hear. "Don't worry – just see what fits."

Several rounds later, after sorting out items that work and trying on more clothes in batches of three, I've picked out an impressive wardrobe that's totally unlike anything Mother would have let me wear. She'd be appalled if she saw me shopping in a place like this. We used to donate clothes I had outgrown to Salvation Army, but I doubt she had ever set foot inside one of their stores.

When the checkout clerk tells me the total price of my purchases, I'm sure I've misunderstood. Sylvia nudges me playfully. "Told you." Even on my meager wages, the cost is easily manageable.

"We'll come back again next week," she says as we set off to walk back to the shelter. "There's always new stuff. You'll need a winter coat and some cold-weather clothes for when we move to Denver."

"I haven't said I'm going."

She leaps in front of me, forcing me to stop. "You gotta come with me, K. I've got a place lined up and it'll be super affordable if we share it. It'll be so cool – it's a large bedroom in this fantastic old house my friend has. There's a big bathroom down the hall and we'll just share it with one other girl. And a monster kitchen for everyone to use. It'll be great."

"But, what about work? What kind of money can I possibly make? You're older – people will hire you for all sorts of jobs. But I'm only sixteen." And pregnant – something I've kept quiet up till now, but I know will become obvious before too long. I'm just lucky I've hardly ever had morning sickness – just some queasiness now and then – or people would have already guessed. Who's going to hire a single, pregnant sixteen-year-old?

Sylvia laughs. "Older? Me? How old do you think I am?"

I flush. I've been thinking of her as sort of a big sister, showing me the ropes. I shrug, unwilling to tell her my guess, which was nineteen or twenty.

"I just turned seventeen," she declares. "I just know my

way around, if you get my meaning." She winks and I plaster a grin on my face, not understanding her meaning but not willing to admit my naiveté.

"Anyway," she says as we resume our walk, "just leave everything to me. I've got it handled. We'll have work – don't worry about it. But it's time to get out of this place and go somewhere *crazy*. Denver, K, Denver! Are you with me?"

I can feel my heart thumping and my mouth has gone dry, but I decide to take the plunge. "Okay. Denver."

I mean, how could it be any worse than living in a homeless shelter and working in a soup kitchen?

***

Sylvia wants to head out next week, so I let my boss know I'll be quitting. He was kind enough to schedule me for extra hours so I can try to build up my savings a bit. While I believe Sylvia when she says we'll be able to find work, I'm afraid to count on it being immediate. She assures me that she can front me some money if needed, but I don't want to be in debt to her or anyone else.

It's been a long day, working all three meals, and my back is aching. Once my cleanup duties are complete, I shuffle back to my room and collapse on the bunk. I spotted Penelope out in the common area, engrossed in a game of gin rummy. Even though we're not supposed to gamble, she's confided in me that she often comes out the winner, collecting cigarettes, sticks of gum, small amounts of money, and a menagerie of other prizes from her opponents. I think she sells some of it when she's out on the street during the day.

I have the room to myself. Most of the women don't

73

hang out in the sleeping areas this early in the evening. Rolling up my blanket, I place it under my knees, trying to ease the discomfort in my lower back. All afternoon, I've felt like I've got cramps, but not quite like I do when I have my period. They're getting worse.

After a while, I roll off the bed and stumble down the hall to the bathroom. When I spot the blood in my underwear, I stare in disbelief. I never bled like this before – something is wrong. Cleaning myself up as best I can in the stall, I create a temporary pad of toilet paper and waddle out to wash my hands, which are trembling.

"You see a ghost, girl? You're as pale as one."

An older woman I've seen before but never spoken to grabs me under the arm as my knees start to buckle. "We need some help in here," she hollers. "This girl needs a doctor!"

***

I'm supposed to feel devastated. Everyone keeps asking me how I'm doing and saying how hard this must be for me. "I didn't even realize you were pregnant," they say. "I'm so sorry for your loss."

I'm supposed to feel terrible, and in a way I do, but not for the right reason. I just can't bring up any sort of emotions about "losing my baby" because it never felt that real to me. All that seemed real was the upheaval in my life. I worried about where I'd be six months, a year from now, but it was only an afterthought that I'd also have a baby to take care of. Mostly, I tried to push my pregnancy to the back of my mind.

What keeps running through my head, though, is how *ironic* my life is. I ran away from home because Father would have beaten me – possibly killed me – if he learned I was pregnant. Steve took me as far as the state line before abandoning me, surely because he didn't want to marry me and raise a child. And here I am, not even two months after I first suspected I was expecting – no longer pregnant. In a matter of months, all my bridges are burned, I'm living in a shelter in a city I chose simply because I could afford the bus ticket. And I'm about to move to another city because another runaway girl wants me to go with her.

Ah, the hell with it. I've got nothing, so what can I lose now? Let's go to Denver.

# CHAPTER 11 - ROBIN

"You been sick?" Lupe asks after we've walked partway around the school yard in silence.

"Kinda." Doris drilled me repeatedly over the past three days on what I can and cannot say to my teachers and classmates, but I'm tired of lying. The absence excuse she wrote said I'd been sick – throwing up and even passing out, which is how I ended up with this swelling on the side of my face and my black eye, just starting to fade from deep purple to splotchy shades of sickly yellows and browns. I hit my face on the edge of a table when I fainted – that's the story I've repeated at least four times already.

She's quiet for a while, but she keeps glancing over at my face. I stop suddenly and kneel to re-tie a shoe that was fine to begin with, then maneuver so I'm walking on her other side so she can't see my bruises so well.

"Somebody hit you, didn't they?"

I respond quickly, remembering Doris's threats. "No. I fainted and hit my face."

Grasping my hand in hers, she stops me in my tracks. "I won't tell on you, Robin. We're friends." She looks me square in the eye, a crease formed between her eyebrows as she stares intently. "I promise I won't tell."

I shift my eyes one way and another, unable to meet hers. "Bad things will happen if I tell. Really bad things."

"Not if we keep it a secret between us."

I want to confide in her so badly it hurts. For three days I've paced my bedroom and sprawled on my bed, only allowed through the door to use the bathroom. I ate my meals there, delivered by my grandmother along with another lecture which was repeated when she retrieved my dirty dishes. By the third morning, I even begged her to let me out to clean up the dishes and do my other chores, but she'd have none of that. The only sign I heard of Clay was the night I came back from running away, after he struck me and knocked me to the floor again. After they sent me to my room, I heard his drill whining outside my door, the wall vibrating as I held my hand against it. Frightened of angering him further, I held back from opening the door to see what he was doing until much later when all the sounds in the house had ceased except for the low rumble of Clay's snoring.

The doorknob turned, but the door wouldn't budge. He had installed a latch on the outside to keep me locked in my room.

I try to whisk away a tear that is weaving its way down my injured cheek, but Lupe reaches up first and brushes it gently with her fingers. "You can tell me. I won't tell a soul – cross my heart and hope to die."

I pull her over to the fence, putting as much distance between us and the other kids as possible and the words spill out of me as if from a breach in a dam, spraying out in a powerful flow that pulls along everything in its path. Somewhere during my meltdown, the recess bell must have rung, because she hands me a tissue from her pocket and leads me toward the school entry. "We'll talk some more after school," she says as we duck into the girl's bathroom where I wash my face with cold water. We slide into our seats just as the tardy bell rings.

When school lets out, we take our usual places together on the bus, but instead of getting off at her stop, she stays on board until we reach mine. "I'll walk you home," she says and we stroll slowly toward my house. Since I always linger as long as possible and search for every conceivable distraction to delay my return home, Doris won't notice anything different today if we take our time.

We find a quiet spot to talk in a tiny park tucked into the neighborhood. I've been unable to concentrate on my lessons all afternoon, my stomach in knots and my mind replaying one miserable scene after another. I didn't realize how desperately I needed to tell someone until I began my story this afternoon. Now, in the shade of a huge cottonwood, I spill it all – my mother's disappearance, the police, Dad's promises to keep us together, the baffling rules in my grandparents' home, Annie stolen away from me, and the "slaps" that weren't at all the same thing as hitting, according to Clay.

"They brought me a book to read while I was locked in my room," I say, trying not to start crying again. "*Oliver Swift*. You ever read it?"

Lupe shakes her head, saying nothing. She's barely said a word since we got off the bus, but never looking away as I speak.

"It's about a boy who lives in an orphanage – a really nasty place where he doesn't get enough food and the adults are really mean. Then, he has to work all day in an even nastier place and he gets beaten and finally runs away. But even then, his life is one awful thing after another."

Wide-eyed, Lupe asks, "So what happens to him in the end?"

I shrug. "I don't know. Every time Doris came into my room, she'd ask me to tell her what was happening in the story and to show her where my bookmark was. Then, when I was most of the way through it, she took it away and I haven't seen it since. But here's the really bad part," I say, leaning even closer to her and lowering my voice to a whisper. "She said if I ever, ever run off from the house again, or leave the yard for even a few minutes without permission, they're going to put me in an orphanage like they did to Oliver Swift."

"They can't do that! You're not an orphan. You said you talked to your Dad on the phone after your sister went away. And your Mom is still alive, too, even though she walked out on you."

Shaking my head, I try to explain. "That's what I thought, too, but Clay says they take kids to places like that if nobody wants them, just like they were orphans. So I'm trapped."

There doesn't seem to be anything left to say. After a while, we get up and make our way to the end of my block. Having no idea if Doris has rules against walking home with a friend, we decide to play it safe and part ways while we're still out of sight of her piercing eyes.

Back in my room, I huddle over my schoolbooks in case Doris walks by the open door. Now that they're not locking me in, she's become a spy who has to peek in at me at least once an hour. Under my report on "Extreme Weather I've Seen" hides my latest artwork. Two figures – one plump with short, gray hair and the other mostly bald, his palm raised in the air, ready to strike – are about to be crushed by a giant boulder falling out of the sky. I listen carefully for Doris's voice, talking back to the television as she watches one of her talk shows, and nod when I hear her shrill voice calling someone an idiot. Grasping my pencil like a dagger, I stab at my drawing, scrawling dark lines from the boulder onto the heads of the two people. The paper tears as I scribble with all my might, covering the figures with bold slashes of graphite. When the tip of the pencil breaks, I crush the remaining tip against the paper again and again until my hand gets too tired to continue. The cardboard beneath the demolished drawing is deeply dented from my attack, but I haven't torn all the way through it yet, so I stash it in the back of my closet to be used again. The rest of the mess I wad up tightly and drop in the trash, feeling a rush of satisfaction.

"Are you done with your homework?" Doris asks, squinting suspiciously at me from the doorway. "What are you doing? If you're just messing around, I have plenty of chores to keep you busy."

"Just stretching for a minute. I'm still working on my essay." I flash a plastic smile and sit at the table again. Without another glance in her direction, I begin to write. After a moment, she retreats.

I can hardly wait to leave for school again in the morning. I wish I never had to come back here.

# CHAPTER 12 - KATHARINE

Sylvia had better be right about being able to find work right away, because after buying my bus ticket and handing over half our first month's rent, I figure I have just enough money left over for food for about three more weeks. Mother always went over the household budget with me, insisting that was a skill I'd need when I became a housewife in several years. I've been running through the numbers ever since we got off the bus and now I'm nervous. I should have thought this through better before I agreed to her plan.

We're sharing a house with four others, each of the three bedrooms accommodating two people. John and Maggie live in the largest room, with their own tiny bathroom containing only a toilet and sink, so they have to share the main bathroom when they want to bathe. Paul and Paulette (I laughed when I heard their names) are next door to us and we can hear their bed thumping against our common wall at all hours of the night. All of them seem a lot older than Sylvia and me – twenty or twenty-one, at least. Our room barely has room for two twin beds and a small dresser, and the closet is about two feet wide. I keep my cold-weather clothes in a duffle bag I picked up at the thrift store, hang my two second-hand dresses and a blouse that tends to wrinkle in the closet and stuff everything else in a single drawer of the dresser. Sylvia starts out doing something similar, but after our first week, her clothes are pretty much wherever she happens to drop them, including on my bed. She doesn't seem to mind – or even notice – that I always toss them back onto her bed.

Paulette seems to be the only one with a job, or at least with any kind of regular schedule. She dresses in dark slacks and a white blouse and heads off to work in a department store downtown three days a week. For the second time since we arrived last weekend, while Paulette's gone, John has taken off in his beat-up Chevy Nova and returned with a large brown grocery bag under his arm. He calls out to Maggie and Paul, and the three of them disappear into his room, closing the door behind them. They don't ask me to join them. Curious, I decide to ask Sylvia about this when she returns. She didn't sleep in her bed last night, but none of the others seem troubled about her whereabouts.

"She sometimes works nights," Paulette said when I expressed my concerns this morning as she was getting ready to leave for work. Nobody else was up yet, even though it was after 9:00.

"She didn't tell me she found a job," I said, irritated that my roommate wouldn't share important information like that with me, especially since that's all I've been focusing on every day since we arrived – finding work.

I couldn't read her expression, but her hesitation in answering and slight raising of her eyebrows made me nervous. "It's kind of a...freelance thing. She takes on a one-time job now and then, you know, whenever something comes along."

Puzzling over her answer, I was about to ask her to be more specific, but she made a hasty exit, claiming she had to get to work a little earlier today because of a training meeting.

With the house quiet, I decide to make some calls before any of the others finally decide to drag themselves out of bed. I set the only phone in the house on the kitchen table in front of me and work through the ads I circled in this morning's paper. Jotting notes when I don't get an outright rejection on the phone, I make a map for myself of the businesses I need to visit for a person-to-person interview. Earlier in the week, I learned that I need to lie about my age to even get people to agree to meet me. I've also become adept at talking around their questions about my experience.

I make just three appointments out of the eighteen ads I've circled. They're all within three miles of each other and I have over an hour between each visit, so I'll walk and save the bus fare. I've already covered the fast food places and convenience stores around the first one, a tire shop that needs someone to answer phones, but I plan to stop into any business I pass if I think there's a possibility they might be hiring.

After walking the six blocks to the tire store, I stand tall before entering. There are two young men in identical overalls behind a counter. One heads through a door into the garage and the other looks up at me, his eyebrows drawn.

"I'm Katharine Gibb," I tell him. "I'm here about the job."

Now his eyebrows shoot up. "Seriously?" he says, but he raises a finger ("one minute") and follows his co-worker through the door. Over the screeching *whirr* of a tool in the garage, I can hear him shout, "Hey, Boss. There's a girl here wants to talk to you."

Soon, an older man, wearing the same style of overalls, but with "Bill" embroidered above a chest pocket, emerges and walks toward me. I introduce myself again.

"How old you say you are, again?"

I had told him on the phone that I was eighteen. I stick to my claim.

"You sure don't look it."

I've got this lie down pat. "I know I look young. I get that all the time."

"Uh huh. So," he says, wiping his hands down his thighs, "you got any experience answering phones?"

"Yes. I answered phone calls in an office and took messages." I leave off the details. It was at our church and I helped out on three different occasions when the regular secretary was at lunch and the lady who usually covered for her wasn't available. I was thirteen at the time.

"What do you know about tires? Know about radial versus bias? All-seasons versus snow tires?"

I'm trying not to look like he's speaking a foreign language, but I don't think I'm succeeding.

"Katharine," he says with a sigh, "suppose you tell me something you do know about tires."

I freeze. All that pops into my head are stupid things like *they're round. They're made of rubber* (I think). "They have tread, and they're filled with air," I offer, anticipating his eye roll before he even has a chance to do it.

Red-faced, I leave and continue my search. The rest of my stops are not as humiliating, but the end result is the same. *Thanks for coming in, but we're looking for someone with more experience.* Or, in the case of places that might need a busser or dishwasher, *Sorry, we're not hiring right now.*

When I walk into our room, foot sore and discouraged, I'm surprised to find Sylvia dozing in her bed. "Sorry," I say, "I didn't realize you were here."

She rolls over, yawning. "What time is it?'"

"Quarter past four." I sit down hard on my bed and pry off my shoes.

"In the morning?" Her voice is hoarse and words are slurred with sleep.

"No. Afternoon." I think about asking her where she's been, but I don't want to start acting like Mother who quizzed me about every place I went and every friend I visited. I refuse to ever be like her.

Sniffing repeatedly, my roommate rolls out of bed. Literally. She lands on the floor with a thud, moaning once but then collapsing with laughter. I catch a whiff of something I can't identify wafting from her clothes – slightly sweet, but not in a flowery sense. I realize she's dressed in a low-cut blouse and remarkably short skirt, which has ridden up around her hips. I've never seen this outfit before.

"Are you okay?" I ask, my voice harsher than I intended.

She giggles and uses the bed to help her get to her feet. "I'm better than okay. I'm fantastic!" At this point, she seems to notice how she's dressed for the first time, and starts undressing, oblivious about the door to our room standing wide open.

I shove the door closed as she strips totally naked and begins pulling out clean underwear from the dresser. Embarrassed, I turning my back to her. "I heard you were working. You didn't say anything about getting a job. What are you doing?"

She laughs, slipping out the door in a bathrobe and carrying a wad of clothes. "Loosen up, K. Don't be such a stick in the mud!"

I'm still fretting over her strange behavior when Paulette arrives home from work. Of our four new housemates, she's the only one who seems willing to talk to me beyond saying hello. After she changes out of her work clothes, she enters the kitchen where I'm chopping up vegetables to add to a soup stock.

"Any luck today?" she asks, nibbling on a slice of celery.

"None. I guess I'm going to have to keep hitting up the fast food places and restaurants and hope somebody's hiring. Everyone else turns me down flat since I don't have any experience." I scoop up handfuls of vegetables and plunge them into the large pot. "How am I supposed to get any experience if no one will hire me until I do? That doesn't make sense."

"Yeah, I know. I just got lucky with my job. A friend's sister knew about an opening and got me an application the day before they started advertising in the paper. Well, speaking of work, I've got to go figure out what to do about the zipper on my slacks. It jammed today and I had to pin it together and wear my blouse untucked all afternoon. My boss was *not* happy. That's the only pair I've got that's good enough for work and I hate spending the money on new pants. They never fit me right – I always have to shorten them at least five or six inches. And I hate sewing."

Paulette is barely over five feet tall and while she's not fat by any means, she has wide hips. I'm not surprised she has trouble finding clothes that fit.

"Can I take a look at the zipper? Maybe I can fix it or put in a new one for you." Mother started teaching me to sew when I was five. Although I don't have a sewing machine to use right now, it won't take me very long to replace a zipper. Or hem a pair of slacks.

"Seriously? That would be incredible if you could do that. I'll get them..." she says, dashing to her room.

I meet her with my sewing kit in hand. After replacing the zipper pull, it's functional but I'm thinking it'll jam again before long. "I'll pick up a new zipper tomorrow and have it ready for you before you go back to work on Wednesday."

By the time I replaced her zipper, word had spread throughout our house that I knew my way around a needle and thread, and John, Maggie, and Paul began talking to me more. They also brought me jeans to patch, buttons to sew on, torn seams to repair.

"You *like* doing this stuff?" Maggie asks with a look of astonishment on her face. "I absolutely hated the one sewing class I was forced to take. I used to have nightmares about mean old Mrs. Bartlett chasing me around the room with a giant pair of *shears* – never call them *scissors* in front of that witch or she'll bite your head off!"

I shrug and smile modestly. "I enjoy sewing. I find it relaxing. Knitting, too. I've even done some tatting and quilting, but I'd really like to try weaving."

John, who is sprawled out on a stuffed chair that's lost much of its stuffing, chuckles. "Hey, kid. Maybe you could take up hooking, like Sylvia." Maggie snorts in appreciation of his comment but Paulette shoots him an angry glare.

I don't get the joke, but with Paulette's reaction, I keep my question to myself. What's funny about weaving hooks? Ever since I moved in with these people, I've felt like they share a secret language that I'm not allowed to learn. Frankly, other than Paulette, I find all of them to be a bit strange. Secret meetings in John and Maggie's room, grocery bags spirited in and out of the house. Sylvia is off somewhere and I have no idea if she'll be home tonight. Plus, I suppose I've just been lucky not to come down with a cold and runny nose like most of them have.

All except Paulette return their attention to the

television where some sitcom I've never watched is playing. John uses the remote to crank up the volume. Canned laughter fills the room as she motions to me to follow her into the kitchen where we can talk.

"I've got a great idea. Since you're so good at sewing and all that, what about applying for a job at a department store in notions?"

"What the hell does that mean, babe? Notions? Like – I've got a *notion* that it's gonna rain tomorrow?" I didn't hear Paul follow us into the room, but here he is, pulling open the refrigerator door and studying its contents.

"Sewing stuff. Like buttons and snaps and sometimes fabric. Depending on the store," she tells him. He grunts in response, pulling a jar of pickles from the fridge, but still contemplating the selection. Turning back to me, she continues. "We don't have notions where I work, but some of the bigger stores do."

"I hadn't thought of that," I say, remembering the times I accompanied Mother to the big city to shop the large department stores and specialty stores that carried so much more of everything than the shops in Markerton. We hadn't stopped in notions, since our local sewing store carried all the essentials, but I had noticed that department listed on the store directory. "Notions. I won't have to sound like such an idiot if they ask me questions about the merchandise." I nod, feeling a hint of optimism. "That's a great idea. Thanks!"

I have a good feeling about this.

# CHAPTER 13 - ROBIN

It wasn't easy convincing Doris to let me go over to Lupe's house on Saturdays, but she eventually called Mrs. Baez ("Like the singer?" she asked) and grilled her about how careful she'd be about watching over us. "I hope you know what you're getting into," I heard my grandmother tell her on the phone. "Robin can be quite a handful, putting it mildly." Apparently Lupe's mother quelled her doubts by relating a few stories about raising her own four kids – Lupe being the youngest – because I was allowed to go visit that same weekend. Mrs. Baez had to come pick me up, however, despite our homes being just four blocks apart.

What Doris doesn't realize is that Lupe's older sister, Sylvia, sometimes takes us on outings. Although Sylvia just got her driver's license, she's not allowed to drive us without one of her parents in the car, so the three of us catch a bus and head downtown or to one of the malls in the surrounding suburbs to shop or go to the movies.

I love riding the bus again, like I used to do before our mother left. I pay close attention to everything Sylvia does – the cost of the tickets, asking for special passes from the driver called "transfers" if we need to switch from one bus to another, and especially how to read the schedules and maps of all the different bus lines. Every time we take a different route, I collect the schedule for that bus number, carefully tucking away my expanding selection in with my school supplies when I return home.

We're taking a familiar route today to the shopping mall closest to our neighborhood. A plan is forming in my mind, but I need more information.

"I guess you can go almost anywhere on a bus," I muse, addressing my comment to Sylvia who is sitting in the seat in front of the one I share with Lupe.

She turns her head. "Pretty much, as long as you can walk a little bit, too. Is there somewhere you think you want to go?"

Remaining nonchalant, I say, "Nowhere in particular. I was just wondering. Like, could you take a bus to Boulder?"

After she explains about the local and regional bus systems, I ask, "What about going farther away? Like Indianapolis or...San Diego?"

Patiently, she offers more details about traveling cross-country – exactly the information I was looking for. Not wanting her to focus too much on why I've been asking, I change the subject, asking her expert, teenage advice on whether I should grow out my bangs or wear my hair shorter. Not that Doris will let me have anything to say about what I do with my hair, but Sylvia doesn't know that.

In the mall I find myself watching for my mother. Not that it makes any sense that she'd be shopping in a Denver suburb a thousand miles from where I last saw her, but she could be anywhere, so it's possible, right? I spot a woman walking away from us with dark hair and a plump figure and I wonder, is *that her*? If I run over and confront her, what will she say? But the woman turns her head and she's nobody

I know, so I look away and watch for another thirty-ish lady with dark hair, just in case.

When I'm deposited back at my grandparents' house at the end of a day spent with Lupe, whether at her house or on one of our outings with her sister, Doris always greets me with the same questions. "Did you cause Mrs. Baez any trouble? I'm not going to hear from her about something you've done, am I?"

Muttering "no" and "no" to each inquiry, I hurry to my room, my refuge and my prison. Saturdays are my days of freedom. Mrs. Baez is satisfied when Lupe tells her we're going to the nearby park to play, giving us a deadline for when to return, but never questioning where we actually go. Usually, we go where we say we're going, but sometimes I convince Lupe to accompany me by sneaking into the backyard with the trampoline. We boldly walk up to the front door and ring the bell to determine if anyone is home. If the lady who lives there answers, I tell her we're taking orders for Girl Scout cookies (neither of us belongs to Girl Scouts, but this woman can't know that, can she?). Or we ask her to sign a petition about adding more equipment to the local playground. I carry a tablet of paper and a pen so these ploys won't seem suspicious, but I think she's starting to catch on.

I continue to beg Clay and Doris to let me talk to Annie on the phone, or to start writing letters to her again. Doris shuts me down with a blunt, "Absolutely not. Stop asking," so I retreat to my room or go huddle under the willow in the front yard, shivering and miserable. With its leaves gone, the winter version of my magical hiding place is more like a giant cage with hundreds of naked branches hanging in a circle around me, offering little of the privacy I relish during the summer. I try wrapping my arms in the branches, like Annie used to do in the few weeks she lived here with me, but the dry twigs break off and the few remaining dead leaves crumble to dust.

I'd mail letters to my sister without Doris's knowledge if I could, but all I remember of Aunt Sophie's address is that she lives in San Diego on a street name starting with "M". Returning home from school one afternoon, I seize an opportunity. Clay is out in his workshop, repairing a snow blower, and I can hear Doris muttering in her sewing room. I peek in and watch her rip out stitches, growling in frustration, and I scurry to the kitchen where she left her purse.

I've stolen money from her before – always in small amounts and never more often than once a month – but this time my target is a little address book I've seen her look at when making a phone call. I'm certain she used it last Sunday to call Aunt Sophie. It was a rare occurrence, her calling her daughter – usually it's Sophie calling here, and generally it's Clay who takes the call, Doris turning the phone over to him as soon as she recognizes her daughter's voice. I was furious that she wouldn't give me the phone and she was furious that I was asking again. The moment she hung up, I was marched to my room and locked in for the rest of the afternoon.

I snatch the address book and shove it into the waistband of my pants before walking nonchalantly to my room. The coast remains clear, Doris's vocal irritation with her sewing project still audible. Thumbing through the book, I locate Aunt Sophie's name and swiftly write her phone number and address on a piece of paper which I tuck inside a notebook. Luck is with me as I smuggle the book back to the kitchen and tuck it into her purse. I hold back from stealing a few dollars, instead returning to my room to curl up with my latest novel from the library.

\*\*\*

"I don't know," Lupe says, her eyebrows knitted. "My parents will figure it out and I'll get in trouble."

"No you won't. If they say something, you can tell them it was all my idea and you had nothing to do with it. That's the truth. If they're mad about the cost, tell them I'll pay for it."

She's still pondering this, so I forge ahead and dial the number, my pounding heart betraying the calm image I'm trying to display.

"Hello?"

Okay. This is what I've been rehearsing for weeks, ever since I decided to find out her number.

I make my voice higher and more childish, imitating the way my little sister talks, or at least the best I can still remember of it. "Is Annie there?" I squeak. I thought of just being myself, saying, "Hello, may I please speak to Annie?" but I didn't think I'd have a chance if I went that route.

"Who is this?" Aunt Sophie asks. Do I hear a note of suspicion, or is it just my fear that's making her sound that way?

"Susie. She's in my class." Keep it as short as possible. Surely there's a kid named Susie in Annie's kindergarten class. There's always a girl named Susie.

I clutch the phone tightly, waiting for her to say something. Is she fetching my sister? I swallow hard, thrilled at the possibility that my ploy is working.

"This is Robin, isn't it. Are you calling from home? There's no way my mother would have caved in on this. She's not there, is she. Is my Dad even around or are you just hoping not to get caught?"

There's no doubt in her voice. I keep opening my mouth

to try to deny who I am, but I know it's not going to help. Maybe a different approach?

"I'm sorry, Aunt Sophie. Please don't be mad. I really, really need to talk to Annie. She's my sister and I love her and I miss her so much and I know she misses me and..." I had promised myself I wouldn't cry, but there's no holding back my tears as I choke out my pleas.

"Robin, listen to me. I know this is hard for you to understand, but it's better that you not contact Annie."

"Better? How can it be better?" I wail.

"It's better for her. She's finally settling in here, making friends at school, feeling like she has a home. Hearing from you is just going to confuse her."

"But—"

"She's young. It's not too late for her. That's why we knew we had to get her away from everything in her old environment, including you, Robin. Grandpa Clay and Grandma Doris are doing their best to undo the total lack of direction your mother gave you kids, the neglect, the things you must have witnessed..." She sighs.

My mouth has stopped working.

"I know my brother should have done more after the divorce, but what's past is past. She's starting to warm up to him now that he visits regularly, so that's a positive sign."

Dad has been visiting them? I feel like someone has reached inside my chest and is crushing my heart in their fist.

"Don't call again, Robin. If you really love your sister and want the best for her, stay out of her life. Maybe in a few years..." she paused. "Don't call. Don't write. There's still hope for her – don't take that away from her."

I don't wait for her to say anything else, not even goodbye. I hang up the phone gently, as if any sudden movement might destroy it and everything else around me. I look down at my body, half expecting to see it broken into fragments.

"Robin? Are you okay?"

It takes me a moment to pull myself back into this room. I'm in Lupe's house. Lupe is staring at me – have I changed into something else, someone else?

Sophie says it's too late for me. Am I poison, destroying everything I touch? Is that why my mother ran away – was it because of me? Was I poisoning my sister? Why have all the people I love abandoned me?

I dash out of her house, covering my ears so I don't have to listen to Lupe calling after me. I don't want to damage her, too. The moment I arrive home, I run to my room. I was sure they'd let me stay if I showed up in San Diego to see Annie, but nobody wants me.

I snatch up every bus schedule I've collected, and rip them up, flinging the pieces into the trash can in my room. When they're all destroyed, I carry the trash out to my refuge under the willow, dumping the contents on the ground. Using the book of matches I swiped weeks ago from Doris's purse, I set the heap on fire.

That was stupid. The ground is covered with dead leaves from last fall and fire begins spreading across the area hidden by the long strands of branches. I stomp furiously, kicking dirt and racing around the growing circle of smoke and flames. It's hard to tell the smoke from the dust raised by my wild dance, but I finally realize that the fire has stopped spreading and I scurry to grab the hose so I can water down the area to make sure my tree doesn't get damaged.

Of course, Doris is furious when she sees what I've done to my tennis shoes.

"You are grounded, young lady. No library visits for the next three weeks. No getting together with your little friend. You'll stay in the house. What did you do to the soles of your shoes? And what were you thinking, thrashing around in the mud like that? Are you stupid?"

I don't care about being grounded. I can't face Lupe. I don't want to see anybody.

# CHAPTER 14 - KATHARINE

"A double date?"

Sylvia grins and tilts her chair back so far I'm sure she's going to topple over any second. "Roger's got this friend – real good-looking guy. Kinda shy, but real sweet. C'mon, K. It'll be fun."

I've only been on one date since I started my job at Pellmans Department Store. I thought we were having a good time – he snuck a flask of Schnapps into the movie theater and we drank it with our popcorn. When he drove us to an empty parking lot and kissed me, I liked it at first, but it became clear that he expected me to go all the way that night – on our very first date! I thought we ended the evening with an understanding that I just wasn't ready to move that fast and he was okay with that, but I never heard from him again.

"So, it's really a blind date, but you and Andy will be there, too."

She laughs. "Double date, blind date – whatever you want to call it. They'll take us out to dinner and we'll go see that movie that opens this weekend. You said you wanted to see it, and this way the guys will pay instead of us."

Since she started going out with Andy, she's been coming home by midnight, except for a couple of nights a week when I know she's out on a date with him. It's been months since she's shown up home mid-day wearing the same revealing clothes she wore to go out the night before.

Paulette told me she thinks Sylvia isn't hooking any more, and I finally figured out what that means. I've also learned why several of my housemates have perpetual runny, and sometimes bloody noses. Paul demonstrated how he arranges the white powder on a mirror laid on the kitchen table, but I declined his invitation to try it out. Too scary. Paulette did convince me to take in a lungful of marijuana, but I choked and coughed for ten minutes and never felt anything. I haven't tried it again.

"This is just a regular date, right? Not like when you were..." I can't find a word that doesn't sound awful.

She laughs and slaps me on the back. "A lady of the evening? A tart? When I was selling favors? Doing the dirty deed?"

I feel my face go hot, and know I must be beet red. She's enjoying my embarrassment. I turn to leave the room, but she grabs my arm and holds me back. "C'mon, K. I'm just messing around. Don't be like that." Her smile grows wide as she ducks her head and positions it in front of my lowered eyes. "C'mon. You can take a little joke, can't you?"

Reluctantly, I raise my head and nod slightly.

"So, Friday night. You and me and Andy and Otis. You'll like him – I just know it. Say yes."

"Otis?" She wants me to go out with a guy whose name sounds like an elevator?

"Is that a yes? He's sweet, I'm telling you."

With a sigh, I give in. I always give in to Sylvia when she insists on something.

***

It's a bit awkward when the four of us arrive back at the house after our double date. Sylvia and Andy obviously plan to spend the night at his place, so they sit in the car waiting as Otis walks me to the door. "I really enjoyed tonight, Katharine," he says, his voice soft and warm. He glances up at the glare of the bare light bulb by the front door and takes me by the hand, leading me to the shadowy end of the porch.

"Me, too," I respond. He seems pleasant enough, even though he didn't say all that much during dinner. Of course, with Andy telling his animated stories and jokes and Sylvia interjecting witty barbs, neither of us had much opportunity to do a lot of talking.

"I'd like to see you again. Maybe next Friday we can try this again? Just the two of us?"

He asks so gently that I'm intrigued. He's profoundly different from Steve, who gave off such an air of confidence that it seemed impossible to say no to anything he suggested. Steve was like a magnet – from the moment we met, I was drawn to him so strongly that it seemed that nothing could pull us apart. It's not like that with Otis, at least not yet. He's nice-looking, sweet (as Sylvia said), and likeable, but I don't feel much of anything when I look into his eyes. But I'm willing to give it a little more time.

"I'd like that. Thank you for dinner and the movie tonight. I'll see you next week."

He leans forward and kisses me lightly on the lips. It's nothing like the devouring kisses I once shared with Steve, but it leaves me feeling just a bit light-headed. As I step inside, I replay his tender kiss in my mind, wanting to remember exactly what I felt.

**99**

Maybe I need to be with someone as different from Steve as possible. I smile as I prepare for bed, imagining more of those gentle kisses when I see Otis next weekend.

***

"It's a bad idea, man. We don't need to be drawing any more attention to this place."

John storms out of his room, Paul on his heels. "You know what your problem is? You don't think big. We could be doing double, triple the business if we bring these guys in." Paul gestures with his hands, spreading them wider and wider to illustrate his point.

"Bigger isn't always better. We're staying under the radar now, but we start dealing with more people, how do we know they're as careful as we are? And having them come pick up product here? You gotta be kidding."

"Listen to me. All we gotta do is—"

Noticing me standing in the doorway to my room, John holds up his hand and Paul stops in the middle of his sentence. John turns to me. "Hey, kid. Uh...hope we didn't disturb you. We'll quiet down."

Paul adds, "Yeah. Sorry. We were just heading out. See ya."

Both men step outside where I can still hear them whispering to each other, their words undecipherable but the mood clearly tense.

When I first came here, I had no idea what was going on in this house. I suppose I lived a sheltered life back in Arkansas under the heavy thumbs of Father and Mother, and I suppose I was pretty naïve. I've figured out a lot since leaving home. I'm not one hundred percent sure of what kinds of drugs they're dealing, but it's not hard to figure out that marijuana and cocaine are almost certainly being sold. I hope there's nothing more, since I'm not aware of other drugs that my housemates use themselves, but I don't know that for a fact.

Nobody seems to suspect that I know what's going on. Even Paulette, who smokes pot now and then but doesn't seem to be interested in the coke, talks to me in careful terms, never actually speaking about the drugs.

"Katharine," she said one time when Maggie and John ducked past me into their bedroom carrying what I assume was a large sack of drugs, "this might not be the best environment for you."

Or, another time, "How did you and Sylvia get to be friends? You seem to come from such different backgrounds." That comment came after my roommate stumbled into the house in the middle of the afternoon, high as a kite, her skin-tight blouse buttoned unevenly, not even bothering to tug down her short skirt so it totally covered her ass. Paulette and I helped her undress and tucked her in bed.

I keep my nose out of everyone's business and they've stopped inviting me to partake of the drugs. When I get home from work, I pop open a beer and unwind, sometimes hanging out with Paulette. Often, I spend part of the evening taking care of whatever sewing tasks I've managed to pick up that week. Between my job in the notions department and my freelance work as a seamstress, I'm starting to put away some savings. In another two months, I hope to finish paying off the sewing machine I picked up at the rent-to-own store. I consider Paulette's comments and what sounds like a possible escalation of the drug sales coming out of this house and begin scanning the newspaper for other places to rent.

"How about dinner at my place?" Otis asks. "I'm a pretty good chef, even if I do say so myself."

I twist a strand of hair, considering his offer. This will be our third date – well, fourth if you count that first blind, double-date when we hardly had a chance to talk to each other. Our conversations have been congenial, sticking to safe, easy topics like favorite movies or places we'd like to visit. I haven't revealed anything about my past and know little about him that goes beyond casual conversation. We've discovered a common love of beer, which he buys for us whenever we go out. Last week, he produced a container of rum and coke, which I thought was even better than beer.

I've discovered that he's a great kisser, though, and we've even taken things a bit beyond kissing. I can just imagine what Mother would be saying right now, as I consider spending an evening with my boyfriend alone in his place.

"Your place?" I echo, uncertain about his motives as well as my own. Is he expecting me to sleep with him? Do I want to? I pace, clutching the phone tightly.

He seems to read my mind. "Katharine, I promise I don't have any expectations. This is just dinner. I'd love to cook up something special and enjoy a relaxing evening with you. What do you say?"

"All right. That sounds good. Can I bring anything?"

"Just your beautiful smile. I'll provide the wine. Pick you up around 7:00?"

Hanging up the phone, I lie down on my bed and close my eyes, remembering the warm rush through my body when we last kissed, the thrill of his hand on my breast. It's still not the tear-off-our-clothes raw passion I felt with Steve, but my body most definitely responds to his touch. It's been a year since I've slept with a man and I've missed it. I only wish I felt something stronger about Otis than simply liking him. I want more. I want to be in love again.

Then again, look how that worked out for me.

I focus on finishing the alterations to a jacket I've promised to complete by Thursday, putting thoughts of our next date on hold.

\*\*\*

Otis seems so intensely proud of himself about the spaghetti dinner he prepared, I compliment him lavishly. The noodles were overcooked and I'm sure the sauce came from a jar, but I focus on the thought that he went to the trouble to do something special for me. He insists on clearing the table without assistance, and we retire to his living room with another glass of red wine.

Like his cooking, the décor of his place is not remarkable. Beige sofa, slightly rickety coffee table, and a well-used recliner in dark brown sit on worn carpet, also beige. A clunky television sits directly in front of the couch, and the wall decorations consist of inexpensive posters of famous works of art– Starry Night (which I love) and that weird one with the melting watches.

"Do you like to dance?" he asks, crossing the room to put on some music. Something slow and melodic, but I've never heard it before.

"I don't really know how to dance." Father thought dancing was sinful. He would no more have allowed me to attend a dance at school than to let me perform in a strip joint. I wouldn't be surprised if the only music he and Mother ever listened to were the hymns the choir sang at our church.

Pulling me up from the couch by both hands, Otis leads me into the open area of the room, pulls me close, and places my hands in the correct positions. He clasps my hand in his and wraps his other arm around my waist. We rock slowly in time to the music and he begins to lead me with subtle pressure and movements. After I step on his toes for the third time, we both kick off our shoes and try again.

"That's it. You're getting the hang of it now," he murmurs in my ear, now holding me so close I can feel him growing hard against my hip.

The song ends but we keep rocking. He lets go of my hand and wraps both arms around me, and I follow his lead. We kiss, tongues exploring, and he lowers his hands to my ass, pulling me tightly against him and thrusting his hips into mine.

I'm excited, but still unsure about where I want this evening to go. I pull away slightly and he lets me, shifting his hands to hold my face gently as we stand and kiss again, softly, sensuously.

"Katharine, I want you so much," he whispers, his kisses tracing a path down the side of my neck. I feel his hand go to the top button of my blouse, and in a moment he is reaching inside, fingers brushing the top of my breast just inside my bra. His other hand snakes up the back of my shirt and deftly releases my bra. We've done this before, and I sigh with pleasure, anticipating his next move to caress my breasts as he did on our last date.

I'm shocked when he grabs my blouse with both hands and rips it open, the remaining buttons shooting off like heated popcorn. Things are moving much faster than I expected and I've never seen him like this.

"Otis, wait. Slow down…"

But he isn't listening. He lifts me in his arms like they do in the movies and carries me into the bedroom, depositing me on his bed.

"Please, Otis. I'm not sure I'm ready to—"

He's shoving up my skirt now, grabbing at my panties.

"Don't give me that. You know you want this."

I try to wriggle away from him, but he's too strong. "Stop it! Stop, Otis!" My own voice sounds like a little girl's to me. I can't believe sweet, quiet Otis is doing this.

My struggles are in vain. As he lies on top of me, forcing himself into me, all I hear is a tiny voice saying again and again, "No. Please stop."

When it's over, he rolls off me, flings an arm across my chest, and snuggles close to my side, kissing me softly on my shoulder. I turn my head away, but not before seeing the sweet expression on his face.

"That was wonderful, Katharine," he whispers gently, as if we were tender lovers.

A tear rolls down my face.

"Oh, now, don't be like that. My God, it's not like you're a *virgin*. You knew exactly what we'd be doing tonight." He rolls away and gets out of bed. "If you're going to be that way, then maybe you'd better go home and pull yourself together. Come on. Get dressed. I'll drive you."

Despite my protests, he insists on lending me a sweater to wear instead of my ruined blouse. I feel too empty to argue any more, so I let him drive me home. Although I jump out of his car before he can come around to open the passenger door, he follows me up onto the porch, standing much too close as I fumble to open the front door. He manages to kiss me on the cheek before I can escape inside.

"Good night, Katharine. Sweet dreams, my sweet."

I head straight for my room, thankful that nobody else seems to be up. I can't face questions about how my date went. My luck holds – Sylvia isn't here either. I dump Otis's sweater in the trash, strip, wrap myself in my robe, and scurry into the bathroom. I stay in the shower until the water turns cold, but I still feel soiled.

Weeks later, I cry in relief when my period arrives right on time.

# CHAPTER 15 - ROBIN

Mrs. Ridgway gives me her sternest look. Some kids burst into tears when they're sent to the principal's office, but I spend so much time here it doesn't bother me one bit. At her worst, Mrs. Ridgway is easier to take than Doris on a good day.

"Robin, we've been through this. You know that kind of behavior just isn't acceptable."

I realize she can probably see my hand as I pinch the side of my thigh through my cotton pants. I can get away with it in my classroom, since Miss Erikson can't see what I'm doing under my desk. If they catch me, they'll send me to the school nurse again and she'll freak out at the array of black-and-blue marks on my upper legs. So I stop.

"Nate was trying to cheat off me. He grabbed my papers," I say, crossing my arms over my chest.

"That's not what Miss Erikson explained in her note. You were doodling again, weren't you?"

I stare her down, remaining silent.

"Robin, you can't be tearing up school books and damaging property that belongs to others. You need to find ways to deal with anger other than destroying things or pushing people or vandalizing property."

I know she's right. The school counselor, Miss Anderson, and I have talked several times about ways to interrupt my reactions and take time to consider consequences. I've tried. I really want to do better – I do.

"I'm sorry. I won't do it again."

She sighs. "Robin, I know this transition has been hard for you. Miss Anderson has suggested a special program for you this summer and we've talked it over with your grandparents, who have agreed to give it a try. It's called Expanding Horizons and you'll be attending three days per week. It's a bit like a day camp, with lots of interesting activities like going hiking in the mountains, horseback riding, and swimming; learning skills like carpentry and cooking; field trips to see how computers are put together or how dairy farms use machines to milk the cows – a wide range of things. Expanding Horizons is for kids who might benefit from getting away from the usual school environment and gaining self-confidence by experiencing new challenges."

Oh. So it's a camp for misfits. I keep my mouth shut. I've been dreading the end of the school year. It's hard to imagine dealing with being under Doris's thumb all day, every day. If this gets me away from her, it's got to be better than the alternative. I manage a bright smile. "That sounds like a great program, Mrs. Ridgway."

***

"Happy birthday, dear Robin, happy birthday to you!"

I'm beaming as Erica, my group's lead counselor at Expanding Horizons, presents me with a cupcake with a candle stuck in the middle. "There isn't room for eleven candles, so that's the one for good luck," she says. I blow it out, wishing what I wish for every day – to be reunited with Annie. Of course, there are plenty of other wishes that are the stuff of my daydreams. Like seeing Dad in person – not just talking on the phone once every month or so and getting a card from him in the mail – and having him invite me to come live with him. Or the one where my mother shows up, thrilled to see me (and Annie, because she's got to be in the picture for these daydreams to work) and telling me about how she was kidnapped and escaped at last, or that she was actually a U.S. spy who had to go off on a secret mission to Russia, or that she was in an accident and had amnesia but finally remembered who she was, and how she'd missed us so much and would be such a great mother to us from now on. Even though that's hard to imagine.

The other five girls on my "team" join me in snarfing down the cupcakes, except for Yolanda, of course, who pretends to eat while inventing ways of discarding bits and pieces in ways she thinks nobody notices. I've never seen her actually eat anything but a few bites of apple or a generous helping of celery sticks – but not if they're stuffed with peanut butter or cream cheese. Erika and her assistant, junior counselor Jeannie, pour cups of lemonade for everyone before handing a trash bag to Francine to take care of clean-up.

"Okay, girls. Back in the van. We're going bowling this afternoon!" Jeannie always tries to make every activity sound equally thrilling, but bowling sounds pretty stupid to me. Then again, I'd rather spend the afternoon launching a heavy ball toward some pins than be pinned up in the house. I grin at my clever play on words. You know, if I imagine those pins as being Doris and Clay, I might really get into bowling.

We bowl two games and I score thirty-two and fifty-one.

Yolanda, who has to use the lightest-weight ball in the place, since she weighs about as much as a toddler, manages to score zero on her first game. No kidding – twenty alley balls in a row. I would have scored higher than I did if I hadn't sent my ball careening into the next lane several times. Jeannie told me I was throwing it much too hard, and I wouldn't be allowed to bowl a second game if I didn't cool it. I thought I wasn't throwing it nearly hard enough, but maybe it's impossible to get the pins to smash into pieces, no matter how hard I try.

Francine solves a mystery for me when she tells me her mother only let her into this program because she didn't have to pay for it – somebody else pays. A guy named Grant, she says. Her parents are divorced, like mine. When I tell her I live with my grandparents, she asks why I'm not with my mom.

"She's dead," I answer. "And my Dad travels for work all the time." One true thing, one possible lie, but who knows? Maybe she really is dead. She abandoned us and I wonder if we both ended up in hell.

"Sorry," Francine says, but the more often I tell people my mother is dead, the easier it becomes to think of her that way.

\*\*\*

I squeal with the joy of being out here and almost scare myself with the sound. My cheeks ache. Can your smiling muscles get weak if you haven't used them in a long time?

Panting hard, I spin in a slow circle, taking in the scenery around me. This is the second time our team has taken a trip up to the mountains, and it's even better this time than before. I'm standing in a grove of aspens, their pale green, heart-shaped leaves fluttering in the light breeze. Surrounding them are the darker greens of pines and firs. If I lean back and look straight up at the sky, the intense blue seems like something a child might paint, not a color that can be real.

When I first started coming to Expanding Horizons, I thought Erika was going to be another adult with too many stupid rules. She's actually pretty okay, though. The first time we came out hiking and I ran ahead of the others, she took me aside and explained why our team needs to stick together sometimes. Explained. No yelling, no telling me I'm a terrible, stupid kid, no locking me away from everyone.

This time, she told me I could run ahead just as far as the trail junction sign that's in front of me now. Here I am, alone for just a few minutes until they catch up, but it feels like I've left everything bad behind me. All I want to do is take it all in – the rich smell of the dirt, the chirping birds, the sparkling light from the creek running beside the trail, the tiny blue flowers, perfectly named, that hang from their plants like tiny bells, the flowers of white and yellow and red and orange – everything! Even the air that I suck into my lungs as I catch my breath feels clean and crisp and unlike the air anywhere else.

"Good job, Robin," Erika says as she and the rest of the group arrive. "Girls," she says, louder now, "always remember to do what Robin did. If you are ahead and come to a trail junction or to a spot where the trail isn't obvious, stop and wait for everyone."

I beam, my cheek muscles getting as great a workout as my legs today.

*** 

Not every Horizons day is filled with a fun activity. Today we're supposed to be drawing pictures of our families. I contemplate depicting Doris and Clay, but surely I'll be kicked out of this program if I show them being hit by a train or hacked with an ax.

I could draw my mother with Annie and me, but since I've told anyone who's asked that my mother is dead, that could be awkward. And Annie's gone, so even the thought of showing the two of us together makes me feel like tearing the drawing pad into pieces.

In the end, I just draw a picture of myself.

"Robin," Erika says when she sees my art, "what about the rest of your family?"

I can't look at her. "I am my family. There's nobody else."

*** 

Three days a week I escape to be with my team. Thursdays are library day, the only thing in my world that Doris and I seem to agree on. She takes me there before lunch and I always check out the maximum number of books allowed. I read almost anything – biographies, teen romance, travelogues, science fiction, classics (but not *Oliver Swift*), flower and tree guides, mysteries, mythology, history. In a surprise move that nearly left me speechless, Doris even bought me a dictionary – a thick, hardbound dictionary – for my very own. At the end of the school year, Miss Erikson called my grandparents in for a conference – Clay didn't go – and told us that I was reading two to three years ahead of my grade, and to be sure to continue reading over the summer. As Doris drove me home, she was unusually silent, but when she turned off the engine, before I could open the door, she turned to me and said, "Don't let this go to your head."

I nodded and looked at my lap.

"We'll go to the library weekly, but only if you behave. No smarting off, no running away. Do you understand me?"

"Yes, ma'am."

So, Thursdays can be great days. Thursday nights, though, can be awful.

I've learned Clay's pattern now. He has a drink before dinner most nights, but doesn't seem to get drunk and nasty except on some Thursdays. That's when he goes to his "club" for "happy hour," a term I find confusing since it sometimes stretches well into the evening. When it does, I make myself scarce. Doris likes to start eating supper at 6:30. Thursdays, she'll push that back to 7:00 or maybe even 7:15. If Clay hasn't shown up by then, she sets aside a plate for him and the two of us eat in silence. Sometimes I think she feels the same dread that I do.

Those are the nights he often comes home drunk. If he seems fairly sober, Doris asks, "Good game tonight?"

He pops open a beer and sighs contentedly after taking a swig. Doris brings him his plate of food and he tells her how much he won, about the hand where he filled an inside straight, or when he bluffed his way to win a large pot with only a pair of nines.

But when he has a losing night, he stomps into the house and heads for the cabinet where they keep the booze. Doris sets his food on the table without a word and retreats to her sewing room unless he stops her with a demand for more ice or criticism of the dinner.

"What the hell do you do around here all day? Can't I get

a decent meal? Is that too much to ask?"

"Sorry," she'll mutter, scurrying around and trying to fix whatever he's upset about. Meanwhile, I do whatever I can to make myself invisible, staying in my room even if my bladder feels like it's about to burst. Anything to keep him from noticing me.

Sometimes that isn't enough. If he's given her an especially hard time, she takes it out on me later. "Don't you see how frustrated Grandpa Clay gets with all the grief you give us? It's no wonder your mother couldn't handle you and your father doesn't want you. If it weren't for us taking you in, you'd be in an institution – you realize that, don't you, or are you too stupid to understand?"

Those times I really have done something wrong in her eyes are the most dangerous because she'll tell Clay about my dropping a glass while washing dishes, or she'll reenact a conversation we had when she didn't like my tone of voice. That's when he'll often take a swing at me.

That leaves Tuesdays, Saturdays, and Sundays. They aren't wonderful days like when I'm at Expanding Horizons, and they aren't unpredictable days like Thursdays. They're just days when I read my books and try to understand why I'm here. Not just here at my grandparents' house, but why I'm here in this world. Why my mother left and my father is like a stranger and my sister was taken away from me and why Lupe moved away this summer and why I'm sure I'll never get to see any of the people from Expanding Horizons once the summer ends.

I dream about the day when I'll be old enough to leave this house. I dream about the people and stories I read, wondering if I'll ever get married and have children and live in a pretty house and live happily ever after. Or does that only happen in books?

# CHAPTER 16 - KATHARINE

"He's looking at you again, Katharine," Julie Ann whispers. Last Thursday she invited me to join her for lunch at a burger place down the street, so this week I figured I should ask her to eat with me at my regular spot. I don't know her well at all, but she's always friendly enough when we see each other in the break room at the store.

I quickly finish chewing the bite of sandwich and swallow before glancing his way. He grins when he sees me looking. I offer the slightest of smiles back and turn back to my lunch.

"How long have you two been checking each other out?" she asks.

"Oh, I don't know," I say, trying not to smile too much since I'm pretty sure he's still watching me. "A while. This seems to be his usual lunch stop during his delivery route." I don't mention that I used to only come here for lunch about once a month, but it's now become my regular spot on Thursdays. Ever since I noticed that his Coca-Cola delivery truck seems to always be parked out back on Thursdays at lunch time.

"I do love a man in uniform," Julie Ann says, grinning. "So, when are you going to stop flirting across the room and go talk to the man?"

I've thought about it, but every time I decide that today's the day, I remember what happened with my so-called fiancé, Steve, or that ugly incident with Otis, and I wonder if it's worth ever getting involved with a man again. I feel my mood darken, remembering how Sylvia just shrugged off my story of what Otis did that night. "That's just how life works, Katharine. Men spend money on you and they expect something in return. What's the big deal? You should have asked him for an expensive present to make it up to you."

As opposed to refusing to see him again or take his calls, which is how I handled it. Panicked for the next seventeen days, I cried with relief when my period arrived exactly on time.

"Hey, I didn't mean to upset you," Julie Ann says, and I realize my face has been reflecting my dark thoughts.

I force myself to relax. "Oh, no – it wasn't that at all. Sorry. My mind was on something else." I look up to see if my mystery delivery man noticed my sour expression, but he's gone.

Next time I'll go say hello, I promise myself.

***

I'm in my own little world inside my head, just walking from the bus stop to the house as I do almost every work day, when I glance down the block and freeze. Red and blue lights flash ahead and they appear to be coming from directly in front of the house where I live. Immediately, I cross to the opposite side of the street to get a better angle on what I'm seeing.

I only have to advance another twenty paces before my

worst fears are confirmed. There are two police cars parked at our house. I see one man in uniform standing at the foot of the front steps, but don't see any other cops. What's happened? Are the others inside? Are my housemates home?

I spin around and walk swiftly away from the house, afraid to even turn my head again to see if anything is happening. It's the drugs. It's got to be.

I hurry to a nearby park and find a bench. What should I do? Are they arresting John and the others? Searching the house? What about Paulette – she's not really involved with the drug dealing, but then again, she knows about it. So do I. But Paulette's over twenty-one and I'm only seventeen, so can they do something to me?

Unable to remain still, I get up and pace to the end of the small park and back again. If they arrest me, will they show my photo on the news? Could my parents possibly see that?

This thought frightens me even more than simply being arrested. I've got to stay under the radar. I can't let them find out where I am.

I continue like this, alternating my pacing and just sitting on the bench, until it grows dark. The options for spending the night in this park aren't great – there are no suitable trees where I can huddle, unseen, the way I did back in Oklahoma City that first night. I need to figure out what's happened back home.

I approach the house cautiously, observing that there are no lights on in the windows and the front porch light is off. After searching for any signs of life and convincing myself that nobody is parked along the street staking out the house, I creep up the stairs and listen by the front door. Nothing. I try the knob – unlocked. Feeling like the stupid teenagers in the horror movies who go ahead and walk into the haunted house, I go ahead and walk into *our* house.

The living room is always a mess, but I've never seen it like this. Afraid to turn on any lights, I make my way through the obstacle course of sofa cushions and overturned lamps, grateful for the streetlight just across the way providing enough illumination for me to manage. New buds are just starting to emerge on the naked tree branches, and the shadows on the wall make me feel like the trees are forming a cage around me. Reaching the bedroom I share with Sylvia, I find more of the same disarray. The mattresses have been shoved off the bed frames, drawers are lying on the floor, their contents strewn around the room.

I pull up the blinds to let in as much light from outside as possible. This needs to be quick – I have no idea if the police will be back tonight or not. Locating my old sewing bag – the one I used to carry all my belongings when I eloped with Steve – I shove some random articles of clothing inside. I'll just have to leave the rest, but I don't care. Except, I have one possession now that I'd hate to part with. With only a couple of payments left on my portable sewing machine, and its crucial role in helping me earn money, I'm willing to lug it along with me. I snap it into its carrying case and head out the door, wondering how many times I'm going to have to run away and start over.

I do know a bit more this time around. By midnight, I'm checked in to a shelter and sitting on a cot in a room filled with the sounds of people sleeping. Tomorrow morning, I'll tote all my belongings to work, where I hope I can fit my sewing machine in my locker and figure out a place to live by the time my shift ends.

I feel lucky. I have a job, a little bit of money saved, and a sewing machine. Starting over at seventeen isn't going to be as hard as it was at sixteen.

# CHAPTER 17 - ROBIN

It's hard to believe a year has gone by since I last saw my mother. Clay and Doris show no signs of being aware of the anniversary, which is a relief. I can just imagine Doris reciting one of her standard speeches. "You don't appreciate how lucky you are that we took you in. Nobody else would put up with all your stupid crap for five minutes. You must have inherited your brains from your mother – why else would you be so stupid?"

*Stupid, stupid, stupid.* That's her favorite word to describe me. Clay leans toward *feral, savage,* and most recently, *incorrigible.* "You think you're such a smart ass with all your books and big, fat dictionary, so you must know what incorrigible means. You're beyond hope."

Although it doesn't happen as often now, I still find myself wondering why she disappeared. Nobody seemed terribly interested in looking for her, including the police, probably because she packed a suitcase. I'll bet Dad and probably my grandparents know something they're keeping from me. Maybe they know exactly where she went and why. I don't have any theories on *where*, but as for *why*, that's pretty obvious. She didn't want to be a mom any more.

The summer's almost over which means Expanding

Horizons will be ending in just a week and I'll be heading back to school. The good news is that we're having a sort of "graduation" weekend – three whole days of activities up in the mountains with campouts and everything! Erika says there'll be some special challenges for each of us, but she wouldn't explain what that really meant. I can hardly wait for Friday!

***

Erika and Jeannie demonstrate how to set up a tent, then collapse it, pair us off, and watch as we assemble the three matching tents. I'm pretty sure they've put each of us with the one person from the team we like the least. Maybe that's the special challenge Erika said we'd be facing. I'll be sharing with Francine who must not have been paying attention (as usual), since she keeps trying to pull the tent poles through the tent sleeves instead of pushing them, which causes the sections to separate and the poles to try to fold up. I reach over to snatch it from her hands, ready to try to break the offending section over my knee, like we did to the twigs and branches for our camp fire, but I stop myself in time. *Count to ten*, I remind myself before Erika has to tell me again to think about consequences before I act.

I close my eyes and count, imagining a ruined pole and a tent that can't be erected. I picture Francine and me crawling into a mangled mess of a shelter and trying to sleep there for two nights.

"Francine," I say, "how about I put in the poles and you pound in the stakes?"

"That's good by me," she says. "Those poles must be defective – the pieces keep falling apart."

Five minutes later, we're tossing our sleeping bags inside and crawling in after them to check out our home for the next two nights.

We emerge when we hear Jeannie call out, "Good job, girls. Now, everybody gather 'round." The opening in the woods is now filled with three identical green tents for our team members, plus a tent in shades of blue, and a yellow tent that Erika and Jeannie must each be using.

"Remember when I told you there will be some special challenges this weekend?" Erika asks. "You just completed one of them, and we're proud of how all of you did. I saw some good teamwork. One team decided to do each part of the task together and the other two split up tasks using the strengths of each person. Yolanda, I know camping out really isn't your 'thing' and I'm proud of you for getting in there and sharing the work with Nan. Francine and Robin, good job in finding a way to overcome frustration and stick with the task. Marla and Jenny, that was great to see you both willing to compromise a little to achieve a common goal."

I'm impressed. Nan is a total tom-boy who's made it clear she thinks Yolanda is a wimp. Marla and Jenny both want to be in charge all the time, and have had their share of screaming matches and even come to blows twice, early in the program.

Erika announces, "Back pats all around." As we've done many times this summer, we form a huddle and pat the backs of the girls on each side of us. I grin, remembering how resistant I was when she first introduced us to the idea. Now it's one of my favorite moments – I crave the warmth of the touch of people who care about me.

Erika steps back from our tight circle and we drop our arms. "Okay, everyone gather up your backpacks and lunch bags and let's hit the trail. We gave one team member her own personal challenge a week ago. We asked Yolanda to plan our lunch menu for today. I don't want anyone peeking inside your bag until we stop at noon, got that? Lunch will be a surprise."

Francine and I exchange wide-eyed looks. Although Yolanda isn't quite as super-skinny as she was at the start of the summer, she now moves away from the group and turns her back to us when we're eating. Jeannie tells us not to talk to her about food and to let her eat by herself if she needs to. So, I'm not sure if she's moved beyond meals of celery sticks and water. I hope we're not all starving by dinnertime.

As soon as everyone is ready, Erika taps me on the shoulder. "You'll be our rear sweep until we stop for lunch."

I suppress a moan. She knows my favorite thing is when I get to run ahead of the group and wait at a trail junction or other obvious landmark for them to catch up. As rear sweep, I'll have to be behind everyone, especially our slowest hiker, skinny Yolanda. If she stops to rest (which she always does), I have to stay with her.

Everyone starts out at about the same speed, but it's only a matter of minutes before Yolanda and I are trailing behind. As I stroll slowly behind her, I fiddle with the whistle Jeannie gave me to wear around my neck. I stick it in my mouth and blow softly with every breath, trying to test its range of sound effects without being loud enough to be heard by one of our counselors.

"Do you have to do that?" Yolanda says, stopping so suddenly that I bump into her. "And don't follow so close. You're making me nervous."

"Sorry." Everything makes her nervous. Still, I let the whistle drop to my chest and gesture to her to continue walking while I stand and let her move ahead. Then I realize that I can still hike pretty much by myself if I just walk in super slow-motion and stop whenever she comes into view.

It's not so bad. I have plenty of time to pick up colorful rocks and examine them or kneel down to smell the wildflowers. Look up and watch an invisible jet draw white contrails that contour across the blue sky. Stop and search for the source of a rhythmic pounding high in the trees and respond, "Who's there?" when I spot a woodpecker knock-knocking on a trunk.

Glancing up the trail, I realize that Yolanda has stopped and is watching for me to catch up.

"Need a break?" I ask.

She shakes her head. "Which way do we go?"

"What the hell?" We've reached a trail junction and nobody's in sight. What about our rule about always waiting for the whole group if there's a split in the trail? I survey both paths, looking for clues about the correct choice and feeling angrier by the moment at our counselors and team members for going on without us.

Yolanda is staring at me, a frightened look in her eyes. "What are we going to do? I don't remember Erika saying anything about another trail." She's blinking rapidly and I'm afraid she may have a melt-down any moment.

"It's okay. Just let me think a sec." I can't see very far along either fork and both seem equally worn. There's an old post holding what may have once been a sign describing the two choices, but it's so worn and weathered that there's nothing left to read on it.

Watching Yolanda sink to the ground and pull her knees to her chest, I know I need to do something soon.

"Everything's going to be fine, Yolanda. You stay here and I'm going to run up this trail a little ways and look for the team. Stay put, okay?"

Now she's wailing. She doesn't cry loudly like some kids do, but the undulating sound is like a mixture of whining and high-pitched squealing. I want to cover my ears, but know from experience that it does no good.

"Don't leave me!"

The urge to just take off running as fast as I can to get away from her is almost overwhelming, but I can hear Erika's voice in my head. *Count to ten.*

We've talked about this. As much as it feels like the exact opposite of what I long to do, I remember our discussions about what to do if we're lost or just separated from our group: stay put.

I run through the mental count a second time before taking off my pack, setting it on the ground, and sitting down beside her. "Yolanda, listen. We'll stay right here. I'll blow the whistle and even if they don't hear it right away, they're going to realize we're not catching up and they'll come back for us. We'll be okay. Really."

When I wrap an arm around her shoulders, I remember how I used to comfort Annie when she was upset. Yolanda is a year older than me, but in some ways she seems like a little kid. Her horrible noises stop and she leans her head against my shoulder.

"Thanks, Robin," she whispers.

Once she's calmed down, I stand and try the whistle. She cringes at the shrill noise, but I'm happy it's so loud. The sooner someone comes for us, the better. I don't know how long I can keep Yolanda calm.

I hear twigs breaking and rustling in the bushes nearby. Something is coming toward us and it's big. I blow on the whistle again with everything I've got, hoping to scare it away, but the noises are getting closer and louder.

I hear a grunting sound as a larger branch cracks. I snatch up a pair of small rocks near my feet, hoping they'll be enough to discourage whatever is coming our way.

"Girls, it's me," a familiar voice calls out as Jeannie emerges from the vegetation. "Good job, Robin."

I stare at her with my mouth gaping open. "What—?"

She sticks two fingers in the corners of her mouth and lets out a pattern of notes that rival the volume of the plastic whistle dangling from my neck. Moments later, I hear voices and laughter as the entire team dashes down the right-hand trail toward us.

"Robin," Jeannie says as the group arrives at the junction, "you have successfully completed your personal challenge. Congratulations!"

"I'm so proud of you," Erika says quietly, kissing me on top of my head as she wraps me in a hug. I cling to her, wanting this happy moment to last. This is what it must have felt like for Annie when I used to hug her tight.

Jeannie turns her attention to Yolanda, somehow coaxing a smile from her. She offers up a bandana from her pack, which Yolanda uses to dry the tears from her cheeks and blow her nose.

"Okay, girls, just another five minutes up the trail and we'll break for lunch."

Oh boy. Celery sticks, here we come.

When I retrieve my lunch sack from my pack and reach inside, I'm surprised to find a turkey sandwich with lettuce and avocado on what turns out to be the most yummy bread I think I've ever tasted. There's a small, crunchy apple to go with it, plus a tiny piece of chocolate. *Dark* chocolate, which I've never tried before, but love after one taste. No celery sticks.

Yolanda sits away from the rest of us, but closer than I've ever seen her before. Everyone makes a point of gushing about the food selection and I notice her sitting up straighter and even glancing our way. When I finish eating, I scrunch up my sack with the apple core inside and slip it back into my backpack. I can't tell for sure, but Yolanda's lunch bag looks pretty small when she puts it away. I think she ate at least half of her food.

The weekend goes by much too quickly. As they have all summer, Erika and Jeannie challenge us with learning new skills and trying things we've never done before – spending the night in a tent and then, the second night, sleeping out in the open where the stars fill the sky like a million glowing crystals of ice and a shooting star streaks through the black sky, disappearing so quickly that I wonder if it was really there or if my eyes are playing tricks on me.

Along with my team members, I gather twigs and branches from the forest floor and build a camp fire. I learn how to cook a dinner by wrapping meat and vegetables in aluminum foil and nestling my bundle among the brightly glowing embers. We roast marshmallows on long, green sticks and I get my first taste of S'Mores. We hike through the woods, not following any trail, and learn to match landmarks with the squiggly contour lines on a map and how to use a compass.

I hate to climb back into the van after we hike out to the trailhead. During the ride down from the mountains, we start off singing the camping songs we've learned this summer, but the closer we get to Denver, the fewer voices join in. We spend the final half hour in silence, each girl lost in her own thoughts.

When the van stops in front of my house, Erika and Jeannie both step out to say goodbye.

"It's been great having you on the team," Jeannie says as she pulls my small duffle from the back. She gives me a quick hug before she closes the double doors.

Erika holds me by the shoulders at arms length, smiling warmly. "Robin, never forget that you are a very special girl. You're smart and creative and strong. It has been a joy to have you on my team." She opens her arms to me and I fall into her, holding on as if she were a lifeline, my only hope to keep from drowning.

"You're late."

I hug Erika as hard as I can for just a moment longer before stepping back. I begin my count to ten before turning to look at Doris, who is standing on the front porch, hands on hips, perpetual scowl on her face.

"Stay strong, Robin. I have faith in you," Erika whispers before waving toward the house. "Traffic was heavier than we expected," she says, taking several steps in Doris's direction. "Your granddaughter has done so well this summer. You should be proud of her."

"Hmmf," she grunts before turning her back and walking back inside.

I pick up my duffle and shuffle toward the front porch, turning around after every few steps to wave goodbye until the van rolls down the street and out of sight.

Now I just need to make it through one whole week at home before I can escape five days at a time at school.

# CHAPTER 18 - KATHARINE

"Mind if I join you?" I stand over my mystery delivery man, lunch tray in hand, and offer him my warmest smile.

The café is busy but not packed. There are several empty tables where I could have sat and eaten lunch alone. His eyes flick quickly around the room, verifying that fact while I hold my breath. Too bold?

His mouth curves up in a slow smile. "Please do," he says, getting to his feet and reaching out to pull back a chair for me. Very nice.

"You got the BLT, too," he says, picking up the second half of his sandwich and raising it like he's making a toast. "My favorite."

"Mine, too." Now that I'm sitting here, I feel tongue-tied. I imitate his gesture with my own sandwich and take a bite, buying time to come up with a topic of conversation. Why didn't I think about this longer beforehand?

"I'm Roy," he says, "Roy Milstead."

"Uh...Katharine Gibb." He offers a hand so I drop my sandwich on my plate and shake it. We both laugh at the awkwardness of the moment.

"Sorry to act so nervous," he says. "I just can't believe

that the beautiful girl I've been admiring across the room for all this time has sat down at my table to share lunch. I'm so glad to actually meet you, Katharine."

Blushing, I say, "Me, too. I hate to eat my BLT alone. Maybe we can make this a habit." I don't mention that I've sometimes come here with Julie Ann, my co-worker and, for the short term anyway, my new roommate.

His brown eyes seem to sparkle as he looks into mine. "Asking me for a second date already, eh? Do I look that easy to you?" He winks and his smile brings out a sexy dimple on his right cheek.

"You better believe it," I answer, grinning and blushing.

"My answer is yes. So, I guess we'd better get to know each other a bit. Do you work around here?"

"Just down the street at Pellmans. How about you?"

I almost hit myself in the face with my palm for asking such a dumb question, but Roy just chuckles. "Sure...about a ten mile radius of stores around here. That's my day, driving in circles delivering beverages. Different route each day of the week, but then it starts all over again the next week. Pretty boring, really, but in a few more weeks I should have my CDL, and then the options open up big time."

"What's a CDL?"

He shrugs. "Sorry – Commercial Drivers License. Once I get that, I can start driving a big rig. Haul freight across the state or across the country. I'm buying my own tractor, so I can contract with businesses that need freight moved from point A to point B. And B to C and C to D. I'll have the flexibility to travel all over, not just keep driving soda pop in circles around Denver." His face lights up when he talks about his plans.

"That sounds exciting."

"You think so? Wow. Most people I tell about my plans say it sounds terrible, driving thousands of miles every month, living in the cab of a truck, eating at truck stops."

"I've always wanted to travel, to see the countryside, visit cities like New York and Boston and Miami and Dallas and Los Angeles. If you don't have strong ties to a place, why not hit the road and see what's out there?"

"Maybe you should become a trucker, Katharine. You just might have the heart for it."

I glance up at the clock on the diner wall. "Oh, oh. I've got to get back. I wish I could stay and talk."

"Well, we do have a date for BLTs here next Thursday, right? But I'd like to see you again sooner than that. Do you have any plans for Saturday?"

I can't believe how this is working out. "Not yet. Do you have something in mind?"

"I'm thinking, since we both seem to like lunch, how about a picnic at City Park? We could also visit the zoo, or just walk around the lake."

"That sounds perfect. Shall I make us some sandwiches?"

He raises his eyebrows in an exaggerated look of shock. "Absolutely not! What kind of jerk asks you out for lunch and then expects you to make it?" He shakes his head and tuts. "I'm thinking BLTs."

Giggling, I say, "BLTs it is."

I pull a note from my purse so I can copy it to give Roy my new address and phone number. "I haven't memorized it yet. I just moved."

Again, he rises when I do. "Thanks for making my lunch break so great, Katharine. I'll see you Saturday at eleven."

He smiles and I can't take my eyes off that dimple.

# CHAPTER 19 - ROBIN

I like the idea of being in sixth grade, the oldest students in our grade school. All the younger kids look up to us. Out on the playground, I show off to a cluster of fourth-grade girls, demonstrating fancy jump rope moves that I learned this past summer. They clamor for pointers on how to master the routine.

"Hey, Robin. You gonna hang out with those little kids or come with me?"

Billie's new to North Elementary this year and she's what my mother used to call a *free spirit*. Just like me. Her mom died in a car wreck when she was eight. Some drunk ran a red light and slammed into her car, killing her instantly. When she first asked me about my family, I told her my mother was dead, too. Kidnapped from our apartment by some lunatic who later murdered her. Billie seemed impressed.

"You've got this," I say to the younger girls and stroll toward the far corner of the playground with Billie. We've got "looking casual" down to a science. As soon as we determine that the teacher watching over recess has his back turned, we scurry to the opening in the fence and duck behind a parked car. After another quick peek to see if we've been detected, we hightail it across the street and down the block to where she stashed her bike this morning. Balancing on the handlebars, I give her the thumbs up to start pedaling.

Our destination is a back door to the local movie theater. Billie discovered that it's propped open most afternoons by a chubby guy with greasy hair who works there, cleaning up the spilled popcorn and empty cups between shows. He takes a lot of smoke breaks and leaves a small trash can in the door so he doesn't get locked out.

It's easy to watch for him from behind a dumpster in the alley. We count out thirty seconds after we see him go back inside before scampering to the door and stepping inside. Billie knows the way to get through the backstage hallways and into one of the multiplex's auditoriums. We emerge near the front row of seats, and slump into two of them so nobody can see our heads above the backs.

We've missed at least the first half hour of the show and it's a war movie, which I don't like, but that's not the point. We're out of school, watching a movie for free.

"Count to ten." Erika's lesson pops into my head, even though this seems totally unrelated to what she called my "fight or flight, impulsive behavior." The longer we sit here, the more I worry about what our teacher, Mr. Jeffries, will say about our sudden absence when we show up in class tomorrow. And what about Clay and Doris? Won't they hear about this?

I nudge Billie with my elbow. "We need to go back."

"No way! We just got here," she says, continuing to watch the screen.

"Seriously, Billie. We're going to get in so much trouble."

She shrugs. "Who cares? So we go have a talk with Mrs. Ridgway. Big deal. So they call my dad and your grandma.

Nobody's going to do anything to a couple of kids who've lost their mothers. Don't you know that?"

Realizing that she's determined to stay, it dawns on me that I've still got a chance to avoid the avalanche of anger and punishment by my grandparents. I'm not due back in Mr. Jeffries's classroom for another twenty-five minutes – I'm normally in music class right after recess.

"I'm going back, but you've got to write me a note from the nurse," I tell her, fumbling in my pants pocket for the small notebook I carry there. I have part of a story I've been writing on the first several pages, but I skip back to a blank sheet and rip it out. All I have to write with is a stubby pencil, which isn't going to look good. "Wait here," I say, and race up the outside aisle to the top of the auditorium and out into the hallway.

I march up to the man behind the refreshment counter. "May I borrow a pen?" I ask, as if there is nothing odd about a kid showing up in the middle of a show during a school day asking for a pen.

"Uh, yeah. I guess." He locates a pen by the cash register and hands it over.

"Thanks. I'll bring it right back," I say, smiling politely before I rush back inside the theater and down to the front row.

"What the hell are you doing?" Billie hisses.

"Write a note saying I missed choir because my throat felt sore and sign it, Nancy Mortenson." Billie is very good at forging her dad's signature and has been practicing Doris's in case I need it.

"I don't know what her signature looks like."

"That's okay. Just write it so it doesn't look like mine. I'll have to take my chances."

She writes the note but keeps it in her lap. "I don't know why you're doing this. It's *stupid*."

Stupid, stupid, stupid. I clench my teeth, snatch the note and pen from her hands, and start counting to ten in my head even while I run to the back of the auditorium and slam through the doors. I manage to calm down enough by the time the guy behind the counter can see me.

"Thanks," I say, setting the pen near the cash register. I race out the front doors and run all the way back to school. I hear the bell ring just as I reach the outside doors, but the clock tells me it's to signal the end of a class, so I'm in time. I take a moment to catch my breath, run my fingers through my hair and re-tuck my blouse, and walk calmly into the choir room.

I walk right up to Mrs. Lieberman, the choir director, and hand her the fake note. "I wasn't feeling good, but Miss Mortenson gave me something warm to drink and says it's okay for me to return to class."

She glances at it quickly, nodding. "Do you feel better now, Robin?"

"A bit." I don't want her realizing I ditched choir. She might be on the lookout in the future.

"Well, I hope you're all better soon." She glances at the clock. "Hurry along, now, or you'll be late for your next class." She smiles and pats me on the shoulder, so I smile back and head to Mr. Jeffries's classroom.

After school, I retreat to the weeping willow tree in the front yard. Many of its leaves have turned yellow, but it is still resplendent and sheltering. Instead of starting with my homework as I do most afternoons, I pull out my little notebook and stubby pencil to write more of the story I've been working on.

It's the story of a wizard – a female wizard – with magical powers that only work when she wears a cape made of willow leaves. With it on, she is able to think about a particular person, chant the magic words, and then she can see them as clearly as if they were standing right in front of her, even if they are really a thousand miles away. One day, a girl comes to the wizard and asks her to think about the girl's mother.

"Can you see my mother now?" the girl asks.

The wizard spins slowly in a circle, her cape flowing out behind her. She says the magic words, "Abra cadabra cadare, I can see you anywhere."

"Yes," she tells the girl. "I see your mother."

"Where is she? What is she doing?" the girl asks.

The wizard shakes her head. "She is very, very far away. Even she does not know the name of the place. She is trying to come home, but doesn't know the way."

The girl starts to cry. "Wizard, can't you help her find her way?"

Again, the wizard shakes her head. "No. I'm sorry, but my powers can not help her."

I chew on my lower lip, re-reading what I've written. "That's stupid," I say aloud. "Stupid, stupid, stupid!"

I rip the pages from the notebook and tear them in half, throw them on the ground and grind them into the dirt under my heel.

As I stomp in angry circles around the tree trunk, I count to ten. Three times.

I know what I have to do. I don't have my maps and schedules anymore, but I remember enough to get started. Peeking out from the safety of my refuge under the weeping willow, I decide the coast is clear. I race to my room and retrieve my stash of money rolled inside a pair of socks – mostly funds I've stolen from Doris's purse over the past year. I add another blouse over the one I'm already wearing, plus a sweater, stuff a clean pair of underwear into my pants pocket and slip back outside. I don't think she heard me and Clay is out in his shed, as usual.

I gallop the two blocks to the nearest city bus stop and slip behind a nearby trash can sitting by the curb. My confidence grows as I mount the stairs to the bus, pay the fare, and ask for a transfer stub. I remember the route!

After changing busses, I sit directly behind the driver so he can help me make sure I get off at the right stop. Feeling triumphant, I march into the Greyhound station and try to tamp down my excitement while standing in the ticket line.

"I'd like one ticket to San Diego," I say, standing on my tiptoes so I can see better over the counter.

A woman with glasses perched on the end of her nose looks down at me and scrunches just one side of her mouth, like she's not supposed to frown at customers but can't help but do it halfway. "One of your parents has to be here to buy your ticket. If you can get them here right now, I'll help you. Otherwise, you'll have to go to the back of the line."

My parents? "My dad is driving around looking for a parking place. He said I'll miss my bus if I don't hurry and get my ticket and that I shouldn't wait for him."

She sighs. "All right, we can get started. Has he filled out a form for unaccompanied minors? He'll have to do that before you can board."

Rats. That's like what we had on the plane trip. "I'm not sure. Can you give me the form so he can fill it out as soon as he comes in?"

Now both sides of her mouth are scrunched up. "What's

your destination?"

"San Diego," I say with confidence. "I'm going home to my mom and sister."

"The next bus to San Diego doesn't leave until 9:40 this evening." She purses her lips and stares straight into my eyes. "Your father didn't bring you here, did he," she says with certainty in her voice.

"Sure he did. I guess he misread the schedule. I'll go find him," I say, backing away and bumping right into the woman in line behind me. I spin away and sashay toward the door, trying to look as calm as can be, but moments after I step outside, a man in some sort of uniform takes hold of my arm and walks me back inside to a small office.

"I think we got ourselves another runaway," he says to the woman sitting behind the desk.

I protest, explaining that my father is parking the car even as we speak, then insisting that they let me go look for him before he gets worried when I'm not in the main lobby. It does no good.

"Oh, geez," a familiar voice says and I slink lower in the chair they've assigned to me for the past hour or more. "Yes, that's her."

Clay doesn't yell at me in front of the people at the bus depot. He takes my hand firmly and leads me to the car, where Doris sits in the passenger seat, sucking on a cigarette like she's trying to inhale the whole thing. I'm deposited in the back seat. As Clay walks around to get in, I grab the door handle, thinking I can escape and come up with a new plan, but the door won't open.

"Child locks," Doris says without even turning around. "Because we knew you'd be stupid enough to try to take off again."

"Goddamn wild animal," Clay mutters as he starts the engine. "Gonna have to lock her in her room again."

Doris snuffs out her cigarette in the ashtray and turns to look at me. "What the hell are we going to do with you, girl?" She huffs, like a threatening bear. "For starts, you are grounded. For a month. You will not set foot outside the house except for going to school, and I'm going to escort you to your classroom in the mornings and back to the car in the afternoons."

Ugh. Kids are going to give me so much grief.

Clay eyes me in the mirror. "If you weren't a girl, I'd beat the living crap out of you."

I barely stop myself before answering him with *you already do hit me, even though I'm a girl.* My father never went into a lot of detail, but I know the beatings he got from this man were far worse than the painful slaps that I've endured so far. I've even managed to dodge him a couple of times, when he was even more drunk than usual. I'm sure I don't want to find out what he can do sober.

# CHAPTER 20 - KATHARINE

Roy seems so different from the other guys. Not that I've had a lot of experience with dating – Mother and Father only let me go to church dances where it seemed like there were more chaperones than kids. My surreptitious late-night excursions resulted in being kissed by one boy before I hooked up with Steve. Of course, he and I did a lot more than kiss, but now that I think back on it, about all we did on our dates was have a drink or two, dance to "sinful" music, and make out. Did we ever really talk to each other?

Roy and I both love BLT sandwiches and walks in the park. He's a movie buff, but I've hardly ever seen anything that wasn't G-rated. I read books, novels mostly, but he's game to check out some of my favorite titles. He loves heading up to the mountains on his day off and I'm anxious to check that out. We both enjoy playing checkers and hearts but not chess or bridge. He thinks the best President ever was FDR. I'd put Abraham Lincoln at the top of my list. He's not close to his parents and has a younger sister. I've told him I ran away from home, but not the real reason why. He's twenty-three. I told him I'm nineteen rather than seventeen, since that's what my fake IDs claim. I haven't told him my real name.

"Penny for your thoughts," Roy says, "or a nickel or a dime. Do I hear twenty cents?"

I squeeze his hand and smile. "I was just thinking how much I enjoy this. Just walking and talking about whatever pops into my head."

"And holding hands," he adds. "Don't leave that part out."

I turn to face him and take his other hand. "Especially holding hands."

He leans closer and we kiss softly. Chills run down my body. "And kissing," I murmur, "and other stuff." Roy holds me closer and I can feel that he's as excited as I am, but we're standing in a public park and there are people around. Taking things any further will have to wait.

He gives me another quick kiss before stepping away. Again I'm struck with the differences between him and the other men I've been involved with. He doesn't push me to move our intimacy along any faster than I'm ready for. Last week, in his car, things were turning quite steamy, but when his hand began to slide up my thigh, I must have tensed up. He sensed it and removed his hand while we still kissed. He didn't try again.

We resume our walk. We've gone out to dinner twice and to the movies once, but my favorite dates are like this one, where we also get to take a long stroll together.

"What are your dreams, Katharine? If you could go anywhere in the world and do anything you want, where would you go and what would you do?"

I don't think anyone has ever asked me that before. "I want to go...everywhere. All over the U.S. and Europe and Asia and Africa and Australia and...everywhere!"

He laughs. "And what do you want to do? Besides

travel?"

That's a tough one. "Do you mean for work? Well, sometimes I dream about designing clothing, but if I'm being realistic, that's probably more of a hobby than something I might want as a career. I'm good with numbers, like budgeting and balancing a checkbook, so I think I'd like to get into bookkeeping."

"That's the one part of becoming a commercial driver that I dread – keeping all the records and books. I'm terrible at that sort of thing. I'll probably have to hire someone to help me if I'm planning on going independent."

We walk on in silence for a few minutes.

"Maybe I could—" "Maybe you could—" we say in unison, then laugh.

"Go ahead," he says, grinning.

"No, you go."

This time he turns and holds me by the waist. I wrap my hands around his neck, as if we're about to dance to a slow, romantic song. "I was going to say that maybe you could help me out with my paperwork and bookkeeping. Maybe we could..." He stops speaking and our eyes meet.

"We could...?" I prompt.

He lets go and takes a step backward, clearing his throat. "Katharine, even though we've only known each other for three months—"

"Three months and five days," I say, my hands clasped in front of me to stop them from fidgeting. Is he going to say what I think he's saying?

"Three months and five days," he echoes and licks his lips nervously. "Despite that, I feel like we've known each other for much longer. We fit together, you know? I'm in love with you, Katharine."

Oh my God. He is going there. I nod and barely squeak out the words, "I love you, too, Roy." There. I've wanted to say it for weeks, but I was afraid of scaring him away.

He drops to one knee and I feel faint. "Katharine Gibb, will you marry me?"

***

By some miracle, my phony papers suffice when Roy and I go to get our marriage license. My old housemate, John, had a friend who had a friend who turns out to be pretty damn good at making up fake IDs and birth certificates. It's a good thing I didn't need anything else, since I have no idea how to get in touch with John since the raid on our house.

We opt for a simple, civil ceremony at the courthouse early on a Monday morning. Two total strangers sign as our witnesses and I change my name again, officially this time, to Katharine Sue Milstead. The department store let me rearrange my schedule so I don't have to be back on the job until Saturday, and Roy used one week of his vacation time so we can enjoy a quick honeymoon.

"My buddy and his wife rent this cabin for a week every summer," Roy says as we load a box of food in his car with our clothes. "We're lucky to get it for this week – the aspens should be at their prime. Wait until you see the mountainsides filled with brilliant gold and deep green. There's nothing more beautiful – except for you."

I scoot as close to him as I can in the front seat and we hold hands as he drives out of the city and we begin the ascent into the mountains. They look so different up close than they do from town. I twist and turn, trying to see every rock outcropping, every colorful stand of trees – towering walls of granite and sparkling streams running through the valley below.

"It's gorgeous!" I say, pecking him on the cheek.

He chuckles. "We're barely into the foothills. Wait until we get to the real mountains."

He's right. As the highway continues to climb, we can see ranges of peaks, those in the distance taking on shades of dark blue in contrast with the green hues of wild grasses, evergreens, and deciduous trees still holding their summer color. The aspens glow as if with their own light source, their golden color almost too brilliant to gaze at, like looking directly into the sun.

Roy steers onto a side road which soon turns to gravel and we bounce along the washboard bumps for a ways until he locates an even less groomed road and turns onto it. "Almost there, sweetheart," he says, slowing the car to a crawl to navigate around protruding rocks and dirt potholes.

Finally, I spot the cabin nestled in a small, cleared area in the forest. It's like something out of a storybook – broad logs separated by white mortar, a wide front porch with a hanging swing chair, and a carved bear with a "welcome" sign hanging around its neck.

"It's perfect," I say, my voice barely a whisper.

Inside, the quaint décor sets the perfect tone for a romantic getaway. The bed looms large with its log-style headboard and thick comforter decorated with moose roaming through the woods. There's a bear-claw bathtub and bear-inspired towels in the bathroom and the living area holds a matching leather sofa and recliner with a bear rug. I kneel to feel the fur and imagine lying naked in front of a roaring log fire, snuggled in Roy's arms. Even the little kitchen matches the mood, with rustic wooden cabinets, pine-green and white checkered curtains and matching towels.

After we unpack our small suitcases and put away the food we've brought, we step onto the porch hand-in-hand.

"Mrs. Milstead," he says, his warm brown eyes sparkling, "I have another proposal for you."

I giggle, still getting used to my new name. "And what would that be, Mr. Milstead?"

Suddenly he seems shy, his eyes lowered for a moment. "I want to make love to you."

It hits me like a brick – does my husband think I'm a virgin? I never told him about getting pregnant by Steve – only that I had a boyfriend when I was sixteen. I didn't even mention dating Otis, much less the horrible night when he forced himself on me. Roy believes I'm almost twenty, which is what my fake papers all say. I was planning on telling him the truth, but this all happened so fast. What was I thinking?

"Sweetheart, are you okay?" he asks, his expression full of concern.

"Oh – yes, sorry. I guess I was just overwhelmed with realizing that this day has really arrived." I smile sweetly and caress his cheek. "I want to make love to you, too, honey."

We take our time, Roy lingering over each button on my shirt, kissing my skin as he exposes a fraction more. I close my eyes and bury my nose in his hair, breathing in the clean scent of him. After helping him remove his own shirt, I press close and enjoy the smooth feeling of his muscular back, the press of his strong chest against my breasts. By the time he lifts me in his arms and lays me gently on the bed, both of us nude, I am more than ready.

Our joining is unlike anything I've experienced. We

seem to find a perfect rhythm immediately, as if we had made love a hundred times before and our bodies were created to fit together like this. The world around us disappears as I discover for the first time what it feels like to reach an orgasm, to lose all inhibitions and cry out in ecstasy again and again.

As we lie wrapped in each other's arms, our legs tangled together, I let out a loud sigh of pleasure. I've never felt so spent in my life. "My God, I feel like I just got run over by a Mack Truck," I say.

We both burst out laughing.

"Well, I warned you, sweetheart. You're married to a bona fide trucker now, so..." He wiggles his eyebrows like Groucho Marx.

"In the future, if I call you Mack, you'll know what I'm thinking about."

I imitate the eyebrow thing and he jumps out of bed, grabbing my hand and pulling me up so I'm sitting on the edge of the bed. "Let's freshen up and get dressed. I want to explore the trails around here. Maybe later we can find ourselves a pretty spot in the woods to see if Mack is ready to come out to play again."

I slap him playfully. "We'd better take along a blanket, then. And you might have to carry me. I'm not sure I can walk to the bathroom, much less along a trail."

Maybe there's no real reason he needs to know about my past. He seems so happy and we're both in love – why risk spoiling it?

# PART TWO
## RUNNING AWAY

# CHAPTER 21 - ROBIN

I stare out the window, watching the landscape far below. This is my second time ever on a plane, but this time I'm traveling alone. Like last time, there's a flight attendant assigned to watch over me, an unaccompanied minor, but she doesn't need to hover over a fifteen-year-old like that "airplane lady" did when her charges were ages five and ten.

While I'm usually ready and willing to take on any opportunity to get away from my grandparents, I have mixed feelings about this trip. I haven't seen my father face-to-face since shortly before my mother disappeared. When he called last month and begged me to come share Thanksgiving with him and "our family," my first inclination was to say no. He's sent photos of his new kids – Molly, who's five and later Matthew, now three years old – and I've torn them up into tiny pieces every time. "Your new sister" and "your new brother." No thanks. I already have a sister, and Dad's done nothing in all this time to keep us together or even let us get in touch with each other. I don't need any other siblings or a step-mother.

If there's any chance I can get him to help me, it's going to have to be in person. Infrequent phone calls haven't gotten me anywhere.

When I reach the baggage claim area, my eyes dart around at all the people, trying to find a familiar face.

"Robin! Over here!" His voice sounds overly excited and he rushes toward me, arms held out for a hug. Seriously, after all these years? Still, I let him wrap his arms around me and give him a perfunctory hug back. I would never admit it to him, but being hugged feels awfully good.

Of course I've seen him in photos these past five years (briefly, before ripping them to shreds), but I'm still a bit surprised to see a glint of silver in his hair. That wasn't apparent in the pictures. Well, he is over forty now, so I guess that's to be expected. He grabs my suitcase from the carousel and I follow him to his car.

"Glenda and the kids are really excited to finally meet you."

I'll bet.

I say as little as possible during the drive to his house, counting on having some opportunity during the next three days to talk to him alone while he's not distracted by traffic. We drive through a fast food place and buy burgers for lunch, which we eat in the car.

When we walk into his house, his two little kids rush into the living room and then freeze like statues, staring at me. A woman who I recognize as his wife, Glenda, approaches from the kitchen, wiping her hands on a towel. She reaches out to shake my hand. I comply.

"It's so good to meet you, Robin!"

If her smile were any more forced, her face would crack open like ice on a frozen pond when you heave a large rock onto it. Little Matthew has approached, peering at me from around his mother's legs, which he's clinging to for reassurance. Molly hasn't moved from her original frozen stance.

"Kids," Dad says, "come on and give your big sister a hug. This is Robin, you guys. Come on!"

Molly, who reminds me so much of Annie from when we were last together that my throat tightens, shuffles across the room and barely wraps her arms around my waist, keeping her body as far away from mine as possible. I place my hands on her shoulders before she makes her escape. Seeing her comply, Matthew throws himself against my legs and gives them a bear hug before dashing away, screeching like he just tackled a scary monster.

Dad shows me to a bedroom with two twin beds – one with a pink bedspread and the other pale blue. "Sorry there's no room in the closet," he says, sliding a door open partway to demonstrate that it's stuffed full of children's clothes and toys. "The kids are both camped out in our room. Literally – we've got them set up with a little tent and sleeping bags. If you want to take a shower, there are towels in the closet right outside the door to the bath."

"I'll be fine."

"Okay. Well," he says, shifting from foot to foot. "Dinner will be at 5:30, so I guess just make yourself at home until then. Do you need anything?"

"No, I'm fine."

This doesn't seem like the right time to try to talk to him about getting me the hell out of his parents' house or reuniting me with Annie. I have three days. Maybe after we've all shared a Thanksgiving feast, things won't feel so stilted.

Meanwhile, what am I going to do for four and a half hours?

He escapes back to his family while I retrieve my toiletry

bag from my suitcase and lock myself in the bathroom. I splash some cool water on my face, run a brush through my hair, and stare into the mirror. I look miserable. No wonder the kids were freaked out. Forcing a pleasant smile on my face, I exit and make my way into the den, where Dad and the children are watching an animated, blue Aladdin on TV. There's enough room on the sofa next to Molly that I could probably squeeze in, but I choose the stuffed chair to the side. Dad offers me a thumbs up, but otherwise I'm ignored.

After what feels like an hour, but was probably more like ten minutes, I retreat and head to the kitchen, where Glenda is chopping vegetables for a salad.

"Can I help?" I ask.

She looks up from the cutting board, her face reflecting both surprise and affability. "Robin! Yes, thank you, I could use some help. Do you mind slicing these tomatoes while I baste the turkey?"

"Glad to," I say, taking the knife from her. Her smile is remarkably warm and natural.

"I know this is awkward," she says as she uses a turkey baster to suck up juices from the bottom of the pan, "but I'm so glad for the opportunity to get to know you, and the kids really are excited to meet their oldest sister, even though it's a bit hard to tell so far."

"That's okay. I'm sure they'll get used to me by the time we've all had dinner."

She wrangles the roaster and the enormous turkey back into the oven. "So, tell me about school. You're in...10th grade?"

"Right. I'm a sophomore. School is pretty good, I guess. I like my English class a lot this year. We get to do a lot of creative writing and we're reading some great books – *To Kill* a *Mockingbird* this term and *Lord of the Flies* next semester. I've already read both of those, but we're also reading *Beowulf* and *Canterbury Tales*, so I have something new."

She chuckles. "Heady stuff. I'm not sure I understood anything about *Beowulf* other than how little the language resembled anything I know about English. Good luck with it."

"Mrs. Greenberg is letting us read a modern translation, so I guess we're safe."

We continue chatting about the usual stuff adults always bring up – what's going on at school (Writer's Club), what do I like to do with friends (visit during lunch hour and on the bus home, since I'm seldom allowed to go over to anyone's house and can't ever invite someone over to mine), do I have a boyfriend (I answer *no*, which isn't really a lie). I tell her what I think she'd like to hear. If I'm going to make any headway at all with Dad, Glenda's going to have to be on board, too.

"How are my girls doing with the feast?" My father breezes in, kissing each of us on the cheek. "I've got the kids down for their nap time. Well, actually Molly's engrossed in her Aladdin coloring book but Matthew fell asleep watching the movie, so he should be out until I get back. See you in an hour or so."

Before I can ask where he's headed and if I can come along, he's disappeared out the door.

"A nap sounds good," I say as I add the slices of tomato to the salad. "I got up awfully early this morning for my flight." And we've run out of topics to talk about.

Glenda glances at the clock. "If you're not up in an hour, can I come wake you? Your father has a surprise for you."

I try to guess what that could be. Maybe he's off to a bakery to pick up a pecan pie – my favorite. Or maybe he's got a present for me, even though he's always just sent cards on my birthday and Christmas. Like a typewriter. Or even a personal computer, so I can type up my homework and print it out like Howard does for English class. He says he can even insert a sentence after he types the whole assignment, and the computer will fix it so the pages get rearranged and nobody can tell the difference.

But that's way too much to expect from my father. Maybe he's just running some errand that has nothing to do with the surprise.

I doze for about twenty minutes. When I wake up, I can hear Glenda reading a Dr. Seuss poem out loud, probably to Molly since her voice is the only other one I hear. I stare at the ceiling and rehearse what I want to say to my father when I get him alone.

"They're here," Glenda announces. She knocks on my door. "Robin, are you awake? Come on out to the living room."

I roll off the bed and head that way, curious if Dad will be revealing his surprise right away or if I'll be kept in the dark even longer.

"Look who's here!" he announces as I step into the room.

We stare at each other, this girl he's brought home and I. It takes me a moment to realize who she is – she's changed so much in five years.

"Annie?" I whoop, rushing across the room to take her in my arms, tears already flowing down my cheeks.

She takes a half step back as I reach her, but I wrap her in my arms anyway. "My God, I almost didn't recognize you."

Her hands barely touch my back as she returns the hug. "Same here," she says, her voice flat.

Her lack of enthusiasm feels like a rock settling in my stomach. I step back and hold her at arms' length, a "let me look at you" pose that she tolerates. "I can't believe how big you've grown. You're ten! That's so hard to take in."

"You look really different, too," she says, eyeing me from head to toe. "I wasn't sure who you were until you said my name."

"I've missed you so much, Annie. I think about you all the time." I want to ask her how things are living with Aunt Sophie and Uncle Brad, but not with Dad and his family all gathered around us listening to every word.

"Annie!" Molly scurries over and gives her a hug. I turn away, my tears of joy turning into tears of pain. Not only has our father been visiting Annie in person since we were separated, his kids know her as well.

Why not me? What makes me so disposable? Am I really such a horrible daughter that it's taken five years to dare let me be near my own sister and Dad's new family? Was I the one who drove our mother away?

I back away slowly and mumble, "Bathroom," before escaping. I'm not sure anyone even notices me leave the room. I put down the toilet lid and sit there, weeping as quietly as possible. Annie never said she'd missed me, too. It dawns on me that she probably barely remembers me or our mother – she was just five when we both disappeared from her life.

I abandoned her just like Mom abandoned both of us. Even though I couldn't do anything to prevent it. I'm a stranger to her now.

# CHAPTER 22 - KATHARINE

"What are you, about fifteen weeks along?"

I pull my hands away from my belly, realizing I've been running my hand over my bulge ever since I sat down to wait for the wash cycle to end. "Fourteen weeks, actually." I smile up at the woman I've seen down here in the laundry room several times before. She has three kids with her – a girl I'm guessing is about six, a boy about two years younger, and a toddler, also a boy. Her own pregnancy is far ahead of mine and I imagine her back must be killing her. "How about you?"

"Thirty-two weeks and counting down. Hi, I'm Abby."

"Katharine. Nice to meet you. Of course, I've seen you around, but..."

She snorts a laugh. "Me and my crew are pretty hard to miss. Sheri!" she shouts as we hear the crash of a large trash can tumbled to the floor. "Don't let him get into that. What did I tell you about keeping a close eye on your brother?"

I help right the can and return the used paper towels, empty containers of laundry detergent, remnants of someone's lunch, and a torn pair of men's boxers to the receptacle while little Sheri tries to distract the two-year-old with a stuffed toy.

"Terrible twos," Abby says as she returns to pulling clothes from the dryer. "He can get into trouble in about two seconds flat. The older kids were just as bad, and I'm sure this next one will be the same," she says, patting her protruding belly.

I stare at the kids, wide-eyed with worry. Is this what I have to look forward to? Abby plops into the plastic chair beside me. "Your first one, right?"

"Yeah. I'm kind of freaked out. I mean, I did a little baby-sitting when I was growing up, but those were kids old enough to be in school. I don't know anything about taking care of a baby."

She laughs. "Don't you worry. I'll be more than happy to give you plenty of pointers. Hands-on, if you want, starting in about eight weeks." She pats her belly again. "And I've got all these munchkins for practice for when yours gets past the infant stage."

I sigh in relief. Truth is, I've been terrified about this pregnancy. After I missed a period, I didn't say anything to Roy, waiting until I got beyond the point when I miscarried before. He still doesn't know anything about that aspect of my life and I plan to keep it that way.

My life has been so full of changes since I left home. I didn't realize it at first, but I had become kind of comfortable living in Denver. After we got married, I moved into Roy's apartment and we began taking trips together. Not the vacation kind, of course. Delivering loads, with him driving his emerald green tractor and me riding shotgun. Denver to Salt Lake City to Twin Falls to Boise to Pocatello to Ogden and back home again. Or we'd head east on an even longer sequence of stops, picking up a trailer here, leaving it there, driving to another city to pick up another load.

We loved it at first. During his off hours, we'd eat at a

diner in a truck stop and I often found myself watching the waitresses, remembering the kindness of Sally who helped me out when I found myself alone and stranded. We usually spent the night in the sleeper in the cab. It was extremely cozy, to put it mildly, but for a while we loved being cuddled up close together after making love. But by the time a year elapsed, we were getting on each other's nerves. In the beginning, I couldn't get enough of watching the scenery roll by, enthralled with mountains and lakes, plains, cities, towns, and the almost-bird's-eye-view of the road ahead. We'd eat in a diner just off the highway, and I'd find myself watching all the waitresses, as if I might run into Sally again.

"She saved me," I told Roy. I modified the story so it was a girlfriend, Stevie instead of Steve, who left me at the rest stop. I claimed that she got cold feet about our plan to run away and move to Oklahoma City, so she left me there, thinking I could hitchhike the rest of the way. "I forgot my purse was still in Stevie's car when she left. Sally bought me dinner and took me home with her that night. Then she drove me to the bus station and bought my ticket to Oklahoma City. I don't know what I would have done without her help. I was terrified of hitchhiking!"

"Geez, Katharine, I had no idea. What did you do when you got there? You still didn't have any money or even an ID, right?" Roy reached across the table and held both of my hands in his.

I take a moment to recall the sequence of events. "Again, it was Sally who came through for me. She gave me the name of a restaurant in Oklahoma City to apply for a job. She must have called them, because they hired me right off. And I found some other girls to room with." I nodded, remembering those times so soon after I left home. "I wish I knew how to get in touch with Sally again. I didn't thank her nearly enough."

The months rolled by and the hours riding in the big rig seemed to stretch longer and longer. My dreams of strolling hand-in-hand with my husband as we visited famous landmarks, or hiking through the brilliant autumn colors of Appalachia, or splashing in the Pacific and the Atlantic Oceans were just that – dreams. Gradually, I become disenchanted with the cramped living quarters, greasy truck-stop food, and never having the freedom to stop and really look around in places that caught my eye.

When I got pregnant, we both agreed it was time for me to stay home. Morning sickness and swollen ankles and an almost constant need to pee didn't seem conducive to long-haul trucking. Out of the blue, Roy announced that "home" would now be Indianapolis instead of Denver. "There are so many more trucking lines using Indianapolis as a hub," he told me. Without any discussion, he had already rented this apartment for us and given notice at our place in Denver.

So here I am. Markerton, Arkansas to Denver, Colorado to Indianapolis, Indiana all within three years. Twice engaged, twice pregnant, once married. I've changed my name twice. I'm twenty years old (although my husband thinks I'm twenty-two). I spend my days sewing, watching TV, and keeping house. The only time I feel like I'm doing anything at all useful is when I work on Roy's mileage fuel reports and update the books for our trucking business.

"Sweetheart, you're a life saver. I hate all that paperwork," he told me when I took it all over. It seems so straight-forward to me. Everything I needed to know was in Roy's workbooks for his CDL school.

Life keeps interrupting my plans. I had just started back to school again to earn my GED before I got pregnant and we moved away from Denver. Roy thinks I should wait until after the baby is born before I try enrolling again. I wonder how old it'll have to be before I'll have any time or energy for studying. I can't get up any enthusiasm for having this child, but I hope I'll feel differently once it's born.

I cringe as Abby's young children scream and laugh and shout as she finishes unloading the dryer, wondering how she can stand all the chaos. "It's different when they're your own," someone told me. I hope so.

***

"How did you two meet?" Abby asks, holding out the platter of crackers and cheese again. We've found the rarest of moments to get together. Roy is home for two days, her kids are all in bed and quiet for the time being, and her husband, Wayne, gave in to her pleas to have some adult company instead of falling asleep in front of the TV like he usually does in the evening.

I look toward Roy and he nods back toward me, smiling. I'll tell the story.

"It was at this café near where I was working, back in Denver. I had seen Roy there several times, but I guess he was too shy to come talk to me. Then, one day, I'm sitting by myself and the place is about half full, but he comes over to my table and asks if he can join me." I smile over at him. "The rest is history." I reach over and squeeze his hand. He stares at me, brows knit. "How about you? How did you meet?"

"I won her in a poker game," Wayne says, straight-faced. Abby elbows him.

Our short visit is interrupted by the wailing of a child. Wayne cringes but shows no sign of moving out of his recliner. Finally, Abby excuses herself, hefts her swollen body off the chair and waddles back toward the bedrooms.

"Just a typical evening in the Kowalski household," Wayne mumbles, taking another swig of his beer. "Need another?" he asks, gesturing with his bottle toward us.

"No, I'm good," Roy says, but I pipe in with, "Sure, I'll take another." Roy squints over at me unapprovingly. "You're pregnant," he whispers when Wayne is out of earshot. "You don't need another beer."

When Wayne returns with a cold bottle from the fridge, Roy reaches for it. "We decided to share," he says. I know he's not going to hand it over to me.

After Abby gets the child settled down, she rejoins us. Talk turns to sport teams and a scandal with a state representative and a hooker and I tune out, munching a cracker as slowly as possible to look like I'm doing something other than daydreaming. I envision myself home alone with a crying baby, Roy out on the road for weeks at a time. Lugging it around as I try to do my shopping or laundry. I picture myself asking Abby to watch the baby so I can get away for even an hour, but then she expects me to babysit her crew, which I can't even imagine.

"Sweetheart, you ready?" Roy's voice brings me back to the present. "I think we've worn Abby out."

Seriously? Like her three kids and looming birth of another wouldn't do it, but our visit would?

We thank our hosts and walk down the flight of stairs to our apartment. Immediately after we step inside, Roy starts questioning me.

"What was with the story of how we met? Are you embarrassed that you approached me?"

I'm baffled about what he's saying. "I didn't approach

you. I was sitting there and you came over to me. Don't you remember?"

He shakes his head, looking at something in the distance. "Katharine, I swear you either have a terrible memory, or too vivid an imagination."

"What do you mean? I just told them what happened."

"Never mind. It doesn't really matter." He swipes his hand across the top of his head, smoothing his hair. "I'm beat. Let's go to bed."

As I listen to his deep, slow breathing, I lie awake replaying our first meeting in my mind. I can see him spotting me at my table and heading straight over, asking if he can join me. Right off the bat, he said he wanted to eat lunch with me the following week, too. I think I remember that he even went back and bought dessert for both of us. Yes, I'm sure of it.

I roll on my side so I can watch my husband sleep. He looks so peaceful. I wish he was home more.

# CHAPTER 23 - ROBIN

I have a plan.

This summer, I've been accepted as a counselor-in-training at Expanding Horizons. Since I'll be working with two different teams, that'll keep me out of this house five days a week, which is great news.

I'll stick with it until just after my sixteenth birthday in July. Then I'll have my driver's license and there's a guy at school who says he can get a fake ID that'll show me as a year older. I won't even have to pay him – well, not in cash, anyway, but that's no big deal.

I've been collecting bus schedules again, but this time I know to check out the interstate schedules as well. If they think I'm seventeen, I can buy a ticket without anyone's permission.

So, Dad, screw your "advice" that I only need to *hang in there* for almost another three years, when I turn eighteen and can get away from Doris and Clay. Screw you and your stupid new family. And Mom? I hope you're dead.

Doris sticks her head in my room. "What's wrong with *you*?" she says, scowling. "No wonder you don't have any friends, with that sour look you always have on your face. Don't tell me you're studying. I'm on to you." She shakes her cigarette at me like an accusing finger. Ashes fall to the floor, but she doesn't notice. "Nobody studies all the time and gets such lousy grades, not even someone as stupid as you. I guess you fooled your teachers in junior high, but it's all catching up with you now, isn't it?"

It's all I can do not to scream at her to leave me alone. "I'm trying," I say, my irritation still coming through loud and clear in my tone.

"You're trying my patience, that's what." She rolls her eyes upward, beseeching God, or more likely the devil, to help her cope. Bitch.

I gesture toward my open textbook and papers. "Can I get back to this now? You want me to study but then you interrupt me all the time."

She turns her head so she can look at me sideways – a sure sign that she's working out how to deal with me. "You've got a smart mouth, girl. That's the only thing about you that's smart. Well, you just wait until your grandfather gets home. Then we'll see how sassy you are." With a final gloating look, she spins around and retreats.

That was stupid of me. I forgot that today is Thursday. Clay is off at his club and all I can do is hope his poker game goes well and that he doesn't show up here aching for a battle.

*** 

When he goes straight for the liquor cabinet, I rush to my room and close the door. Maybe Doris won't tell him about this afternoon.

Who am I kidding? Of course she will.

I pick up the novel I started yesterday and try to read,

but I can't focus. I turn back a few pages, attempting to pick up the story again, but it's no use. I can hear Clay cursing and Doris talking in a calming voice – the only situation where I ever hear her use that tone.

My bedroom door hurls open and crashes against the wall. "Get your smart ass out here!"

It feels like everything is moving in slow motion. I set down my book on the bed and slowly drift across the room toward the doorway, edging myself past Clay and bracing for a blow. It doesn't come – yet. I ease down the hallway to the living room where Doris is standing, seemingly frozen in place. Instead of the gloat I expect to see on her face, I see fear. Or maybe I'm projecting my own expression onto hers.

"I'm too old for this shit!" Clay shouts as he follows me into the room. "You think I wanted to raise another brat after I retired? Huh?"

I remain silent, staring at the carpet.

"You little smart-ass savage. You think you can talk back to your grandma and get away with it? Huh?"

He takes a swing at me and I leap backwards, feeling only a glancing blow. Clay crashes into the wall, roaring with rage and possibly pain. "That's it. You ain't getting away with this shit any more," he says as he rushes toward me, crouched like a football player going for a tackle.

"Clay!" Doris screams, "Don't! Please..."

He knocks me off my feet and we both crash into the dining room table before I end up sprawled on the floor. He reaches for me, but I scramble under the table, trying to find shelter with chairs and table legs between us. With another roar, he shoves a chair away and grabs for my foot. I scamper further away.

Doris tries again. "Clay, please. She's just a girl. We can

deal with this some other—"

"Shut up!"

Seeing him turn to look her way, I seize my opportunity. I squirm to the far side of the table and leap to my feet, shoving the table as violently as I can toward him. A chair tumbles, the full momentum of the table adding to its power, and strikes him forcefully in the crotch. He goes down hard, howling.

My rage is even greater than my terror. I barrel to the liquor cabinet and with a single sweep of my arm, send the entire contents flying and shattering on the tile floor. Glass flies everywhere and sticky liquids run down the walls and cabinet doors, pooling into an eye-watering mess around my feet.

"Never hit me again!" I spit out each individual word like shards of glass shooting across the room and cutting him to shreds.

Doris looks like a marionette that can only repeat the same movements again and again. She turns toward Clay, still curled up on the floor, moaning but then turns toward me and the mayhem of the kitchen. Then back again.

I step carefully through the debris, my shoes growing stickier with each stride, but shielding my feet from countless cuts. By the time I reach the kitchen door, I feel like I'm walking on tap shoes instead of tennies. I step outside, carefully lever each one off using the toe of the other foot, and carry my shoes delicately as I plod barefoot across the chilly, still-brown lawn and scramble over the back fence, wondering if I've finally put an end to his violence or if I've just thrown my life away.

# CHAPTER 24 - KATHARINE

When they hand me my baby girl, I stare at her in wonder. How can this entire human infant have formed inside my body? It was almost impossible to believe she could squeeze out through my vagina without ripping me apart, but somehow she managed. Thank goodness for epidurals.

I stare into her face and wait for that feeling of unconditional love to overwhelm me, but all I feel is relief that she's here and not inside my uterus any longer, solace that she appears to be healthy, and curiosity about what she's going to look like as she gets older. I've never understood when people declare that a baby has its mother's eyes and its father's mouth when it's this young.

Will she have Roy's adorable dimple when she smiles? Will her nose be long and thin like mine or more like his?

I want to be a good mother. I do. But right now I don't feel much of anything beyond the wonder of seeing an infant come into the world. Shouldn't I be crazy in love with her right from the first moment?

"She's so beautiful," Roy says, gently stroking her head. "And so are you. I'm so happy, Katharine."

I look up into his eyes and they're sparkling with tears of

happiness and with love. Why can't I feel like that?

"Do you want to hold her?" I ask, and help guide her into his arms. I just want to sleep. Maybe that's all this is – exhaustion. I'll feel that thrill when I see her again after I get some rest.

***

Right from the beginning, Roy was sure we were going to have a boy. He didn't even want the doctor to tell us. Still, he doesn't seem disappointed.

Robert if it's a boy. That was his choice, but I thought it seemed boring.

"There are so many Bobs. How about something less common, like Eugene or Byron?"

He shook his head. "We'd call him Rob or Robby, not Bob. That's not as common. Rob Milstead. Doesn't that sound great?"

I agreed to that, but only if I got to choose a girl's name.

"Maybe Marguerite," I said, "or Genevieve. Those are so elegant, don't you think?"

"Seriously? Can you imagine calling a baby Marguerite?"

I stuck out my lower lip. "She could be Margie when she's little. Or Genevieve could be Genni."

He just grunted. "It'll be a boy, anyway, so it doesn't matter."

When they ask what name to put on our daughter's birth certificate, I'm not surprised when he balks at both my choices.

"How about a compromise?" he says, rocking gently from foot to foot as he holds the baby in his arms.

Since he hasn't put forth any names for girls, I'm puzzled about what the compromise might be. "Go on," I prompt.

"Instead of Robert or a name she won't learn to spell until she's twelve, how about...Robin?"

I turn my head to look out the window and consider his suggestion. I swear at that very moment a robin lands on a branch of the tree growing in the courtyard outside my hospital room. I burst out laughing.

"What?" he says, and I point to the bird.

"Then we're all agreed," he says, laughing with me. He leans down and holds our daughter so we can both look at her. "Hello, Robin Milstead. Welcome to our family." She blinks her eyes and drools in response.

\*\*\*

One week old and Daddy's already back on the road. "If I don't drive, I don't get paid. If anything, I'm going to need to take on a few extra runs each trip now that we have another mouth to feed."

Speaking of feeding, it's not going all that well. The nurses reassured me that it isn't always a success right from the get go, and with their assistance and a lot of patience and discomfort, we managed to get Robin to suckle. Here at home, it's a struggle and I dread it. I'm sure the baby senses my frustration, as she seems to be less willing to even start to latch on every time I try to feed her. I consider asking Abby for advice, but that brings back my feelings of embarrassment the time she demonstrated breast feeding with baby Kenny. She was so nonchalant about exposing her bare breast with me sitting right there. I know Mother would have denounced her as an exhibitionist, even though this happened in her own apartment.

I set Robin back in her crib and hurry to warm the pumped milk we've stored in the fridge before someone comes to the door, thinking her cries mean I'm torturing her. "Mommy's going to feed you in a minute, Robin. Hang on." Roy was so good about getting up during the night to feed her. Why won't she accept the milk when it comes from the original source?

Thankfully, she accepts the rubber nipple and sucks eagerly, her little fists opening and closing in rhythm with her jaw movements. "See. I wasn't trying to starve you."

By the time another week passes, I just go straight to the kitchen when she wants to be fed. If it weren't for the cost, I'd give up the pump right now. Maybe I'll talk to Roy about that when he gets back from this trip.

The phone rings and though I snatch it up in the middle of the second tone, it wakes Robin who immediately starts wailing.

"Oh, shoot," Abby says on the line, "Did I just wake her? I'm sorry. Nothing wakes Kenny up other than his own bodily needs. I could drop a stack of dishes right next to his crib and he'd just scrunch up tight and snooze away."

"Lucky you." I cringe at the tone I've taken with her. I don't consider her lucky at all, cooped up with four rug rats all day. At least *her* husband comes home every night after work and is there weekends to take some of the load.

"Do you feel up to a visit? I can come down there or you can come here. It's just me and the baby," she adds quickly. "Wayne's taken the rest of the gang to the playground."

Oh, yeah. Today's Saturday. With no job and few friends, each day just blends into the next and I lose track. "If you don't mind, come on down," I say, thinking about the lengthy list of items I had to pack and tote when I took Robin to the neighborhood grocery store with me. What normally takes me a half hour round trip took close to two hours. Not that I'll have to deal with the car seat when I'm just going up a flight of stairs, but having her come to me sounds so much simpler.

I'm holding the baby against my shoulder as I answer her knock. She's still crying. Kenny twists in his mother's arms to check out the fuss and starts to whimper.

"You're okay," Abby tells him as she steps inside, sets him down on the floor, and wiggles a squeaky plastic duck in front of his nose. He beams and takes it from her, squeezing it and laughing with pleasure when it makes noise.

"How do you do that?" I ask, patting Robin on the back.

Abby reaches for her and I gladly turn her over to the expert. Within seconds, Robin settles down and looks like she's ready to doze off again. She hands my baby back to me and I manage to lay her down in her crib without disturbing her.

"See. That wasn't so hard," Abby whispers from the door to the nursery.

Yeah, right.

# CHAPTER 25 - ROBIN

The house looks just like it always does when I come home from school. Quiet. I've been standing halfway down our block, partly hidden by a large, bare bush in a neighbor's front yard, trying to get up the nerve to walk in the front door.

Manny offered to sneak me into his basement again tonight, but I've got to face this at some point. Or run away for good. But with no money, one pair of ill-fitting shoes and an outfit borrowed (or stolen – I didn't ask for details) from Manny's younger sister, what are my options?

I still don't know what inspired me to call Manny after I tried reaching Greg. Football practice night – I remembered the moment Greg's mom answered the phone. That eliminated Kyle as well. Anyway, both of my "boyfriends" would have wanted something in return for picking me up and I really wasn't in the mood last night. So I grabbed the phone book and looked up my writing critique partner's number instead. Manny was a gentleman, even though I'm sure he's heard the stories about me. He held me close while I cried and we whispered for hours and he never made a move on me.

Glancing at my watch, I realize I've been standing here

for twenty minutes. *Either go in or turn around now*. I walk toward the house, focusing on keeping my head high.

The first thing I notice is that everything looks perfectly normal. The dining room table and chairs are all in their normal positions, the floor is clear of broken glass and booze, and all I can hear is the ticking of the clock hanging in the living room. That and the hum of Doris's sewing machine from down the hall.

I tiptoe into the kitchen and look out the back window. It's a cool afternoon, but pleasant, and the door to Clay's work shed is half open. I unlatch the window and slide it open just enough so I'm able to hear a rhythmic clanking sound. He's working on some contraption.

"Where were you last night?"

I jump at the sound of her voice and slam the window closed. "I stayed with a friend," I say, straightening my back and looking directly into her eyes. I raise my chin slightly for good measure.

"You staying here tonight?" Oddly, she sounds quite matter-of-fact. I expected fury.

My eyes swing to the kitchen window for a moment. "Depends."

She nods. "Your grandpa and I had a long talk this morning." Walking over to the kitchen cabinet where Clay kept his liquor, she swings open the door. A large crock-pot and set of giant mixing bowls fill the space – items that used to reside on a shelf in the garage. "Now I won't have to clean them every time I go to use them."

She shuts the door again and stares out into the back yard. "Maybe he'll hold to it and maybe he won't. For the time being, there's no booze in the house."

"Okay," I say. She doesn't turn around. After a few more

171

beats, I head to my room. "I've got a paper to finish," I say before quietly closing the door behind me.

At dinner, Clay never once looks at me or speaks directly to me. Which is fine. Doris is quieter than usual as well, making it one of the most peaceful meals I've ever had in this house. By the next morning, she starts grousing again after spotting the glint of another fragment of broken glass in the corner of the dining room, under the china cabinet.

"You know, I had to clean up that entire mess myself. Glass everywhere, liquor stains on the cabinet doors and table legs. You're young and limber. Get down and crawl around. I'm sure there's more I can't get to."

I'm actually happy to comply. If creating all that disarray means Clay won't take a swing at me again, it was well worth it.

Just before lunch, Manny calls.

"You doin' okay? Can you talk now?"

Clay is out in the shed but Doris is fussing about, in and out of the kitchen where I've answered the phone. "I'm okay, but I can't talk for long. Hey – thanks again for the other night."

"No problem. So, Robin, I was wondering if you might like to go to a movie or something tonight."

Or something. I guess he figures it's time I pay him back for rescuing me Thursday night. One good thing about Manny is that he at least *pretends* he wants to be with me for reasons other than what I'll let him do and what I'll do for him.

Before I can answer, he pipes up. "Oh, wait. That didn't come out right. I mean, I really just want to go to a movie and, like, dinner? Or something? Not like – you know. 'Cause I really like you, Robin."

"Oh." Like a regular date. Not a drive to some make-out spot but an actual date. "Yeah. That'd be nice. But I have to ask my grandmother and I don't know how that'll go. Can I call you back in a bit?"

A regular date. No sneaking out after they go to bed and bunching up clothes under the covers in case they look in my room. After a few close calls with the squeaky floor board by the front door, I've become pretty adept at climbing out my bedroom window, but...a regular date!

"Grandma Doris," I say, intercepting her as she enters the kitchen, "I just got asked for a date. For tonight. He's taking me to dinner and a movie. Is that okay?"

"Tell me about this boy."

So I do. Of course, I don't tell her that he was the one who held me in his arms all night as we talked and slept and cried and talked some more. I tell her about how he walks with me to some of my classes and carries my books. That he sits with me at lunch – but I leave off the part about him telling off the guys who try to come on to me when he's there, or grab their crotch as they walk past.

"All right. You can go out with him. But I need to talk to him when he comes to pick you up. And you need to be home by ten – no later. And next time, tell him he should ask you earlier in the week. It's rude to call a girl and ask her out that same night."

"Thank you. I promise I'll be home on time. And I'll tell him about calling earlier."

"Tell him he's not the only boy who might be asking you out for the weekend."

I'm sure he's aware of that. There are probably very few boys at my school who don't know that. "I will."

A hint of a smile forms at the corner of her lips. "You're

growing up, Robin. Almost sixteen. I knew the boys would start getting interested in you soon. This is a very special day for you."

Maybe it is.

***

Apparently, Manny passes inspection when he comes to pick me up and has to sit and talk to Clay and Doris before we go. His *yes, sirs* and *yes, ma'ams* sound sincere and smooth.

"I expect her back by ten," Clay says, as if I'm not sitting right here.

"Yes, sir."

"And don't try any funny stuff. You know what I'm talking about."

"Sir, I was raised to treat women with respect. You have nothing to worry about."

Clay snorts at the term *women*, but seems satisfied.

At the curb, I reach for the handle of the car door, but Manny beats me to it.

"Allow me," he says, opening it for me.

I realize my mouth has dropped open and close it, hoping it wasn't obvious. Greg and Kyle and the others would never have opened a door for me. "Thanks," I say, slipping into the seat.

Dinner is at a grill that makes incredible hamburgers. "Sorry it's not some place fancier," he says after the waitress takes our order.

"No, really, this is great. Everybody's always saying how good the food is here, but my grandparents almost never eat out." I realize how lame that must sound. The girls I've heard talk about eating here come with each other or with boyfriends, not their parents or whatevers. If I had any girlfriends, maybe I would have been here before. Or boyfriends who wanted to spend time with me other than making out.

"It's my first time, too. I'm sure you've noticed that I'm not exactly Mr. Popularity around school."

"Me, neither. Um...I guess that would be Ms. Popularity in my case." Then I feel my face flush, because I'm pretty popular among a certain male population and I'm sure Manny knows it.

"Then people are fools, because you're smart, clever, talented, and pretty."

Now I'm sure my face is crimson. "Me? Are you sure you haven't confused me with someone else, like Nancy Grandenberg or Cher Miles?" *Smart?* As much as I study, my B average just proves how stupid I am. Maybe *clever* at sneaking out of the house, but *pretty?*

"No way. You don't give yourself enough credit. You're... unique. Yourself, not some clone of all the other girls. And you write like nobody's business. I've told you before, you're going to be a famous author someday."

"And you'll be a Pulitzer-prize winning journalist." His fiction is kind of flat, but let him loose with writing about the real world and he's amazing.

"Who had the bacon burger?" our waitress asks and the conversation pauses while he sculpts a pyramid of ketchup beside his fries and I load up my burger with lettuce and tomato and pickles and mayo and onions.

For the next several minutes, we eat in silence, other than grunts of pleasure at the taste of our food.

"About the other night..." we both say, as if a choir director just gave us the signal for our duet.

"You first," he says.

"No, you."

He dabs his mouth with his napkin and looks at me – really looks at me. He doesn't say anything for a moment, then leans across the table and lowers his voice. "I've never even held a girl in my arms before. Before you."

"Really?" I say before I can censor myself. "I guess I thought all seniors would have...I mean...not that there's anything wrong with..."

"Hey, it's okay. I guess you haven't heard the rumors about me."

I shake my head. The kids in our Writing Club are a pretty different group than the ones I see in my classes, other than a couple from English Comp. Manny's crowd and mine don't overlap other than at our monthly Club meetings, and even then we both seem to prefer critiquing each other's work rather than being part of the larger group readings.

He leans even closer and I do too, after sliding my plate to one side so I don't get grease on my blouse. "I'm supposed to be gay," he whispers.

I sit back, puzzled. "*Supposed* to be? According to...?"

Manny chuckles. "Ah. There's the rub. The sixty-four thousand dollar question."

"Okay, I'm lost here. You asked me out, so the rumor is false. Hey," I shrug, "I'll bet more rumors are wrong than right."

He blinks several times and looks away for a moment. Have I said something wrong?

"So, I have a question," he says, dipping a french fry into

his ketchup mound. "In your story about the girl on the airplane, was that based on something real, or was that purely fiction?"

I guess we're moving on from the gay thing. "Totally something I dreamed up. I've never even *seen* the cockpit of a jet."

We finish our meal and stroll over to the multi-plex theater in the same shopping mall. During the show, we hold hands. I'm not sure if he made the move or I did – it was like that simultaneous talking we did earlier. We both got the idea at the same time. After a while, he puts his arm around my shoulder, but doesn't do that dumb thing of letting his hand slowly creep down toward my breast like some guys do. What do they think, that the girl can't feel their hand move or notice how totally awkward and uncomfortable it gets to be?

He just holds me and rubs my shoulder once in a while, like when something emotional happens in the movie. When it ends, we walk out to the parking lot hand in hand and get in the car.

We sit quietly for a moment and Manny makes no move to start the engine. I watch him, then the other people from the theater getting into their cars and driving away. We still sit.

Out of the blue, he says, "I might be gay. Or not. I don't know yet."

"Oh."

I'm not sure what to say, so I decide to just go ahead and say the first thing that pops into my mind. "I'm confused."

He turns to look at me. "So am I. That's the problem. I feel an attraction to you, Robin. I want to get to know you better and spend time with you. I even think about kissing you."

Lowering my gaze, I can't help but smile. Because of him and because it's pretty funny, if you think about it, that a girl like me who's been okay with dry-humping any number of different guys and letting them feel me up and strip me from the waist up, is now getting all shy. "I feel like that about you, too," I say, my voice shaky and girly. Not like normal at all.

He reaches out a hand and lightly strokes my cheek. We lean closer and his lips are soft and gentle against mine – nothing like the teeth-banging, tongue-down-the-throat assaults the other boys call kisses.

"Wow," I say, looking into his eyes from inches away. "That was amazing."

We start again, this time with tongues softly exploring each other's mouths. I feel like we're melting together.

"You sure don't kiss like you're gay."

He smiles at this, but only for a moment. "Can I be honest with you?"

"Of course."

He takes my hand and our fingers entwine. "You're not the first one I've kissed like that."

I give an encouraging smile. "That's okay. I don't need to be your first girlfriend."

"You don't understand. I had a boyfriend. Last year. That's what's confusing. I still find guys attractive, but I'm attracted to girls, too. Well, to you. I needed you to know that. So, if you don't want to go out with me again, I understand."

Even though I don't really know what to make of all this, I feel like Manny really cares about me. He gave me exactly what I needed after the melee at home – someone to hold me and listen. Someone who didn't demand anything in return.

"I'd love to go out with you again."

# CHAPTER 26 - KATHARINE

"Uh, oh. Mommy, you threw up again. Are you still sick?"

Rinsing my mouth with cold water, I close my eyes for a moment. My parents would say that God is punishing me for all my past bad deeds. It's bad enough that I got pregnant again. Why do I have to be suffering with morning sickness, too?

"I'm not really sick, Robin. Remember what I told you about the baby growing inside me? Sometimes the baby squirms around and that makes me throw up."

"Ew."

I don't correct her assessment.

When I missed my first period, I told myself my body was just changing, since I couldn't possibly be pregnant. When it still didn't arrive after another three weeks, I called my gynecologist.

"Something's wrong. I've never been late before."

Something was wrong, all right. At my appointment, she declared, "Congratulations, Mrs. Milstead. You're pregnant."

"But I can't be! I've been taking the pills."

Dr. Bronstein nodded. "Although the pill is very

effective, no contraceptive is guaranteed 100%, even when taken exactly as directed."

When I got home, I dug my current dispenser of birth control pills from their hiding place behind the sheets in the linen closet. I knew I had gotten out of kilter on the schedule a few times, but once I did some calculations with a calendar in front of me, I realized I had probably missed taking several over the last few months.

I know Roy would never agree to an abortion. If you were to ask him about having more kids, he'd say he wanted at least one, maybe two more. Easy for him to say. He's only here a few days at a time before heading out again for another two or three weeks. I've never told him about the pills.

Just when I was starting to see the "starting kindergarten" light at the end of the tunnel, dim though that light would be, this happens. I had it all planned out that I'd start classes *again* to earn my GED once Robin wasn't underfoot all day long. Instead, I'll have a new infant demanding all my attention right when she starts school.

"Mommy, you said we could go to the playground. I wanna go now!"

I still feel like shit. "Hey, kiddo, let's see if Kenny can go." I pick up the phone and dial. Please, please let Abby be available to take the kids to the park so I can just sit and put my feet up and bask in silence for a while.

Plan A doesn't work – Abby's youngest addition to her madhouse has diarrhea – but Plan B does. Now eleven, Sherri is experienced at taking charge of her younger siblings and Abby was just telling her to get them out of the house so the three-year-old can get some rest. What's one more kid to look after with what she's used to?

"Have fun, kids," I say as I virtually shove Robin out the door to join the others. "Let them get totally worn out," I tell Sherri.

After I shut the door, I consider all the housework I could catch up on. Toys scattered around the apartment, the hamper full of Robin's dirty clothes, a sink piled high with unwashed dishes since I haven't gotten around to emptying the dishwasher to make room, dried mud on the carpet, dust everywhere, fingerprints and nose prints on the windows.

I manage to gather up all the books strewn about and put them on the bookcase in Robin's room. I don't know if she's just memorized all of them or if she's learned to read on her own, but I can't skip a word when I read them to her without being corrected. That's about the only thing I feel like I'm competent at when it comes to spending time with my child – our daily reading time.

Instead of tackling anything else, I fix myself a cup of tea, add a generous splash of bourbon, and curl up on the couch. It goes down so smoothly, I treat myself to seconds, skipping the tea this time around.

***

"But what if it comes a week early? I need you here, Roy."

He signals me to keep my voice down so I don't wake our daughter. I take a slow breath before continuing. "Abby's going to watch Robin while I'm in the hospital, but once we come home, I can't handle them both. Not right away."

He reaches for my hand, but I yank it away. "I told you I'll be home by the nineteenth. You're not due till the twenty-third and you were a whole week late last time."

I push my plate away and glare at him. "You promised me—"

"We need the income, sweetheart. Longer trips mean bigger bucks. Besides, Robin will be off to kindergarten by then, so you'll just have the baby to deal with. And I'm going to be here starting the nineteenth for almost two weeks. I can't take off more time than that."

*Ten days is hardly two weeks and even two weeks doesn't feel like enough and what if I go into labor early?* But the baby is doing calisthenics and I'm exhausted and I'm tired of arguing, so I don't say any of this out loud.

It's moments like this when thoughts of Mother flash through my mind. If we were a normal family, she'd be here to help with the baby for a week or so. She'd probably be good at it, too. But in real life, we're not a normal family. I'm sure my parents have no idea where I am, or that I'm married and about to have a second child. After nine years, they no more want to find me than I care to reconnect with them. I'm a sinful and damned embarrassment to them and their church and best forgotten.

As with my first pregnancy, Roy is certain this one's going to be a son, but doesn't want to know what the doctor says. I asked anyway. He'll be disappointed again.

"Anthony, if it's a boy," he said.

"Julianne for a girl," I answered.

"It'll be a boy. Anthony. But we won't shorten it to Tony – just Anthony."

I figure once our daughter is born, he'll be willing to turn *Anthony* into *Annie*, like we adapted *Robin* from *Robert*. Maybe I can even get him to go for Julianne if we call her Annie for short.

Annie punches me in the bladder and I leave the table,

waddling toward the bathroom.

"I'll get the dishes, sweetheart, and look in on Robin," he calls after me. "You just go get comfortable and get some rest. I've got this."

"Don't strain yourself," I mutter under my breath.

***

The nurse brings in little Annie and places her in my arms. "I'll be back in just a bit," she says and I barely hold back my tears until she steps into the hallway. This isn't how it's supposed to work. I feel so alone – how could Roy not be here with me?

The rational part of me knows he's trying his best to get here. "I've found a guy to pick up my load in Baltimore tonight, sweetheart. I'll drive all night and be there when you wake up."

But our baby is here right now and he isn't. He wasn't here to drive me to the hospital, so I had to ride in a goddamn taxi with an idiot driver who wouldn't shut up the whole way about his three kids and how his wife almost died in labor with the last one.

Despite the tedium of hour after hour after hour of riding in the cab of his tractor, I miss that time we had together. I miss making love in the too-small sleeping compartment and I miss the greasy diners. I miss laughing at his stories about the crazy conversations he'd overhear when he was loading up soda pop to deliver to businesses on his old route, how he just became invisible to people so they'd say and do anything right within earshot. Like the woman freaking out about her boyfriend bringing a snake into the bedroom and wanting it to slither around them while they

183

were screwing. Or the one-liners he'd pick up as people walked by, like "How could that *not* be illegal?" or "We both saw it. It was definitely a kangaroo." We'd make up stories to fill in the gaps and laugh until our sides ached.

That seems so long ago. Much more than six years.

Annie starts to fuss so I open my gown and hold her face close to my breast, hoping for a better outcome than with her sister. As I reposition her again, the nurse returns and tries to help. "I know it feels frustrating," she says, possibly thinking my streaked face and puffy eyes are a reaction to my failure to get her to latch onto my nipple. "Let's give both of you a rest and try again in a little while. Maybe get you back in bed partially reclined. That might be more comfortable for both of you."

I nod, not trusting my voice, and hand the infant back to her. Two daughters, and neither will nurse. The common factor is me. They can sense that I'm not overjoyed that they're in my life. I do feel a sense of love for Robin, as I'm sure I will with Annie once a little time passes. But it's not that all-encompassing, mother-bear, no-limits sort of emotion that other mothers describe and I don't know what's wrong with me that I can't feel that way.

# CHAPTER 27 - ROBIN

It's a beautiful campus, with buildings adorned with pale sandstone walls and deep red tile roofs, large grassy areas, towering trees, and astonishing rock formations plastered against the foothills just a few miles away – enormous, towering upheavals of stone called flatirons. Although most of the students have retreated for summer break, the walkways are still buzzing with young people, most of them several years older than Manny and me.

"That's going to be my dorm," he says, pointing to one of several blocky buildings with uniform rows of windows facing the grassy field we're standing in. I scan the windows, wondering if anyone is looking out at us at this moment, imagining the view Manny will have from his room when he starts school here in August.

"We can see each other every weekend," he assured me weeks ago when we planned this visit to Boulder. "It's not that far."

"But you'll have homework," I said. "And new friends. You'll want to go places with them."

He squeezed my hand. "We'll both have homework, but it'll work out. Maybe we'll just see each other one day a week, but we'll make it happen."

We drive to a parking area near the base of the peaks so we can hike closer to the giant slabs of rock visible from throughout the city. I want to touch them and watch for rock climbers creeping up their faces. I squeal like a teeny-bopper spotting her favorite boy band singer when I spot two people ahead of us on the trail with a climbing rope and helmets dangling from their backpacks.

"Look! They must be climbers!"

We follow them as they turn off the main trail and head directly toward the bottom of one of the flatirons. When they stop and drop their packs, I put out my arm to signal that we should stop as well. I feel like we would be intruding on a sacred ritual if we move closer. Manny smiles with a puzzled wrinkling of his forehead, but complies.

"Let's watch from here," I whisper, as if we've spotted a pair of rare birds and don't want to spook them.

The young man and woman pay us no heed as they don their harnesses and helmets, arrange the rope, change into the sort of colorful climbing shoes we used when Horizons visited an indoor climbing gym, and begin their ascent. Only after the man follows his partner a hundred feet or more up the rock do I move.

"I want to learn to do that," I say at a normal volume.

Manny chuckles and shakes out a leg. "We can come out of hiding now?"

Ignoring his question, I scurry to the spot where they started and press my body against the rock so I can look straight up its surface to them. "Don't you? Want to learn to rock climb?"

"I've never even considered it before."

I turn to look at him. "Have you ever climbed in a gym?"

"Nope."

I roll my eyes. "Well, we need to do something about that."

"Not necessarily. It doesn't really appeal to me."

I try not to let my disappointment show. "I'm going to see if Horizons will add a rock climbing session to the schedule. Real rock climbing, not just the indoor kind."

He nods and turns back toward the trail. "Ready to go back?"

He's probably getting bored with all this. "Sure," I say, my voice flat, and I follow him back the way we came.

We don't speak as we're hiking this time. As the parking lot comes into view, he breaks the silence.

"Robin, I know you're worried about me moving up here, but I swear we'll still see each other and we can talk by phone every day. If you're ever having a rough time at home, you know you can call me. You're my girl." He caresses my cheek and I manage a smile.

We move into each other's arms and hold tight, his hand rubbing in a circle on my back.

"Hey, get a room!" someone shouts and I open my eyes to see three guys hiking toward us, laughing and jostling one another. Manny and I separate and he gives them a friendly wave.

Maybe it's just my imagination, but as they pass, one seems to lock eyes with Manny and they watch each other much too long before he turns away and jogs up to catch his buddies.

There are several reasons I don't believe Manny's prediction about our future and that's just one of them.

***

Meanwhile, we each start our summer jobs – me at Expanding Horizons as a counselor-in-training, or CIT as we're known, and Manny mowing lawns for a landscaping company. With evenings and weekends free, we usually see each other two or three times a week, often taking walks or attending a free outdoor concert, no matter what type of music. Clay basically ignores me other than to remind me every single time I go out that my curfew is at 10:00. As if I could have forgotten since a couple of nights earlier.

In Doris's eyes, however, I can still do nothing right. She keeps assigning me more and more household chores, despite being perpetually dissatisfied with everything I'm already doing. Like ironing. I hate ironing. I can never get the collars of Clay's shirts to come out right and apparently the creases in his sleeves aren't perfectly matched up. Or dusting. There's the original list of surfaces that need attention, but it grows every week to include the tops of doors and the cracks and crevices of cabinets and the heat registers and the window screens and blinds and curtain rods and even the leaves on the houseplants.

She follows me around as I work, dreaming up new tasks for me or tallying up anything I skip. "You missed the top of the toaster, girl."

"But I wiped that when I did the kitchen after dinner."

"Don't give me that back talk. That was last night. Look at it – there are crumbs all over."

So I dutifully brush the half dozen crumbs that obviously came off her toast this morning – nobody else had any – and deposit them in the garbage can.

"Attitude, girl. Don't give me that sour look. You missed

the back corner of the refrigerator. You know, if you weren't so stupid, I wouldn't have to watch over your work like this. You can't get anything right."

I try to put on a neutral expression, but the effect is probably lost since I can't seem to unclench my jaw. She never cleaned this thoroughly when I was younger and couldn't manage some of these tasks. Now she barely lifts a hand to do anything around the house and Clay never has. If this house were any cleaner, you could perform surgery in here.

When I'm not at work, I escape to be with Manny whenever I can, or to spend time alone, something I'm quite adept at.

He and I attend a huge fireworks display on the Fourth of July. As we sit in his car afterwards, waiting for the traffic to die down, he says, "I've got something special in mind this weekend for your birthday. Do you think your grandparents will let you stay out past ten on Friday night?"

"I kind of doubt it, but I've never asked. What time should I try for?"

"At least eleven. But midnight would be even better."

No way they'll agree to midnight. I'll be lucky if they go with eleven.

He must see the doubt in my face. "Here's an idea. What if I call them and tell them where we're going and the timing. Then they'll understand why you need to be out later."

"Why not just tell *me*?"

He laughs. "'Cause it's a surprise, dummy."

I spin away from him and stare out the passenger window. I know he doesn't mean it like that, like I'm dumb, but my throat has grown tight and my eyes are burning and I want to rewind the world just a few seconds and have him say that again without calling me names.

"Hey, what's wrong?" He tries to take my hand but I pull it away. "Robin? Please talk to me. You know you can tell me anything."

I've told him so much that I've never shared with anyone else, except maybe years ago when I was friends with Lupe. No, I've told him much more. About my mother disappearing without so much as a note and them taking Annie away from me and Clay hitting me and Doris always belittling me. We've never really talked about all the other boys, but I know he knows. But I can't bring myself to say the words out loud about how much that word hurts coming from him. If I try, I know I'll start crying and he'll feel terrible and my birthday surprise will be ruined. Although I really shouldn't let him go through with whatever he's got in mind.

"Can you take me home now?" I say, my voice gravelly and small.

I can feel him watching me. Finally, he starts the engine and pulls out into the street.

"You can try calling them," I say after several minutes. I turn forward again and attempt a smile, reach over and give his hand a squeeze.

"It's okay?" he asks, trying to read my expression and watch the road at the same time.

"It's okay."

*** 

The surprise turns out to be tickets to a live performance of a musical in a cozy theater downtown. The bigger surprise is that Doris and Clay agreed to a midnight curfew, since the play doesn't get out until ten o'clock or so and it's a good half hour drive back out to their house in the suburbs. Manny told them he wanted to take me out for a late dessert after the show.

"Don't be getting any ideas, girl. This is a one-time thing and only because so far your young man has gotten you home on time," Clay told me after Doris informed me of their decision.

"When your Aunt Sophie turned sixteen, we held a party for her. Remember, Clay? I made her Sweet Sixteen dress and she acted so embarrassed when most of her girlfriends showed up terribly underdressed for the occasion. I told her there was no reason for her to feel bad, other than it showed the poor upbringing of her friends."

Clay's only response was, "Midnight. Sharp."

Thank God she didn't decide to make *me* a dress for my birthday. I can just imagine a frilly, lace-decorated costume that looks like something Shirley Temple wore in the movies back when she was about five years old.

I do try to look special for the theater, though. With the advice of Laura at work, I select my simple, pale yellow dress and add a beautiful scarf she loaned me and showed me how to tie. The color enhances my early-summer tan. Her long, dangling earrings add a touch of elegance.

"You look gorgeous," Manny says when he picks me up. He's looking sharp in a suit jacket over a solid blue shirt that brings out the blue in his eyes. Only, I think he's going to be much too warm in that outfit.

The theater is small and intimate, with skinny tables in front of each row, not at all like the auditorium seating I expected. As the show begins, I take a final sip of my Coke and forget about it as I'm drawn into the performance. The actors are steps away and at the intermission, I find myself humming the theme melody.

"What do you think?" Manny asks as we wait for the play to resume.

"It's wonderful! What a great birthday present. Thank you so much."

The second half goes by much too quickly and we exit the building feeling excited and upbeat, both singing the theme song at the top of our lungs as we head for the parking lot. Other patrons look our way and a few join in, laughing.

We end up in a restaurant that serves nothing but pie and beverages. He orders peach and I opt for dark chocolate peanut butter, which is so rich I can't finish it. Back in the car, driving toward home, we both realize we have over forty-five minutes to spare before my curfew.

"Let's stop somewhere quiet," I say. "Maybe over by Windsome Lake." It's a lesser-known make out spot I visited one time with a guy whose name I can't remember at the moment. We were the only ones there and I cross my fingers, hoping what's-his-name won't be there tonight with a different girl. With luck, we'll have the place to ourselves.

It's hardly large enough to deserve to be called a lake, but the water is pretty at night, reflecting the moon. Surrounded by cottonwoods with massive trunks, we're able to find a secluded spot to park.

Despite my days as the class slut, the term I heard bandied about at school, I'm technically a virgin. Thinking back on my activities, I realize I was more interested in snuggling after getting the guy off than anything else. Boys who wouldn't hold me for a while before taking me back to crawl through my bedroom window didn't get another chance with me.

Although I didn't plan this ahead of time, and even with

the limited amount of time available to us, I want to change that tonight. Manny's been the perfect gentleman every time we've been together – maybe too perfect. We've kissed for hours, yet he's never once made a move to feel my breasts. It's time I let him know that I'm ready for more and he doesn't have to hold back any longer. I'm ready to go all the way with him.

As always, his kisses send an electric current through my body and I feel myself getting turned on. His arms are wrapped around me, so I reach up and caress his face with one hand, knowing he'll respond by doing the same to me. I wait a moment once he does, my tongue deep inside his mouth, exploring. He moans with pleasure and I take his hand, guiding it to my breast.

He pulls away and sits up straight, staring at his hand cupped around me as if he'd never seen it before.

"It's okay," I say softly. "I don't want to hold back any longer."

He withdraws his hand and grasps mine instead. Have I made a terrible mistake? He doesn't want to have sex. *Remember, stupid?* He thinks he's probably gay.

"I...didn't expect this."

My head lowered, I shake it from side to side. "I'm sorry, Manny. I shouldn't have pushed you. Just forget that happened, okay?"

His hand gently lifts my chin. "Don't be sorry. You just took me by surprise, that's all. I don't want to forget. I'd like to...are you sure that's what you want?"

We stare into each other's eyes, illuminated by the moon but our faces striped with shadows from the trees. A cricket chirps a rhythm that matches the thumping of my heart. "Do you have a blanket?" I ask.

We settle on the ground, a warm breeze ruffling our hair and kissing our skin as we undress. The dappled moonlight spills across his body and he looks like a beautiful, marble statue. He looks down at me, lying naked on the blanket, with both tenderness and desire.

Our joining is painful at first, but soon I'm lost in the feel of skin against skin and the primal dance of our bodies as we make love. I don't have to beg him to snuggle and hold me close afterwards and he kisses my hair as I lie with my head against his chest, listening to the whoosh-a-whoosh of his heart pumping blood through his body.

I wish we could stay like this all night, but we rouse ourselves and dress quickly, realizing the time. Manny speeds the rest of the way to my house, pulling up to the curb just one minute before midnight.

"Made it," he says as I notice a gap in the front curtains of the house close up. He gives me a quick but thrilling kiss before hurrying around the car to open my door and escort me to the front porch.

"Goodnight, Robin," he whispers as he strokes the back of my hair. "I'll see you soon."

"Goodnight, Manny," I answer, checking myself just in time before saying "Goodbye" and giving away my secret.

***

I mail the letters at the downtown bus depot just before boarding the bus to Flagstaff. It's better this way. I know Manny will meet another girl – or maybe it'll be a guy – this fall when he goes off to college. I couldn't face telling him in person that I'm leaving and this way, once Clay and Doris realize I'm never returning home from work, he won't have to lie to them about where I've gone, since he won't know. As for the letter to my father, I just told him I'm starting a new life and not to worry. I'll be in touch.

Once we're rolling along the highway, I pull out a ten-day-old classified section of the Flagstaff newspaper that I sneaked out of the library on the way to the station and begin circling ads for roommates and jobs. I've got a fake youth hostel membership card, so I'm set for a few nights, but I'll need to figure out something else quickly.

# CHAPTER 28 - KATHARINE

"Watch the baby for a few minutes, Robin, and don't take her out of the playpen," I say as I scurry out the door. Annie has started walking and is a proficient crawler, but if her sister will let her stay put, she shouldn't get into anything. I'm toting my surprise for Roy stuffed into a black garbage bag. When he gets home from a long trip like this one, he always likes to take a long shower, bring up a shave, and heaven knows what else in the privacy of the bathroom. I know I have enough time.

I climb up into the cab of his truck, realizing I haven't been inside in at least six months. That's when he started insisting on stripping the bed and bringing all his laundry in, rather than have me do it. "It's not fair to dump all these chores on you, sweetheart," he told me, his broad smile bringing out his dimple. "I do my own laundry on the road. You shouldn't have to be my maid."

He also insisted on making up the bed again once the laundry was clean. I almost got the impression that he didn't want me inside the truck, but I was probably just being paranoid and negative. I get that way sometimes.

Before I start, I take a moment to perch in my old seat and remember how things used to be before the kids. How I loved every minute of our travels together. Maybe when Annie starts school...

I sigh. That's what I told myself about Robin and then, boom, pregnant with Annie. Well, that's not going to happen again. Getting my tubes tied while Roy was away was one of the best decisions I've ever made.

I tidy up a bit, gathering a crushed paper bag and beverage container from McDonald's from the floor, checking several receipts stuffed into one of the cup holders to see if they need to be entered into my ledgers, and scrounging through the large glove box, pulling out more trash, a used drinking straw, a plastic fork with only two tines, and a pair of pink sunglasses, which he probably found and planned to give to Robin. I suppose he doesn't realize that she hates pink. I leave them.

Glancing at the clock on the dash, I realize I'd better get moving. I pull the new sheets and bedspread I made for Roy from the bag and quickly make the bed. After I add the colorful throw pillow and matching sheers to hang over the black-out blinds, I survey the effect of the sleeper make-over. He's going to love it!

I've been working on this surprise during his last two trips, hoping to set a better tone for our time together than how it's been going. Bring back some of the tenderness and the romance to our marriage. I've promised myself to keep a positive outlook while he's here – no complaints about being stuck at home for weeks while he's on the road, no nagging about how he's taken on more and more hours, no questioning about how he's spending the extra income. As Abby says, you can catch more flies with honey than with vinegar.

As I open the blinds so sunlight streams through the sheers, something shiny on the floor just under the bed catches my eye. I kneel to examine it and come up with a lovely earring – a single pearl dangling from a short, golden chain. It's not mine.

I sit on the bed that I've just smoothed, the earring in my hand, and stare at it. Maybe there's an innocent explanation. I try to imagine what it might be, but nothing comes to mind. Pulling open a drawer, I sort through his remaining clean socks and underwear, a single t-shirt, and a baggie filled with earplugs. And an open box of condoms.

I remain frozen in that spot for five minutes. Or maybe it's been an hour. Either way, Roy is undoubtedly out of the bathroom by now and wondering where the hell I am.

*Honey, not vinegar.*

If I storm in there to confront him with the evidence, what then? He leaves me with a one- and a six-year-old, very limited income as a seamstress, and no prospects for employment. Abby and her husband are talking about moving to a bigger place, so there goes my only close friend. There are a couple of other women in the building who've traded off with me to babysit for short spurts while one of us goes shopping or manages a doctor's appointment, but I know I've worn my welcome thin. They've helped me out a lot more than I've helped them.

It's just sex, right? He's gone for such long stretches at a time...men have needs, right? It's just sex. With me, he has a history, someone who loves him, two beautiful daughters.

That's all this is about. Sex. I'm not going to throw away my marriage and the rest of my life because Roy needs someone to screw during those long trips. And he's being safe about it, using rubbers to help protect both of us from anything those hookers may be carrying.

I need to stick with my original plan for this week.

*Honey, not vinegar.* I'll show him how I've spruced up his sleeper and I'll finish preparing tonight's special dinner. I won't say anything. I'll put the girls to bed early tonight so Roy and I can enjoy a quiet evening. Light candles, pour some wine, set the mood. Instead of waiting until his last night home, I'll wear my new nightie tonight and we'll make love like we used to – slow and sweet.

I dab at my eyes and blow my nose. *It's going to be all right.*

***

As I watch from the window, Roy's truck disappears down the street. Things didn't go quite the way I planned this week, but I hung in there. Maybe he picked up on my fears, no matter how hard I tried to be loving and upbeat. When we did connect, our lovemaking was tepid. He claimed to be too tired to even try that first night, despite my sexy new nightgown. Another night, his back was bothering him.

If I face the truth, this week wasn't much different from how things have been for a while now. I still haven't managed to shed the extra pounds from my last pregnancy. Or even from my first, for that matter. Maybe he just doesn't find me attractive anymore. Which isn't fair at all, since I don't care at all about the weight he's put on since he starting driving the long routes. More of him to love, and all that.

Still, I think he appreciated the extra attention I lavished on him. We had some laughs, especially with the girls when we all visited the zoo and Robin became so fascinated with the panther pacing in its cage. She would slink back and forth with him, staring into his eyes. Annie squealed in delight at the monkeys, pointing and babbling at them.

"Mommy, what are those monkeys doing?" Robin asked after watching a male dashing in a frenzy around the large display area only to fly up a tree-like pole and start humping a female that had been lounging quietly in the branches.

"Playing," I said at the same time Roy answered, "Hugging." We both tried to keep a straight face, but whenever we glanced at each other for the next ten minutes, we'd both burst out laughing before forcing it down again.

"Why are you snorting, Daddy?"

We just lost it, our laughter coming out as *guffaws*, tears streaming down my face. At least for that little while, I forgot all my worries.

*****

For the past four weeks I've been working on a list of special things to do when Roy comes home again. Favorite dishes, places to take the kids that we'll also enjoy, alternate ideas in case he's not crazy about something I dreamed up. I've mended his favorite pants that wore through the butt, but first I made a pattern from them and just put the finishing touches on an identical pair. Whenever an image of him with another woman creeps into my mind, I push it away and focus on some project, like cleaning the apartment from top to bottom or coaching Annie to say *Dada* in response to her daddy's photo.

"Who's that?" I say, pointing to the picture.

If I'm lucky, she'll point at me and say, "Mama!" Robin often pitches in to help, but I fear that all we may accomplish is to get Annie to associate *Dada* with photographs, not with her living, breathing father.

"When's Daddy coming home? I wanna go to the zoo

again."

I've convinced her that we can only manage big outings like the zoo if he's with us. Truth is, it's damn hard to manage both kids without another adult to help. Robin loves to run off if I don't keep a close eye on her. Annie often turns fussy in her stroller and she's getting too heavy to carry a long way. And of course there's finding a place to change her diaper while Robin is antsy to get going, and trying to feed both of them, and on and on.

"I told you, kiddo. Tomorrow." She's asked daily for the past two weeks. I've tried having her help mark off the days on the calendar in the kitchen and I *know* she understands this – she's crazy smart. She's just being a pain in the butt. "Tell you what. Why don't you run down to the playground?"

I send her out the door. She's fine with riding the elevator down by herself and making her way to the swings and slide which I can see from the girls' bedroom window if I press my cheek against the pane. Gloria, who has a six-year-old of her own, let me know that she was appalled that I let Robin play down there by herself, but almost a third of the apartments have windows overlooking the playground, so it's not like nobody's around if she falls off a swing or something. And there are usually other kids and a parent or two down there on a nice weekend like this. It's just too complicated to take Annie down there too, plus I've got to get dinner started so I can't be hovering over Robin every minute. Besides, she's very independent – she loves being free to go play on her own.

When Roy arrives the next afternoon, Robin races downstairs to greet him. He helps her climb up into the cab, one of their rituals whenever he comes home. I'm surprised when she bursts into the apartment again without him.

"Daddy says we need four batteries," she declares. "C

batteries. He bought me a big rig just like his!" She holds her hands about two feet apart. "But I have to play with it on the sidewalk, not inside."

"How cool," I say as I rummage through a kitchen drawer, hoping we actually have four C batteries on hand. "We're in luck. Here you go."

She's out the door again in a flash. Ten minutes later, Roy makes an appearance without her.

"She sounds thrilled with her present," I say. "Maybe she'll grow up to be a trucker like her dad."

He doesn't return my smile, but stands just inside the doorway, his jaw muscles twitching.

"What's wrong?"

Without a word, he takes a step toward me and hands me a large manila envelope.

My hand trembles as I take it from him, but I try to maintain my smile. *Honey, not vinegar.* "What's this?" I say and my voice cracks, betraying me.

"I've filed for divorce," he says as if he were telling me the time of day. "I'm not asking for anything but the tractor so I can make a living. The lawyer told me I shouldn't even offer child support, but I couldn't do that. I think the amount is reasonable, but if you want to get a lawyer and turn this into an expensive fight, I guess that's up to you."

My mouth doesn't seem to be working. I hold the envelope using both hands at arms' length, as if it might bite me if it gets too close. "But..." I manage. No other words seem possible.

"I'm just gonna pick up the rest of my clothes and go. I'll call tomorrow to see if you've signed those papers or you're going to make this harder."

"Aren't you even going to go see your other daughter?

She's down for a nap."

This finally draws some emotion from him as his eyes grow moist and he looks toward the girls' bedroom. "I don't want to wake her. She barely knows who I am anyway." He turns to leave. "I'll tell Robin I have to hit the road again. Unless you want me to try to explain this to her right now."

Whether she learns the news now from him or later from me, I'll still be the one to comfort her and help her understand, and that's going to take a hell of a lot longer than he's going to be around for her. Better to just let her be mad for the moment that he's leaving before taking her to the zoo.

"No. I'll talk to her."

He nods. "Right. Read that over and we'll talk tomorrow night."

I drop the documents on the table and clench my fists, trying hard not to cry in front of him. "Who is she?" I choke out.

Roy glances at me one more time before walking away. When I hear the *ding* of the elevator and the sound of its door closing, I slam the apartment door. "God damn you, Roy!" I scream, anger coursing through me like lightning in a storm. "You bastard!"

Annie's cries from the bedroom break through my rage and the tears I've been holding back escape, my sobs competing with hers in an ugly chorus.

"Why?" I weep, "Why are you abandoning me? Why don't you love me anymore?"

# CHAPTER 29 - ROBIN

Trying not to get my hopes up, I slide the letter opener carefully across the top of the envelope. I've had so many rejection letters – why should this one be any different?

"Oh my God!" I shriek when I spot the word *Congratulations!* "Sandi! They're publishing my story!"

My roommate rushes into the kitchen, half her hair neatly styled and the other half still frizzy from her shower. "Which magazine?"

"*Cloudshadow.*" I'm sure she's never heard of it, but it features three short stories in each quarterly issue. "And they sent money!" I wave a check high above my head, dancing in circles around the room. It's less than I usually take home each week in tips from Highpoint Bistro, but this is the first time I've received *payment* for a piece I've written, so it's a big deal.

She throws her arms around me. "I knew it. I told you you'll be a famous author someday. You're on your way."

Folding the check carefully before slipping it into my purse, I smile as I shake my head. "I've got to get to work. Enjoy your date." I grab a light jacket from the closet, expecting the night to be chilly by the time I get off after the dinner shift, and head out.

I work through two problems on my math homework while riding the bus. With my work schedule, I'm taking only three credit classes and no electives this term as a junior. At this rate, assuming I manage three more per term, including two summer school sessions, I may be able to graduate only six months later than my high school class back in Colorado. The problem is finding time for things like sleep or doing anything with friends.

Dating? No way.

Pamela, my counselor at SafeTeen Place, *suggests* (they're all very careful not to tell runaways what we *must* do) that I give myself one extra semester to graduate and not push myself so hard. While I'm grateful for all she and the staff have done to help me since I arrived in Flagstaff, I want to get my diploma as soon as I can manage. I've already contacted a college about their creative writing program, but I can't go anywhere with that until I finish high school. With great grades, since I'm going to need all the financial assistance I can get.

I share my exciting news with Jake and Rose during our shift. Jake wants to be an actor and always earns great tips from his tables with his flair for entertaining the customers.

"I told you, I expect you to write me a play next," he jokes.

"Now you're famous," Rose says, frozen in place holding a tray of beverages. "I guess you won't be working here anymore." I think she's serious. She's a hard worker and the diners seem to like her, but she's not the sharpest knife in the Bistro. I assure her that I'm neither famous nor rich now, just the same old Robin waiting tables and praying for decent tips.

As I finish wiping down the tables at the end of my shift, I consider calling Annie with my news. It's an hour earlier in

California, so she should still be up. It's been over a month since I last phoned her and I'm not even sure why I keep trying to connect with her again. Last Thanksgiving was heartbreaking for me and I dread the thought that Dad might invite me again this year. Of course, he can't do that unless I call him, since I haven't given him my phone number or address yet. After Annie's cool reaction to seeing me, for the rest of that day I kept hoping it was just the shock of it all that made her seem distant. Waiting for our opportunity to talk once we headed to bed was all that kept me going through Thanksgiving dinner.

Our half-siblings weren't sent to bed until nine o'clock. I feigned sleepiness a half hour later, hoping that Annie would follow me to our shared room shortly, but it was after ten before she walked in, changed into her pajamas, and crawled into the other bed.

"Hey, Annie. Remember that drawing you sent me with the sun and the pigtails? I still have it."

Long pause. "I don't remember that."

"It was soon after you went to San Diego. You drew our aunt and uncle and cousin Billy, and then you drew pigtails on the sun, so I knew that meant you were thinking of me."

"Bill. He doesn't like to be called Billy anymore."

I bit my lip. "Okay. How about that time we ran after the ice cream truck for like three blocks before he stopped, but he didn't notice us and we had to race after him for another two blocks. And I got there first and begged him to wait so you could catch up. And when he saw how hard we were both panting, he gave us our cones for free. Remember?"

"No."

"No?" I asked, beginning to feel desperate. "How about the time Dad came to visit and brought us that doll playhouse and you used to put Bunny in it and we'd make up stories about —"

"No! I don't remember any of that stuff, Robin, so stop asking and let me go to sleep."

I lay awake for what seemed like hours, listening to her deep breathing and staring at the glowing numbers on the alarm clock, watching the minutes advance. The second and final night we spent in that room together, I tried to coax her to share something she did remember from when we were together.

"I remember falling off a swing and scraping my knees. You tried to brush the dirt off, but it hurt so I ran away from you. And I remember..." she trailed off.

"What?" I said as gently as I could. "What else do you remember?"

She was silent for a long time and I thought she wasn't going to tell me, or had fallen asleep, but finally she spoke. "I remember Mom didn't come home and I was hungry and you made me eat a gross sandwich."

"There was hardly anything there to eat. I did the best I could." Did she have any happy memories of me?

I realized then that she had been so young when we were separated that she barely remembered our life together. She had few memories of our mother and almost none of Dad prior to her move to San Diego. Mom often charged me with watching over my baby sister while she did whatever she needed or wanted to do, but during that last year or so, I was ready for any opportunity to take off and run around with my friends or find an adventure of my own.

I decide not to call Annie with my exciting news. She won't care and our conversation will be just as awkward and one-sided as always. Maybe I'll just mail her a copy once the publication comes out.

# CHAPTER 30 - KATHARINE

It's still dark out when Roger drops me off at the apartment. Robin has started asking questions about the noises in my bedroom when he stays over, so we've both found it more comfortable if we go to his place. At ten, after a special school program about the birds and the bees, she's already asking for a better explanation about *how* the sperm gets from the man's penis to the woman's uterus. I've tried to explain things so she doesn't connect my answers with the mystery of our bedroom activities, but my daughter is no dummy.

I remove my shoes and tiptoe to my room, trying not to wake the girls. Annie sometimes gets distressed if she realizes I didn't spend the night here. This reminds me of my days of sneaking out of the house and crawling back in through my bedroom window when I was a teenager, trying not to alert Father and Mother about my overnight outings. At least the consequences of getting caught now by my kids are very minor.

After changing into fresh clothes for work, I turn on the coffee maker, sprinkling the top of the used coffee grounds with a teaspoon of fresh grounds. I'll have a decent cup or two at the office, but this will have to suffice for now. Either that, or skip it until I get paid again on Friday.

At least it's hot.

"Hi, Mom."

Robin shuffles into the kitchen, her eyes half closed and her hair sticking up on top. I think about offering to brush it out and fix her hair in pigtails, but she knows how to do it herself now and she's so independent that she probably prefers doing it herself.

"Hi, kiddo. You're up early. Sorry if I woke you."

She simply shrugs. "Nothing from Dad," she says, pointing to a stack of mail on the counter.

*Shit.* We really need that check. "Maybe it'll come tomorrow," I say, wondering if it'll do any good to call and lay a guilt trip on him. Or try to find a lawyer who'll help squeeze child support payments out of him without charging me a fee that I can't possibly pay. But I know I'll just try to hang in there, hoping the checks will resume in another month or two, like they have in the past.

"What does *Final Notice* mean?" she asks, flipping through the envelopes and retrieving one with a huge, red stamp across the front. It's from the phone company.

I close my eyes for a moment. Can we get by without a phone, at least until Roy decides to start sending money again?

"That's just something they put on there so I won't think it's junk mail and throw it away."

"So...they want you to be sure to *notice* it?"

"Yeah. You got it, kiddo." My so-called coffee has cooled and is too awful to finish, so I pour it down the sink. "I gotta get moving. Be sure to hold Annie's hand crossing the streets on the way to school."

She looks at me like I'm an idiot. "I know. You don't have to tell me."

She's right. She's been walking her little sister to and from her preschool class all year. "Sorry. Just one of those 'mother' things I thought I should say. I'll see you later."

"Are you going out with Uncle Roger again tonight?"

"Probably," I answer. Actually, Roger's busy tonight, I suspect with another woman. That doesn't matter. With my bourbon supply even lower than my coffee stash, I might try my luck at Finnegan's later. It's a rare evening when I can't find a gentleman there to buy me a drink, maybe even treat me to dinner.

When I arrive at the office, my in-box is loaded with invoices to tally. Armed with a tall mug of fresh, strong coffee, I hunker down at my computer terminal to enter them and produce the daily reports for my boss. Darlene is leaving at the end of the month, so I've been coming in early and offering to take on even more bookkeeping tasks, hoping they'll promote me to her position as accountant when she leaves. Surely that will make more sense than hiring someone from outside the company, even if they do have formal training. I'm self-taught, but after three years here, I know exactly how they like things done.

I heat up some ramen for lunch – the same lunch I've eaten for the past two weeks since Roy's last support check was supposed to arrive – and eat it at my desk so I can get back to working on the aging analysis report for Darlene. She seems pleased to shift more and more responsibilities to me as she winds down, which I take to be a positive sign.

Before I head over to Finnegan's, I swing by the apartment to change to something flashier than the simple dress I wore to work. The girls aren't home, which makes things easier. They're probably playing with some of their other friends in the building – Robin will look after the little one. I flip through the latest stack of mail that she's piled with yesterday's, see nothing that warrants immediate attention, and head out the door to walk the three blocks to my favorite bar and grill.

\*\*\*

I smile sweetly over at William as I take another sip of wine. He's a step above the usual breed of men whom I've met at the bar. Make that an entire flight of stairs above. No deluxe burger or chicken-fried steak at Finnegan's, no sir. He's brought me to a true restaurant, complete with fabric napkins and tablecloths and waiters dressed head to toe in black. He paid my tab at the bar and brought me here for the fanciest meal I've had since my honeymoon.

I shove that thought away. "And your company paid your way for the whole trip?" I ask, trying to imagine the wonder of flying to London and staying at a Bed & Breakfast, all expenses paid.

He chuckles. "It was a lucky break. My supervisor broke his ankle four days before he was supposed to go meet with his counterpart at our sister company in England, so I got to go in his place. Now mind you," he says, carving another bite of steak, "I was in meetings for six hours a day for the entire week, but in the evenings some of the *gents*," he says with a British accent, "took me around to the local pubs and showed me places like Buckingham Palace and Big Ben."

"That sounds so exciting!"

He finishes chewing before speaking again. "Unfortunately, I never got to visit the museums or see Madame Tussauds or take any of the tours, but maybe I'll get to go back some time and just be a tourist."

"I'd love to do that someday," I say, before realizing how I sound. *Get a grip.* I just met this man and here I am, daydreaming of traveling to faraway places together. Isn't that exactly how things started with Roy and me? And look how that turned out.

"I mean, to have a job where I'm paid to travel the world."

"Yeah, I'd like that, too, but I can't see it happening any time soon. That was a one-shot piece of luck. Unless, of course, I shove Frank down a flight of stairs just before his next trip. You think anyone'll suspect foul play?" he asks, a glint in his eye.

Laughing appreciatively, I shake my head. "You can count on me – I won't tell a soul."

"Nope. They just send me here to Indianapolis once a month. Cincinnati, too. That's my three-state region, since I get to count the home office in Chicago. Pretty exciting stuff, isn't it?"

It sounds better than my life, which seldom extends beyond a six-mile radius of the apartment. Home, office, grocery store, Goodwill, Finnegan's, doctor's office, bank branch, library. That's about it.

I steal another glance at his left hand. No, I don't see any signs that he might sometimes wear a wedding ring, so I think he's told me the truth. I didn't lie, I just kept my answer as short and simple as I could, labeling myself as single with no mention of divorce or children. He didn't press for details.

William insists on ordering brandy at the end of our meal, which I've never tried before but fall in love with immediately. Somehow, through the haze of all the booze I've imbibed tonight, I start to worry about how the evening is going to end. Unlike at Finnegan's, where I can refuse to go home with a man who's treated me to a few drinks and possibly a meal and get some help from Les, the barkeeper, if my new friend wants more than a goodnight kiss, here I am, miles from home, with a man who has spent far more on me than I'm used to. He drove us here. I can hardly declare that I'm walking home and not getting into his car again, since he's – so far – given me no reason to send him packing.

"Penny for your thoughts," he says, and I swear I can hear Roy's voice saying the same thing twelve years ago, when we first started dating.

"Just thinking about how early I have to get up for work tomorrow," I answer, glancing at my watch. "This has been lovely, William, but I'm afraid I'd better call it a night. Shall we?" I add, pushing my chair back from the table.

"Allow me," he says, hurrying to help me with the chair. Like Roy used to. Now there's an old memory.

We listen to music on the radio as he drives and I pay close attention to our route. So far, so good – he's heading right back toward Finnegan's and asks me to give him directions from there to my apartment building.

When he pulls up in front, he turns off the engine and turns to me. "What a lovely evening, Katharine. Perhaps we can do this again when I get back into town next month?"

"I'd like that," I say. Reaching into my purse, I retrieve a pen and scrap of paper where I jot down my phone number. "I'd like that very much."

He leans across and touches my cheek softly. I move toward him and we kiss – nothing with fireworks and bells ringing, but a warm, gentle kiss. "Goodnight, then. I'll call you soon."

He doesn't try to manipulate an invitation to come up to

my place. That's good, because I told the truth when I said I'd like to see him again. That would have been the end of things if he'd pushed me – I don't go for that.

The apartment is dark except for a light on over the stove. Robin is often thoughtful like that. I notice two clean bowls in the rack next to the sink. The girls must have eaten here, then. Sometimes Robin finagles a meal from one of our neighbors if I'm not around.

She's a very clever, independent girl who has no trouble taking care of herself and her little sister. That cow, Helen, who thinks she's better than me, had the nerve last week to call me a "negligent mother." Just because her eleven-year-old brat clings to her like a wet rag doesn't mean my kids need me hovering over them every minute. Negligent, my ass. I'm not going to turn into my mother, who had rules for every little thing and watched me like a hawk. I'm not going to break their spirits like Mother and Father tried to do with me. No way.

# CHAPTER 31 - ROBIN

"Remember the exercise we did with building the scene around the dialog?" I ask Brianna.

She nods, gnawing on the end of her pencil. We make her use the chewed up ones each week, since none of the other kids want to touch them. "Like describing where they are and what they're doing while they talk?"

"Exactly. You've done a great job with capturing how Bonnie and Carla each speak, but are they just standing like this while they have this conversation?" I plaster my arms to my sides and straighten my back. "Or are they walking down the street? Are they in Bonnie's house or at school?"

Brianna removes the pencil from her teeth and squints in concentration. "Okay. Got it!" She snatches her notebook from my hands and scurries back to her desk.

She's got talent and seems far less anxious than she did at the start of the program. I feel my smile spread across my face. My internship with this writing program for "troubled youth" has turned out better than I could have ever dreamed. When my school counselor recommended working at Youth Writes this summer, I was a bit taken aback. How stupid it was for me to write an essay about my experience at Expanding Horizons. I had no idea that Miss Eastgate would

215

pass that information along to anyone else, even get it added to my school record. I should never give away details like that which might link me back to my grandparents. Stupid, stupid, stupid.

But it turned out great after all. I'm earning school credits plus a small salary, I get to help kids like Brianna with their writing, and I'm managing to squeeze in a history class three nights a week that counts toward graduation as well.

At four o'clock, after the kids head for their busses, I help Carlos gather up supplies and close up the room. Mr. Karn, a soft spoken, giant of a man, meets us in the hallway.

"Hey, Winston," Carlos says, amicably. I'm comfortable addressing Carlos by his first name, since we work together every afternoon and he's not all that old, maybe twenty-five, but I can't bring myself to address the head of our program as anything but Mr. Karn.

"Hey, Carlos. How'd the session go today?"

"Not bad. Anthony wrote a poem without a single swear word, if you can believe it."

That earns a chuckle from all of us. "Good. Maybe we can let him read it out loud for the others. Finally."

"Well, not quite yet. There's still a stanza that's R-rated for violence. But we're making progress."

"Keep up the good work." Mr. Karn turns to me. "Robin, can you stay a few minutes. I have something I'd like to talk to you about."

Carlos waves as he heads toward the door. "Uh, sure," I say, and follow him to his office. Is something wrong?

After we both sit, he gives me a broad smile, the white of his teeth gleaming in contrast to his dark complexion. I ease my grip on the arms of my chair. "We want to update our program brochure. We've got a team doing the design work and layout, but we need to really polish up the content. Take what we've been using and bring it up to date with what our program is now and bring some emotion into the descriptions."

My eyebrows twitch as I suppress a smile, remembering how dreadfully dull the informational document seemed when I first read it. For a program emphasizing writing composition, it was a pathetic effort. But why is he telling me this? Does he want the writer to talk to some of our most promising kids?

"I know you've got a pretty full plate, what with your hours here plus your night classes, but I have a proposition for you. Would you be willing to be part of the team?" he asks.

"Me?" I stare into his face, trying to decide if I've misunderstood.

"Yes, you, Robin. I've been hearing great things about your work. Congratulations, by the way, on having another story published. How many does that make for you now?"

"Three," I say, lowering my eyes.

"Three. That's excellent. So, what do you think?" He slides a copy of the current publication across his desk to me. I'm quite familiar with it. "We'll be keeping the brochure to eight pages, like it is now. Most of the topics will stay the same, but we're scrapping the piece on page six entirely. We want more photos of the youngsters in the workshops and some excerpts of their writing." He flips through the pages, where someone has planted sticky notes with comments on graphics and layout.

"Oh, I almost forgot. We can offer a flat payment of $250 and we're shooting for getting this ready in the next six to eight weeks."

I nearly fall out of my chair. That'll pay my share of rent for a month. Plus, I'll still be getting paid for working here afternoons.

"Yes! Thank you, Mr. Karn. I'd love to take that on."

"Winston. Please call me Winston."

He's asked me several times before, so I make the effort. "Thank you, Winston. I won't let you down."

He smiles as he rises and offers his massive hand to shake. "I'm confident you won't, Robin. Now, you just remember old Winston Karn when you become a rich and famous author and I come asking for your autograph, okay?"

Riding the bus back home, I find myself whistling "Girls Just Wanna Have Fun." Even though I was just five when it first came out, it's been one of my favorites ever since. The older woman in front of me twists around briefly and gives me the evil eye, but the twenty-something gal across the aisle with a baby smiles and raises the child under his arms so he's standing on her lap, then bounces him in time to the tune as if he were dancing. He burbles in delight.

I'm allowed to be happy. I am. Leaving my grandparents' house was the best decision I've ever made.

# CHAPTER 32 - KATHARINE

I glare at the calculator as if it's to blame. Maybe if I run the numbers one more time...

My stomach hurts. I've gone through the bills and my checkbook so many times I've memorized each entry. There's no way I can pay both the rent and the utility bill, never mind buying anything but day-old bread and some sort of hyper-processed lunch meat, but only if it's still on sale. There's a late notice from the doctor's office from when Annie was running a high fever three months ago, they've shut off the phone, and Robin can barely squeeze her feet into last year's shoes, which are so worn out they'll probably fall apart before school starts again. We couldn't find any in her size last time we stopped by Goodwill, but we'll just have to keep trying.

Darlene, the former accountant at work, was replaced by Larry, whom they hired last week from outside the company. When I approached our department head today to ask why they didn't promote me instead, he cited exactly what I was afraid he would – my lack of a formal degree. I hit him up for a raise, and he dumped another load of bad news on me. "I was planning on waiting until Friday to tell everyone, but since you're here..." He frowned, and I knew things were about to get worse in my life. "You've seen the numbers,

Katharine. We're going to be cutting back across the board. I'm afraid your position is on the list of layoffs."

He went on to tell me about the packet I'd be receiving from personnel in a few days, but all I could do was run the numbers through my mind.

"Mommy, something's wrong with the TV."

"Then find something else to keep yourself occupied, Annie. I'm in the middle of something very important."

"But you told me to watch TV," she whines.

"Damn it, Annie! I just need you to get out of my hair. Go find your sister."

"She left and said I couldn't come with her."

I slam both hands on the table and the calculator slides off and crashes to the floor. "I said *go*! Get out of here and stop interrupting my work."

She stands there and stares at me as I bend over to retrieve the calculator, relieved to find that it still seems to be functioning. The moment I sit up again, she flees, grabbing her shabby stuffed rabbit and racing down the hall.

"The door, Annie," I shout after her, but she's already headed to the staircase rather than wait for the elevator to come. I rise and slam our apartment door shut.

In the silence of the room, I let out a long breath. What the hell am I going to do?

Maybe if I still had a phone, I'd try calling Roy and give him an ultimatum to send me last month's support payment along with the one coming up. That's not a conversation I care to have on the pay phone in the corner of the convenience store, next to the beer coolers. Chances are his whore of a wife would answer the call and I'd have to leave a message with her.

That's not going to happen.

Or maybe I should call William.

That first month after we met, he called me at ten p.m. sharp every Tuesday from his home in Chicago or, one week, from his hotel in Cincinnati. By the time his Indianapolis stint rolled around again, I felt like we'd been together for a long time. After taking me to a delightful dinner theater, he invited me to his hotel room and we made love. He had to leave early the next morning for meetings, but had room service deliver a scrumptious breakfast of Belgian waffles and smoked bacon. He's continued calling this month, until, of course, my phone service was canceled. I told him I had a new number – this pay phone. I walk down here on Tuesday nights after putting the girls to bed and hang around until he calls. Fortunately, there are seldom any customers in the place at that hour, and the night clerk – a greasy-haired, skinny guy who's so pale I wonder if he's ever been outdoors in sunlight – never looks up when I arrive or when I leave.

I scrounge through my purse for change, but don't come up with enough coins for a long-distance call. For a second, I consider asking the creepy employee behind the counter for change, but I'd rather he keep reading his girlie magazines and ignoring me. I'll call collect.

A minute later, I'm listening to the operator putting through my call. I eye the cold beers lined up like soldiers on parade in the cooler, wishing I could afford a six-pack.

"Go ahead, ma'am," the operator says and I huddle close to the phone, hoping my voice won't carry if I talk into the Plexiglas barrier which was somebody's idea of a privacy wall.

"William, hi. Thanks for taking my call."

"Well of course I accepted your call, *love*." He says *love*

221

just like I've heard in British movies. Like one of the Beatles. I grin every time I hear him say it. "Is something wrong?"

Where do I begin? "I'm losing my job, Will. They're laying a bunch of us off tomorrow. And the bills are piling up..." I blink back tears, but I know he can hear it in my voice.

"Whoa, whoa there, Katharine. Don't you cry, love. Maybe I can help you out for a bit, just till you get back on your feet. You know?"

I sniff and grab a wadded tissue out of my pocket, dabbing it to my nose. "Really?" My voice sounds like Annie's when her sister calms her down from some five-year-old's crisis and wipes away her tears.

"Of course. Listen, can you hang in there until a week from Monday?"

Rent isn't due for a week after he arrives. "Yeah," I answer, my voice sounding tentative.

"Ah. Tell you what – why don't I send you a little something right away. Would $300 help?"

Combined with what I've got in checking, that will keep the wolves from my door, at least until the end of the month. "Oh, William, I can't tell you how much I appreciate that. Thank you."

He pushes on. "I've got something special planned for my next visit. A little getaway for the two of us. What do you think of that, love?

Someplace special by his standards should be spectacular and the thought of getting away from all this stress for a night sounds like a dream. "Really? That would be wonderful."

After I hang up, I realize have my hands pressed to my chest. This man came into my life at just the right time.

But as I walk back home, a newspaper tucked under one arm, the other swinging a six-pack of beer by my side, I wonder if I should have told him the whole story. He's never once asked me if I was ever married, much less if I have kids. Our late evening calls have been after the girls were asleep, so he's never heard them crashing around the apartment, squealing and giggling, shouting and whining and crying. I've never asked him if he's been married or has kids, either.

After this special getaway, if it still seems like we might have something good going on together, maybe I'll bring it up.

***

"Two nights?" I take another few sips of wine, trying to imagine such a magnificent stretch of time nestled in a private cottage several hours away from here.

William reaches across the table and takes my other hand as I finish off my glass of wine. "My friend at work assures me it's a lovely place. There's a large Jacuzzi, fluffy towels and a towel warmer, beautiful décor, views of a small lake from the front porch, and you can't even see the other cottages through the forest. They'll deliver meals to the door, or we can dine in the main lodge. If we get tired of their menu, there are several fine restaurants in town, which is only ten minutes away."

Up till now, I've only left the kids for one night at a time. Well, there was that time when Roger and I stayed up all night partying at his friend's place. We didn't wake up again until early afternoon, crashed out on his floor with half a dozen others. Somebody ran out to the liquor store and restocked, and before we knew it, it was almost midnight and we were too wasted to even think of leaving, not to mention trying to drive back. The girls seemed fine when I did show up, although Robin managed a pretty accurate impression of Mother lecturing me on my responsibilities. She's like a miniature adult sometimes.

Another occasion when I was out two nights in a row comes to mind, but I push aside that distraction. A cottage by a lake!

"It sounds perfect, Will. When do we leave? Don't you have to be back in Chicago Thursday night?"

A sly grin grows on his face. "Nope. I had some personal time built up, so we'll head out Thursday afternoon after I wrap up a few things with work. How about I pick you up at one?"

"I can hardly wait! Will, you are a life saver."

I'll make a point of being out by the curb with my suitcase by 12:45 so he won't come up to see my place. No matter how hard I might try to straighten up and hide all the toys and kids' clothing, it's too big a risk. Even so, I'd better make sure the girls are far away when he arrives. I can't have one of them come running up to me to ask for money for an ice cream or to deliver some momentous bit of news, like letting me know that little Johnny wet his pants or Susie's mom died her hair orange.

My delightful boyfriend orders champagne to celebrate our upcoming adventures. Cheers!

***

"I'll be out late, kiddo. Take care of supper," I tell Robin, handing her a five-dollar bill.

She stares at it in her hand, her mouth pulled into a little "O" like a cartoon character. In a flash, she stuffs the money in her pocket. "Thanks, Mom!"

"Now, go fetch your sister and get on over to the mall. You can buy lunch at the food court."

She races out the door, slamming it behind her. I can hear her running, her feet drumming the floor all the way to the end of the hallway. I move to the window and watch for her to emerge from the building. She's still on fire, dashing around to the walkway that leads to the playground.

Change of clothes, underwear, my best earrings, the sexy nightgown I sometimes wear for Roger...it all fits in my smaller overnight bag. William promised the cottage would supply shampoo and soap, even big, fluffy white bathrobes. I check my purse for a few other necessities – a small hairbrush, the few items of makeup I use on a daily basis.

Glancing at the clock on the stove, I hurry into the girls' room and press one cheek against the window, searching for them on the playground. Good – they must have already headed to the bus stop to ride over to the mall. I gather up my suitcase and handbag and depart, my excitement at getting away for a few days bubbling over.

William is grinning from ear to ear when he steps out of his car to help me with my tiny load. "You look excited, love. That makes two of us."

"I was too eager to wait in my apartment. I would have worn out the rug with my pacing," I say, still giddy.

Once we're on our way, he launches into stories about his travels. Before he started work at his current job, he was a sales rep for a line of vacuum cleaners.

"You went door-to-door selling vacuums?" I ask.

"Oh, no. I called on businesses to try to get them to carry our brand. That involved far more travel than I'm doing nowadays and it got to be tedious, living out of a suitcase most of the time. But it looked good on my resume when I talked to Garrett and Greaves. Been with them ten years now. It's not very exciting, but the pay's good and the benefits aren't bad, either."

"I wouldn't mind finding something with decent pay, no matter how boring it is."

He reaches across and squeezes my hand. "You'll find something, love. A smart girl like you? Your phone'll be ringing off the hook with job offers soon, you mark my words."

If only I had a phone.

He's silent for a while and I sense that he's working through something he wants to say, so I keep my mouth shut and focus on the scenery. We've left the main highway and are passing through scattered small towns, past vast seas of green crops, the flat horizon broken by clusters of trees that haven't yet been removed to make room for more farmland.

I'm startled when he does speak again. "I was engaged to be married once, just before I started at Garrett and Greaves. Ten years ago. I was just thirty-one."

Uh, oh. It's true confession time.

"We hadn't set a date yet, thank God. The more we talked about the future, the more I realized I'd made a mistake. Turns out, we'd never talked about having children, not when I asked her to marry me. I suppose I figured a gal her age – oh, did I mention that she was two years older than me? Anyway, she had never once talked about kids and had seemed in no big hurry to get married. So I didn't think she cared one way or another about having children. So, when she brought it up, that was a shocker."

I paste an expression on my face that I hope conveys interest and not dread and nod at him when he glances my way. Mostly, I keep my head forward and stare at the blacktop stretching in front of us.

"Turns out, she was all caught up in the whole 'biological clock' thing, but had never breathed a word to me about it up to that point. And we'd been seeing each other for over a year – that's what was so shocking. She had her heart set on having two, maybe even three kids as soon as possible."

There's no way out of this. He's going to ask me how I feel about having kids. What am I going to say?

"I've just never been all that excited about children. Now, don't get me wrong, Katharine. I don't *dislike* kids. I have two adorable nephews and I love them to death. But the thing is, when I get tired of playing with them or telling them stories, I can turn them back over to my sister and go home. But to come home to them every night and make all my plans around what to do with the little ones? Well, that wasn't what I was looking for. We broke off the engagement."

He slows and turns right onto a narrow road lined with shrubs and trees, their branches forming a canopy overhead. "How about you, love? Ever thought about wanting children?"

*Wanting* them? Had the thought ever formed in my mind that I might choose to have kids or choose not to? It was a *given* in my parents' household. Mother taught me to cook and sew and keep house, all with the assumption that I'd grow up and marry a boy from our church, have babies, and take care of the home while hubby earned the money. It never dawned on me to consider whether I *wanted* children. It was just part of what I was expected to do. Not get pregnant at sixteen, run away from home, and get left by the side of the road to fend for myself.

Even after marrying Roy, I never gave it any thought. Still, after Robin was born, I didn't consider having another until Annie came along as a big surprise.

If I had really asked myself what I wanted, would I have ever chosen to have a child? The answer hits me like the doctor's slap on a newborn's rump, and I gasp a huge lungful of air at the realization. No. I never *wanted* children. I just let them happen.

Abuzz with this epiphany, I toss aside any concerns about what I say next. "No. I've never wanted children." I lean over and plant a kiss on his cheek. "And I don't care that you almost married someone a decade ago. Let's just enjoy ourselves! Are we almost there?"

His smile filling his face, William points at a sign coming up. "This should be it, love." He turns onto the gravel drive and stops in front of a lovely old house with a large, wrap-around porch and shutters painted an appealing dusty-turquoise blue. A sign over the door reads *Check In*. "Are you ready for another little surprise?" he asks as we walk up the steps.

"What else do you have planned, Will?" I say as I feel like I'm floating on air already.

He holds up one finger and then turns to the man behind the counter. "Brydon," he says.

"Ah, yes, Mr. Brydon. And Mrs. Brydon. Congratulations to you both." William smirks and gives me a wink. "We've got the honeymoon cottage all ready for you. That's four nights, leaving on the 19th, is that correct?"

Four?

"That's right," William says, wrapping his arm around my waist and pulling me closer. "Four nights."

"But I hardly brought anything to wear," I whisper to him as we're shown to our building. "You said we'd be here two nights."

"Don't worry about it, love. I'm told there are several wonderful ladies shops in town where we can find you anything else you want or need."

Alone in the bungalow, William takes me in his arms. "Katharine Milstead, would you care for a cocktail before dinner, my dear?"

We kiss deeply and I sigh in delight. What am I getting all ruffled about? This charming man is treating me to four nights in a romantic cottage, paying for all my meals, and even offering to buy me some new clothes. I feel like I've won the lottery.

# CHAPTER 33 - ROBIN

Rotating the box on the kitchen table, I consider it from all angles. When my father told me he was sending me something for my eighteenth birthday, I dismissed it, remembering the many times he had broken his promise to be home for my special day when I was little. Phone calls took the place of visits and later, when I was living with Doris and Clay, cards took the place of promised phone calls. When I actually turned eighteen last month, I decided it was finally safe to let him know my address and phone number, since I don't think he can force me to go back to his parents' house at this age. During his first call to me, he declared that he had something special that he'd been saving for me.

I'm not sure if I should be feeling excitement or dread.

Finally, I pick up the small kitchen knife I've been fingering and slit the tape along the edges of the cardboard. Opening it, I discover a hefty scrapbook wrapped in newspaper and a folded note. I examine it first, recognizing my father's distinctive handwriting that is part cursive, part print.

*Dear Robin,*

*I found this photo album when I went through your apartment after your mother left. Now that you're 18, I thought you should have it. I don't think Annie will mind as she's never shown any interest in old photos I've shown her.*

*I'm glad you seem to be doing so well on your own. You always were a smart, independent kid.*

*Love,*

*Dad*

I toss the box onto the floor to make room on the table to spread open the pages of the book. The first group of photos shows my parents when they were younger than I can remember, my father's arm around Mom's shoulder, both beaming at the camera. There are also individual shots of each of them, probably taken during that same period. Flipping to the next page, I find images of my parents in a wooded setting with snowy peaks in the background. These remind me of my Expanding Horizons days spent on hikes in the mountains of Colorado and I have a vague recollection of Mom telling me that they lived in Denver for a short while when they were first married.

Flipping through the album, I discover photos of my parents with a baby – me, I assume. As I move through the pages, the baby grows into a toddler. In one photo of all three of us posed in front of a building I recognize as our apartment from when I was little, my mother has her arm around my shoulder and I'm gazing up at her, my face a study in unabashed love. She looks happier than I recall ever seeing her. I lean close and study her expression, her eyes, wondering if it was all a lie. How could she have ever looked so pleased with life and later walk away from it? From *me*, the innocent three-year-old who adored her mother.

I continue flipping pages, re-visiting Dad's first truck, Mom at her sewing machine, observing myself growing older and a new baby appearing in the photos. Again, I search for clues in my parents' expressions – were there hints of their pending divorce? Clues that my mother would abandon us? I fail to solve any of these mysteries.

Did Mom lose interest in preserving family memories or was it Dad who added items to the album before he left? Either way, there are no pictures of us after their divorce.

I close the cover and sit quietly for a long while, lost in my sparse and scattered memories of my life before our family fractured and dispersed. Dad flitted in and out of my world throughout my early childhood, and I'm unable to distinguish one of his home visits from another. I don't think of him as ever having actually lived with us – he was simply a regular visitor. Sometimes he brought me a toy, although I couldn't say if that was a frequent occurrence or rare.

Although my mother had a permanent presence in our home, most of my memories are of my adventures roaming around the city by myself or with a co-conspirator, sneaking into movies or the zoo, riding a bus to the end of the line just to discover what was there. When I was alone and filled with so much energy I felt like I might explode, I remember overturning trash cans all along a city block or throwing garbage against a building to watch it turn into a work of abstract art.

I'm jarred from my meditations when the kitchen timer begins beeping. The banana bread I'm baking to take to a potluck at Sandi and Larry's place is ready. I hope the rest of their guests aren't all couples, or even worse, that she's invited some single guy to pair up with me.

"You need to start dating, Robin," she tells me almost every time we see each other. "Think how fun it would be for all four of us to go out together."

"I'm too busy to get involved with anyone," I answer. I wouldn't want to trade places with my ex-roommate for anything. Pregnant and married at nineteen? Forget it. Besides, I really am too busy. I've loaded up with an extra class this semester and have just one more to go until I graduate. I was just given another assignment to write copy for the new line of women's workout clothes my employer is introducing soon and I'm working on a story I hope to sell to a literary magazine. When would I have time to go on dates? I don't need the distraction.

Fetching the box from the kitchen floor, I carefully pack the photo album back inside, slap a few strips of tape on top to hold it closed, and stow the box on the top shelf in my bedroom closet. I should probably call Dad to thank him for sending it, but not tonight. My emotions feel raw and exposed and I don't trust myself to keep a steady voice if he starts reminiscing about what's in the photos.

Instead, I jot a quick note.

> *Dad,*
> *Thanks for the photos. They arrived safe and sound. I'm keeping them in a special place.*
> *Love,*
> *Robin*

I'll mail it on the way to Sandi's get-together.

As I stand in front of my bedroom closet, deciding what to wear tonight, I break down. Tears streaming from my eyes, I shout in a quivering voice as my entire body heaves in despair. "Why did you leave me? Why didn't you love me?" I sink to the floor and wail like a child lost. Grabbing a shoe from the rack on the floor in front of me, I fling it as hard as I can against the wall. I scoop up another shoe and another, hurling them against the upper shelf of the closet, the walls, my bed, anywhere and everywhere, hearing the crash of my lamp as it topples to the floor, each throw accompanied by my choking shouts of *Why? Why?*

My energy spent, I sprawl on my back and stare at the ceiling, seeing images of her smiling face. Did she love me once? Ever?

Finally I rise and head to the bathroom, where I stand in front of the mirror staring deep into my eyes. "Forget her. Forget all of them," I tell myself. I cover my face with a cool, damp washcloth and breath slowly and deeply. Checking again, I see that the puffiness around my eyes is dissipating. With a bit of makeup, I don't think anyone at Sandi's gathering tonight will realize I've been crying.

I stand tall, my chin raised. For a moment, I consider fetching the album from my closet and depositing it in the dumpster outside. No. That means touching it again and holding it in my hands for several minutes. No.

From this moment forward, it simply does not exist.

As I apply cover-up beneath my eyes, I practice a bright smile for this evening's party. As they say, fake it until you make it.

God, I hope Sandi didn't invite some guy to try to fix me up with.

# CHAPTER 34 - KATHARINE

William extracts another bottle of bourbon from the large box of booze he brought along for our special long weekend, opens it, and pours us each another shot. The last two days have been a blur of cocktails and nightcaps, lovemaking and strolls by the lake, gourmet restaurants and shopping at boutiques. Just now, that nagging voice in my head is telling me I should somehow check on the girls, but with no phone in our cottage, I'd have to go ask the front desk to let me place a call from there. Someone on the staff would hear me asking a neighbor to check on my children. And that's the other problem – who, exactly, could I call? Helen Duckworth? No, she'd probably report me to some child protection agency. Naomi Barolo? Possibly.

Of course, there's another reason I haven't tried calling. I still haven't told William about the kids. I keep looking for a good opening for that conversation, but every time I start to say something, I chicken out.

When he pulls me close and kisses me again, I relax into his embrace. The girls will be fine. This will be good for Robin, helping her grow her confidence and independence even more. She'll take great care of Annie.

Our fourth and final evening at this marvelous retreat has arrived and we're enjoying a walk before dining at *Tutti a Tavola,* an Italian restaurant we've discovered with extraordinary food matched by mind-boggling prices, which don't seem to concern William one bit. As we pass a bench, I notice a girl of about five or six – near Annie's age – sitting alone, her face streaked with tears, her head turning back and forth rapidly as she searches for someone along the walkway.

Pulling my hand from William's, I approach the child. "Hi. Are you lost?"

She shakes her head. "No. But my mommy is. I can't find her anywhere."

I sit beside her. "Where was she when you last saw her?"

The girl stares at her lap. "I don't remember."

"That's okay. I'm Katharine. What's your name?"

After a pause, she answers. "Valerie."

"What a pretty name. Valerie, let's go into this store," I say, pointing to the clothing shop just behind the bench, "and make a phone call so we can find your mommy."

William, who has been quietly standing close enough to hear this exchange, breaks in. "Katharine, I don't think that's a good idea. If someone sees us walking off with some kid we don't know, they could get the wrong impression. We should just go. Her mother will find her if she stays put."

I'm not sure if Valerie's expression means she's about to cry again or if we've frightened her. "I'm not supposed to talk to strangers," she mutters, probably reminded of that rule by William's comments.

With a sigh, I say, "Fine. But we can at least make a call to the police so they're aware of this lost child." With that, I rise and head toward the store's entrance. William doesn't follow.

After I explain to the shopkeeper what's going on, she picks up the phone. "Don't worry," she says as she dials, "This happens a lot. Our local security folks usually reunite families quickly."

As she talks on the phone, I realize this may be my chance to phone home. I pull out my little address book from my purse and locate Naomi Barolo's number. The woman finishes her call.

"Could I possibly use your phone? The cottage we're staying in doesn't have telephone service, and I really need to check in with the babysitter. I'll be glad to pay for the cost of the call."

She smiles and hands me the phone. "Not a problem."

I tuck the handset against my shoulder and start to dial.

"Who did you say you're calling?"

I hang up quickly and turn to William who is standing right behind me. "Did you say *babysitter*," he says, his voice lower than normal and a frown on his face.

"I...uh..."

"Excuse us," he mutters to the woman behind the counter as he takes me by the arm and escorts me out to the street and down the block, away from little Valerie, who is still perched on the bench.

"What was that all about?" he demands, spinning me around to face him.

I blink back tears. This is certainly not how I'd hoped to have this conversation, but I've got to tell him at some point.

"William, I'm so sorry I didn't tell you. I tried to bring it up several times, but I just didn't know how to say it." I swipe at my face, wiping away the first tears trying to flow down my cheeks.

"Stop whining and answer my question." He folds his arms across his chest and glares at me.

Just say it.

"I've got two kids. Daughters. I've been divorced for four years and trying to raise them on my own."

He stands silently, shaking his head. With one hand, he wipes his face and turns away from me, walking a short distance and turning back. He continues pacing for what seems like forever before he stops and faces me again.

"You lied to me."

"No. I never said I didn't have children."

"But we talked about not ever wanting them and you agreed. You lied."

Now I shake my head. "That wasn't a lie. I didn't want kids – that was my ex-husband's idea."

"Then why aren't they living with him instead of you?"

"Oh, you know. He was on the road all the time, his new wife didn't want to be stuck with someone else's kids to raise, and I was the mother, so everyone seemed to think they should be with me. I guess it never even occurred to me to say, 'I don't want them either.'"

He resumes rubbing his face. "This changes everything. What was your plan, Katharine? Reel me in and get me to take care of you *and* your kids?"

I don't have an answer, because he's mostly right. In my dreams, the girls didn't even exist – William and I would ride off into the sunset together and live an enchanted life, just the two of us.

"Okay, look," he says, his arms now drooping to his side. "I'm not going to be an asshole about this. We'll have dinner, spend one last night in the cottage, and I'll drive you back home first thing in the morning. But that's it. I..." He pauses, his eyes turned away from me. "Maybe if you had been honest with me from the beginning, I might try to see if it could work out, with your kids and all. But keeping such an important fact secret all this time? That's what I can't deal with. That's it. We're through."

I swallow a few times until I think I can trust my voice. "I understand."

I barely touch my food and we don't speak at all during dinner, except to the wait staff. Now what am I going to do? I don't have enough money to pay next month's rent and also afford groceries. They'll be cutting off our electricity any day now. I plan to start job-hunting seriously as soon as we get back to town, but the prospects in the want ads look slim.

I hoped to start classes again toward earning my GED this fall when Annie starts kindergarten, but that's out. I'll try calling Roy, even if I have to speak to his new wife to get through to him. But I know what he'll say. "Things are tight. With the new baby, I just can't afford to send anything this month."

"But what about your other children? Do you want to see them out on the street?"

"Okay," he'll say, like he's done before. "I'll see what I can do."

And then I wait and wait and no check arrives, so we act out our little scene again.

It's painful picturing our drive back to the city tomorrow. Will William speak to me at all? The girls are going to be upset. All I told Robin was that I'd be out late, and here I've been gone four nights.

"Oh, shit," I mumble. William lowers his eyebrows and frowns at me. I didn't mean to say it out loud, but I just realized I never made it to the grocery store before I left. My oldest daughter is resourceful, but undoubtedly she had to go beg food off one of our neighbors long before now.

What if the girls told an adult that I haven't been home all this time? If that gets back to someone like Horrible Helen, she might call the authorities. Hell, by now even Naomi might decide I've been kidnapped or killed in an accident and call the police.

Could I be arrested when I return? Thrown in jail? What would happen to the girls then? Could they force Roy to take them? Probably not, but if he were faced with giving his own children a home versus sending them off to some sort of foster care, wouldn't he finally step up and do the right thing?

A minute later, it hits me. Maybe I don't have to face jail. If I were out of the picture – if I disappeared – wouldn't the result be the same? Roy would take the girls. I could go somewhere, start a new life. Without them, I could rent something small or even get a roommate. I've done this before. It'll be easier this time. Without kids, I'm sure I can earn enough to live on while I get my GED. I'll find a bookkeeping job and get into a business school. In a few years, maybe I'll have the educational credits so I can move up.

In fact, I think I'll move back to Denver. I've missed having the mountains nearby and I know my way around the city. Roy's folks live near there, but it's a large place. I'll never run into them and I doubt they'd even recognize me after just meeting them the one time before Annie was born.

Tomorrow morning, when William drives me back, I'll have him drop me off within walking distance of the train station. I'll disappear and everyone's lives will be better.

# PART THREE
## COMING HOME

# CHAPTER 35 - ROBIN

"We'll need you to fill out these forms," the woman behind the desk says as she hands me a pen and a clipboard loaded up with papers.

I glance at the questions on the top sheet and flip to the next. "Dr. Sorensen's office has all this information. Didn't they send it over? All of this should be on the web or something."

"We got new software recently, so we have to ask these questions. Be sure to sign the privacy notice and the insurance release." She turns back to her computer and speaks into her headset, "Better Health Surgical Associates. How may I help you?"

With a sigh, I find a seat in the waiting area and start to tackle the sheath of forms. When I first approached Dr. Sorensen, I thought she could do the procedure herself as an OB/GYN. Instead, after a prolonged interrogation in her office, she referred me here to Dr. Newmann.

I'm still on the first page when I encounter a question that ticks me off. "Marital status: Single, Divorced, Married, Domestic Partnership." Defiantly, I select "Single." What the hell? Are they going to track down Jeffrey after all this time and ask him if it's okay for me to be asking for this procedure? Our marriage didn't even last two years and I haven't heard from him for the last decade, thankfully.

Moving on, I get to the section that always trips me up. Medical history for myself and my immediate family. Dad's never mentioned any heart disease or cancer, so I mark "no" on those questions. I can only assume the same about Annie, although I doubt she'd even tell me if she was having health issues, we talk so infrequently. As for my mother's health, I haven't a clue. I take the easy way out and fill in 1988 as the year she died. She might as well have died that same year she disappeared. Cause of death? I write "accident." That's much better than leaving the section blank or saying "unknown." Far fewer questions from the nurses or doctors.

After I've completed all the pages and turned in my homework to the woman who is still focused on answering phone calls, I amuse myself by inventing stories about the others in the room. Some of my best characters in my short stories and novels originated from my people-watching hobby. I decide the woman who checked me in is named Ruth. She has three sons, all in their twenties, and a husband who cheats on her on a regular basis. She's just decided to divorce him.

The old couple sitting across from me I name Harold and Betty. They've been married fifty-two years and never had children. Lately, they've stopped having sex, but not for the reasons younger people like me often assume. She and her old friend Peggy recently realized that they are in love with each other, although they've both lived conventional, heterosexual lives up until now. She hasn't told Harold yet. She's waiting until he recovers from his upcoming hernia operation.

Before I move on to the twenty-something guy who just entered the waiting area, my name is called and I'm escorted to an examination room where I entertain myself for another ten minutes by reading every sign and informational poster on the walls. With a light rap on the door, the surgeon enters.

"Hello, Ms. Milstead," he says, offering a hand to shake. "I'm Dr. Newmann." He looks to be just a bit older than me – late thirties, early forties I'd guess. His light brown hair is starting to recede and a trace of crow's feet extend from the corners of his eyes.

"So, you are here to talk about a tubal ligation." He glances through whatever papers migrated from the clipboard to the file he's holding. Or maybe all the information really did get sent to him from Sorensen's office. "I understand you are thirty-two and single. No children. Tell me," he says, focusing on my face, "why are you seeking what is essentially a permanent form of birth control?"

Here we go again. "Because I know I don't want children and I don't want to keep taking the pill for another twenty years. Or going back to an IUD. Or relying solely on condoms."

"When did you first decide you didn't want children?"

In retrospect, it could have been even before my mother left. If I tell him that, he'll surely send me to a shrink. "I've felt this way all of my adult life."

"Are you in a relationship currently?" he asks.

"No, not at this time." I haven't been involved with Leonard anywhere near long enough for him to be a part of this decision. Just because I've slept with him a few times doesn't mean he gets to chime in on something this important and personal. We're not at that point.

"Have you thought much about the long-term? When you get older, you won't have grandchildren to—"

I interrupt. "Listen, doctor. I've thought about this for

years, but thought I'd get a lot of resistance from people if I tried to get my tubes tied when I was younger. I don't want to wait any longer. Can we please just move on to talk about the surgery and the medical aspect of all this? Dr. Sorensen already gave me the third degree. I know I don't want children and I think this is the best answer for me. All right?"

His mouth turns down and he flips through the chart. I hope I didn't just blow it, but I'm tired of being questioned. I count to ten and try to breath slowly. I'm not that crazy about kids and I know I have a temper. I'd be a lousy mother. I don't even know how a good parent acts – I've only seen glimpses in other families.

He breaks the silence in the room. "All right. Let's talk about the procedure."

***

Claire reaches for my elbow to help me into her car, but I pull away. "I'm fine. Just a little sore and tired," I say as I ease into the passenger seat.

As she pulls away from the loading area in front of the hospital, I reach over and squeeze her arm. "Hey, thanks again for chauffeuring me around."

She flashes a smile. "No problem, *feygeleh*. That's what friends are for, right?"

If she hadn't been able to take me to and from the hospital, I don't know who else I would have felt comfortable asking. It's not that I don't have any other friends, but none that I'm close enough to for me to share something like this with. Claire's special. She was there for me when I decided I needed to get out of my relationship with Jack last year. While he was at work one day, she helped me load all my things into the back of both our cars and let me stay with her for almost a week while I found a new apartment. She disagreed with me about taking off without telling him, but once my mind was made up, she stuck by me.

"Are you afraid of him, Robin? Is that it? Do you think he'll try to stop you from leaving?" she asked.

"No, it's not that at all. Why have another argument about how much he's gone? It's just a matter of time before he comes home some evening and tells me he wants out of the relationship. I'm making it easier for both of us. It's over. He'll feel relieved when he discovers I've moved out."

Jack knew I had a close friend named Claire, but without having ever met her in person or knowing her last name, I never had to dread a phone call or even a letter from him after I left. Unfortunately, I did run into one of his buddies several months ago, so that was awkward. He tried to make me feel guilty, telling me that Jack was "devastated" by my actions, but I was reassured to hear that he's involved with someone else now.

Claire jumps out of her car after pulling up in my driveway, retrieving a large covered bowl from a cooler stashed behind the driver's seat. "Chicken soup," she explains. "My Bubbe's special recipe."

I chuckle, but stop quickly because my stomach muscles ache. "I'm not sick, Claire, just a little sore. All I need is a little rest to finish shaking off the anesthesia and I'll be good to go. I've felt this sore from overdoing it in my Pilates class — it's no big deal."

"Never pass up an opportunity to eat chicken soup made by a genuine Jewish grandmother. Believe me, it helps everything."

"Okay, but only if you share some of it."

She grins. "I thought you'd never ask."

After re-heating the soup in my microwave, we settle at the kitchen table and both slurp contentedly. I've gone with Claire several times to visit her grandmother, the first time quite reluctantly. I quickly realized, however, that Donna Rubinstein is as different from my grandmother as anyone could imagine. She's petite and upbeat, like Claire. At eighty, she's healthy and active, involved in so many volunteer activities and hobbies that I can't keep track. It's no wonder that her granddaughter adores her.

As for my grandparents, I was relieved when Dad informed me first of Clay's death five years ago followed by Doris just a year later. Needless to say, I didn't attend either funeral. Instead, once there was no possibility of ever running into one of them again, I seized the opportunity to move back to the Denver area to return to my beloved Rocky Mountains.

"No falling asleep in your soup!"

I snap my head back up, realizing I've started to nod off.

Claire rises and clears the table. "I'll get these. Why don't you go lie down and take a real nap? I'll catch up with you later, *birdie*."

I barely kick off my shoes and collapse onto my bed before I pass out.

*** 

Awakening from my nap feels like a struggle to swim to the surface from the bottom of a deep ocean. I gasp for breath when I open my eyes, disoriented for a moment in the late afternoon light in my own bedroom. Parts of my dream still float through my mind, resisting the draw of the real world around me.

I dreamed about my mother. She was upset with me for taking her photo album – the one I now remember is tucked on a shelf in my closet. Or maybe it's in with the boxes I never unpacked since I bought the house. I'm not sure. In the dream, I'm an adult, but she looks like I remember her from when I was ten years old.

Geez – I'm a few years older now than she was when she disappeared. What a crazy thought.

As happens in dreams, our similar ages don't matter – she's still the adult and I'm the child.

"I've been looking for you everywhere," she tells me. "Why did you disappear?"

I'm astounded at her claim. "No, that's backwards, Mom. You're the one who disappeared! Why did you leave me?"

She breaks down crying and sinks to the floor. Suddenly, I realize she and Annie are huddled there together, sobbing. I try to comfort them, as if they were both frightened children, but they shove me away.

"Where are you, Robin?" my mother cries, looking frantically around the room but somehow not seeing me standing a few feet away.

"I'm right here!"

"Where are you? Why did you abandon me?" she cries again. Annie has disappeared.

"Mom – I'm here. I'm right here. Can't you see me?" I'm in a panic, reaching for her but unable to touch her. And then she's gone as well and I'm alone in a vast, dark space.

"Where are you?" I wail. "Why did you abandon me?"

Finally fully awake, I stagger to the bathroom and splash

cool water on my face. I've hardly thought about my mother for years, other than being reminded of her when I filled out the forms for the surgeon's office. I shouldn't have tried to look up her name on the internet after that appointment. I'll bet that's why I'm having nightmares about her again, like I did during the early years after she ran away.

Finding her old photo album turns out to be quite easy – it's in the first box I look in. I tote it to the living room and curl up on my favorite easy chair. I flip through the pages at random, watching her grow older until she is almost my age today. I stare at her images and search for the truth of her feelings back then. Was she unhappy? When she posed with me or Annie for a picture, was her smile a fake?

She'd be in her early fifties now – assuming she's still alive. I remember her fondness for alcohol. Maybe she drank herself to death, or got into a car wreck and died. If not, what does she look like? Has her hair turned gray? The image I form in my head is of a stout woman – even heavier than she was twenty-some-odd years ago, with gray hair and a ruddy complexion.

Would I recognize her if I saw her? Probably not.

Would she recognize me? I'm certain she would not.

I flip to another page and a photo slides into my lap. The glue or tape is getting old – many of the photos are barely attached. Maybe I'll try to fix them up later. A few pages later, two more pictures have come loose. As I stick them into the crease between the pages to preserve their location, I notice that both have something written on the back.

"Robin – Fletcher Ave. 1980"

I have only the vaguest memory of it, but I'm pretty sure the apartment we lived in when I was very young was on Fletcher Avenue. In the photo, a toddler sits in Mom's lap, a look of astonishment on her face. My face.

The other photo is of my father posing beside a big rig, the sign on its door reading "Roy's Trucking." The only thing on its note is the year, 1981.

My internet search is a failure. I try looking for both Katharine Milstead and Katharine Gibb, thinking she might have gone back to her maiden name. Sure, there are plenty of hits on both names, but even after digging through the first dozen pages or so for each, none seem like the right person. Too old, too young, different race – I never even find a likely candidate.

Could there be any other clues written on the backs of these photos?

Only one way to find out.

# CHAPTER 36 - ROBIN

Standing in front of the mirror in my bedroom, I practice reading my short, short story aloud again, trying to remember to glance up at the "audience" from time to time rather than bury my head in the three-page manuscript. Why did I agree to do this?

Once a month, Claire holds an open mic night at her gallery, All About the Arts, back in the large room she rents out for other artists to give classes. She often gets thirty or so people in the audience and features poets, mostly, but she wants to encourage other writers to participate. Her latest idea is to feature one local author and publicize heavily, stapling flyers to telephone poles, running a small ad in the entertainment section of our local paper, and posting announcements on social media. This month, I'm her "opening act." Before and after the show, people mingle over coffee and cake and browse through Claire's sculptures and the other artists' works on display, sometimes purchasing a piece before the evening ends.

Writing a very short piece is new for me, but I didn't want to use one of my longer stories and read just an excerpt. And I'm definitely not ready to lay open my soul by reading something from the novel I've been working on for almost as long as I can remember.

My story features a character inspired by a man I spotted one day in the sandwich shop during my lunch break. He was quite elderly, sitting alone, seemingly staring at nothing. A folded-up walker leaned against his table. Then I noticed the cords dangling from his ears, leading beneath his jacket. A smile formed on his lips and he began moving his head rhythmically, mouthing the words to what I guessed was a song that he was listening to through ear buds.

I decided to make him be a former rock star and imagined him rising slowly to his feet and performing an air guitar rendition of his one and only hit right there, his voice remarkably strong and steady. Only I changed the setting to a nursing home dining room and turned the scene into an impromptu flash mob-like scene of singing, dancing, and drumming.

It's kind of a stupid story, but I'll go with it anyway. If the audience at Claire's doesn't like it, hopefully she'll never ask me up to the mic again.

*** 

They loved my little story.

Before I went on, I was too nervous to listen to the poet before me. After all the applause and cheers (and laughs), I'm too high to listen to any of the readings after mine. Instead, I glance around the room, doing my people-watching thing again, seeking inspiration for another ultra-short piece. I try to be inconspicuous about it, knowing I'm being rude to the people standing at the front of the room reading their work.

The teenage girl with shocking pink hair and an abundance of black makeup around her eyes is a possibility. I could make her parents be extremely strict and have her sneak out of the house and change into this wild persona, like Clark Kent changing into Superman.

The older woman wearing oversized sunglasses is intriguing. How can she see anything in here with those on? With a scarf covering her hair and her face tucked behind the brochure of artwork on display in the main room, I decide she should either be a spy – Muslim, perhaps? – or a housewife turned private eye. She could be the basis for a whole series of humorous cozy mysteries featuring an incompetent version of Miss Marple.

"Hey, Robin. I loved your story."

I look up from my meditations to a familiar face. Dustin straddles an empty chair in the row in front of mine, facing back toward me.

"Thanks. Could you tell I was nervous?"

"Not at all."

He's lying, but I don't mind. My knees were shaking so badly when I first stepped up to the mic that it's impossible that he didn't notice. "So, Vance couldn't make it tonight?" he asks.

I shrug. "We're not seeing each other anymore."

"Oh. Sorry to hear that."

I'm not. Vance was turning into a paranoid, jealous pain-in-the-butt. He didn't want to go hiking with me, but would interrogate me about any men who were part of an outing. It got so he was sure I was hiding the fact that some guy was along unless it was just Claire and me going, which made no sense whatsoever. I wrote him a "Dear John" letter and blocked his number on my phone.

"Listen, I'm putting together a trip to go climb San Luis Peak the weekend after next. Claire says she's in and I've got a guy from my office going. Can you take off early from work that Friday so we can drive down there? We'll camp Friday night, do the hike Saturday and camp again, then drive back Sunday."

"Count me in."

Claire and I are kinda-sorta working on climbing all the fourteeners in Colorado – the mountains over 14,000 feet in elevation. San Luis is quite remote to drive to, but the hike itself is supposed to be straightforward. If we add this mountain to our lists of those completed, I'll be at thirteen and she'll be at twelve peaks.

"Excuse me," a slim, well-dressed woman says as she inches closer, "Sorry to interrupt. You're Dustin Overkamp, aren't you? I have a question about one of your pieces."

"Go," I mouth when he glances back at me. She strikes me as someone who might be able to afford one of his larger wood carvings. Perhaps even the magnificent bighorn sheep that greets visitors as they enter the gallery. He retreats with the lady, his fingers crossed behind his back for me to see as they walk away.

\*\*\*

Claire and Dustin are engrossed in taking photos from the top of the peak, trying different angles and perspectives as Dustin's friend Rick and I remain content to simply sit on adjacent rocks and relax. I'm shocked at myself for how forthcoming I've been with Rick after having just met him yesterday afternoon. Instead of dodging his polite questions about where I grew up and where my family lives, I served up honest answers. I never do that with a new acquaintance. Hell, I rarely talk about my family with people I've known for a while. Of course, Claire knows quite a bit of my background. Before our car ride to the trailhead, I don't think Dustin had ever even heard me mention my mother. For the first time that I can remember, the story just spilled out of me, sounding calm and matter-of-fact, as if I were recalling the various places I've lived or listing the names of the schools I attended since I was a child.

"I must say I'm intrigued by your story about your mother," Rick says as he holds a plastic bag filled with almonds out for me to share. "You said you hit a dead end on the internet when you tried to find anything about her?"

I scoop up a handful of nuts and pop one into my mouth. "I got nowhere. Scanning in all the photos from her album, front and back, took much longer than I expected, and not a single date or name led me anywhere. I even called my father to see if there was anything he could add to help in my search. All he came up with was a theory that she ran away from home a few years before they met. He wondered if she might have changed her name before he knew her. So, you see what I'm up against. I don't even know if her maiden name was really Gibb. Hell, maybe her first name wasn't even Katharine."

"You know, I'm into genealogy, tracing my family history. And I'm a bona fide computer geek, as Dustin has probably told you."

I snicker. "He told me you're in the IT department at work, but he promised you could also speak a form of English that ordinary mortals can understand."

"Oh, great. Remind me later and I'll tell you a few stories about him and the rest of the graphic *artistes*. But anyway, back to your mother. Now, tell me honestly if I'm poking my nose in where it doesn't belong, but I'm intrigued by a challenge. Would you mind if I tried my hand at doing a little research about her?"

The thought of finding out anything at all about my mother is both exciting and frightening. I don't hold out any hope of actually locating her currently. I've imagined her as being dead for so many years that I'm almost certain I'm correct. But to know just a bit about her – did she really run away from home in her teens, like I did? Why? Where did she go after she disappeared? Why hasn't she ever tried to contact me or Annie?

I realize I'm nodding my head. "Thanks, Rick. Maybe you can get somewhere. I'll send you all the scans of the pictures, if that'll help. And my notes, not that they amount to much."

"Do you think your father might have any old records that might show your mother's social security number? Like an old tax return or maybe something related to their divorce?"

"Her social security number? I think I have that, or at least all but the last two digits. She had an old card in the album from before she got married to my father, but the right edge is totally rubbed away. I tried googling the number, filling in '00' through '99' at the end, but then I figured out that I wasn't getting any names to go with the numbers even when there was a hit."

He's nodding and grinning. "I may be able to get somewhere with that," he says, giving me a thumbs up.

I swear to myself that I won't get my hopes up.

"Well, gang," Claire says as she tucks her camera back in her pack, "we've got a long hike back to the trailhead. Shall we?"

Hiking back down the mountain, I start whistling without even realizing it. Just some random song running through my head. Rick begins to sing along.

*"Have you seen her? Tell me, have you seen her?"*

I freeze, embarrassed, but his reassuring smile puts me at ease. Claire catches up with me and gives my arm a squeeze. I'm all right – I'm among friends.

Just when I think I'm going to have to take a break and massage my aching feet, Dustin asks, "What's that I hear up ahead?" as he cups one ear with his hand.

Rick, the newbie in our little hiking group, falls for it. "I don't hear anything."

The rest of us shout as a chorus, "It's Miller time!" and manage a stumbling, slow-motion race for the final hundred yards or so back to camp to celebrate our successful summit climb with a few cold ones from Dustin's cooler in the trunk of his car.

\*\*\*

I force myself to stop folding and refolding my red paper napkin as I wait for Rick to arrive. Taking another sip of cappuccino, I try to distract myself by making up stories about the people in the coffee shop, but my mind won't cooperate.

"Hey, Robin. Sorry I'm late. Did you have to drive past that accident on Colorado Boulevard?" he says as he sets a large envelope on the table.

Staring at it, I manage to answer. "No. I was coming from the west. So, you've got something." I nod at the envelope.

"Well, like I said on the phone, it's not much, but..." He steps toward the counter. "Back in a sec."

Somehow I refrain from tearing into the envelope by resuming my origami attempts with my napkin while he waits for his order.

Once he's settled and had a chance to taste his coffee, I prompt him again. "You found something about her."

"Yeah. I've been focusing on the Social Security Death Index, and I'm fairly confident that she's not dead."

"That sounds like something out of 1984. A 'Death Index'? Is that for real?"

He chuckles. "I'm not making that up. Social Security keeps a giant database of deaths of people who had Social Security numbers. Some of that information is accessible online, mainly through some of the genealogy sites. Unless your mother died using both a different Social *and* a name I haven't tried, I'd say she's still around. I've checked using all the possible final digits on the number you found and also searched for every spelling of Katharine I could think of combined with Gibb and Milstead, also with spelling variations."

"That must have taken forever. Sorry – I didn't realize how much time you'd put into this."

He waves me off. "It wasn't that bad. I put together a little script and ran most of the queries automatically. Anyway," he says, pulling several papers from the envelope, "some of these I found online, and others came in the mail the day I called."

I examine each document, reading the familiar names. There's the copy of my birth certificate that I sent him along with the photos. New to me are my parents' marriage license, their divorce decree, and my father's birth certificate.

"You managed to find all these in just a month?" I feel stupid. I never even thought to search for any legal records related to my family.

"Well...I may have dodged a few rules here and there to get ahold of some of those. The problem is, I'm kind of stuck unless I can get someone to go spend time in Arkansas to go through older newspaper archives that haven't been digitized."

"Arkansas?"

"That's where she must have been living when her number was issued. You can tell using the first three digits."

"You're a regular Sherlock Holmes. How do you know all this?"

He winks. "Magic. Anyway, I've got some feelers out for someone who might be willing to do some research there, but that could take time."

"I've gone twenty-five years without knowing what became of my mother. Time isn't really an issue." I slide the top sheet aside to see what else he's found and my eyes widen. "You found a current photo of her?" I ask, staring into a face that's familiar but far older than when I last saw her.

"No, but this is how I'll start. I used aging software to generate that image of what she might look like today. The original photo is on the next page."

Setting the two shots side-by-side, I study the differences. The simulated photo shows typical wrinkles around her mouth, eyes, and forehead. Her neck and jaw show more sagging. Her eyes have sunken slightly, her eyelids drooping a bit. I'd still recognize her, maybe.

"Sorry I don't have more yet."

I put the documents aside. "I'm impressed with all you've done so quickly. You know, even if we find out more about her, I'm not sure what I really want to do with that. I'm curious, of course. Where did she go? Why didn't she at least leave a note or make an anonymous phone call to tell someone that there were two little kids left alone in that apartment?" I stop, feeling a familiar anger start to rise, my throat tightening.

"That's the part that really made me want to try to dig around for some answers," he says. "I know there are mothers and fathers who walk out on their kids every day. But I tend to think that's more about a failing marriage than about the children."

"Right. Like Kramer vs. Kramer – you ever see that movie?" He nods. "For a long time after I saw it, I had this fantasy that my mother would show up at my grandparents' house because she finally changed her mind and wanted us back. Stupid, right?"

"Hey," he says, laying his hand on top of mine, which had resumed messing with my napkin. "That's not stupid at all. What your mother did? Now *that* was stupid. And irresponsible and cruel and horrible. I can't even imagine what that must have been like for you – how strong you must be to have something like that happen when you were only ten years old and to wind up as an independent, talented, successful woman with so much going for you."

I'm sure my face has turned as red as my mutilated napkin. I pull my hand away from his and cover my face. "Stop," I beg through my hands.

"Come out, come out, wherever you are," he says softly. Peeking through my fingers, I see that he's leaning across the table, a playful smile on his lips.

"Only if you promise not to embarrass me anymore." I know I'm acting childish, but now it's turning into a game.

"I promise."

Lowering my barrier, I can't help but smile back at him.

He inches even closer, looks furtively from side to side, and holds a hand beside his lips, indicating that he's going to tell me a secret. I laugh, but lean forward until our foreheads are nearly touching.

"You're also fascinating and beautiful," he whispers.

With a muted shriek, I slap at his hand and fall back in my chair, covering my face once again. But I can't hide the fact that I'm laughing.

# CHAPTER 37 – ROBIN

I drop the mail on the kitchen counter, my briefcase on a kitchen chair, and my purse beside it so I can hurry to the bathroom. Jeez, the traffic was horrible coming home from work today. Sighing in relief, I flush and wash my hands.

"Honey, where are you hiding?"

I trot out to the kitchen to greet him. "Howdy, handsome. How was your day?" I raise up on my tiptoes for a kiss.

Like a magician, he produces a beautiful bouquet of roses. "Happy anniversary!"

I inhale their aroma. "Okay, I give. Which anniversary is this? Our first date? First kiss? First f—"

"—time we made love?" he interrupts. "No. C'mon – what happened one year ago today?"

"Oh! I moved in with you."

He rewards me with a kiss that weakens my knees. "Now that's a special anniversary to remember."

I fetch a vase and arrange the flowers. "They're gorgeous. So, Mr. Romantic, you were going to tell me about your day."

"The client signed off on my design," he says as he wraps

his arms around me from behind and nibbles on my ear.

"Of course they did. It was perfect."

Pleased with how lovely the roses look on the table, I turn back to the mail. Catalog. Junk postcard about a deal on some obscure internet provider. Envelope – hand-addressed to me. No return address.

"More junk?" Rick asks, plugging his phone into the charger.

"I'm not sure." I run the letter opener across the top of the envelope and extract its contents.

"Hmm. Someone sent me a photocopy of my piece from *The Story, The Word*," I say, shaking my head. "That's pretty weird. Did they think I wouldn't have a copy of my own?"

"Or fifty or a hundred copies," he teases. I only bought ten. "Or maybe they thought we wouldn't know how to make a copy," he adds, grinning.

I flip to the second page, then the third, looking for a sticky note or something written in the margins – some explanation of why this person mailed me a copy of a story of mine that appeared in a magazine three weeks ago.

Then I reach the final sheet. "What in the world?" I say, my mouth hanging open.

Rick moves closer so he can see what I'm seeing. "That's wild," he says. "You've got a serious fan, there. That's exactly how I pictured your character."

The top half of the page is a photo of a woman fixed up with oversized sunglasses, a scarf covering her hair, and in her hand, raised in front of her mouth, the top edge of *The Story, The Word* magazine – the issue with my short story featuring a character I named Aurora Perkenbristle, inspired by that "incompetent Miss Marple" lady I observed at Claire's gallery the night I gave my reading. Beneath the photo, in the same neatly-printed handwriting as on the envelope, there's a note.

*I loved this story. I feel like a celebrity.*

"Shit. Sounds like she's a delusional fan." He leans closer to the page, squinting at the woman in the photo. "I wonder if she usually dresses up as fictional characters and takes selfies to send to the author, or if you're her first."

I'm still speechless. This woman doesn't just look something like the lady at the open mic night, she looks *exactly* like her. The sunglasses and the scarf are identical to the ones I remember. But I never got into enough detail about either object in my story for someone to imitate them this precisely.

"Are you okay, sweets? Maybe you should sit down." Rick guides me to a chair. "I'm sure she's harmless."

Pulling my thoughts together, I shake my head. "One: how did she get this address? I can understand someone finding my old address online or something, but this house is in your name. How would she know to associate me with you?"

"Well, maybe this lady really does have some sleuthing talents. I admit, it's not simple, but I'm sure it's not impossible to piece together."

That doesn't exactly ease my mind, but I continue. "Two: I'm almost sure this is the same woman who I saw at the gallery. Not just someone playing dress-up – the same person."

He stands behind my chair, massaging my shoulders and upper back as I continue staring at her photo. I don't have much to go on, but my gut tells me that this woman is stalking me. Is she simply an over-zealous fan? That's ridiculous – I'm not famous, not by a long shot. I've had a dozen stories published in fairly obscure magazines, a self-published novel that's sold fewer than 1,000 e-books over the past three years, and I write uncredited copy for company brochures and websites.

"Don't worry about it, Robin. She's just letting you know that she loves your work. Maybe she sent this to all her friends and they'll look up your name and buy your novel. This is probably a good thing."

What really makes me nervous is not knowing what she looks like. What if she actually is following me around? Unless she shows up in her odd outfit, I won't recognize her. All I can make out in the photo is the tip of her nose.

Too weird.

***

Nothing peculiar has happened for months following that odd letter from the Miss Marple lookalike, and I realize I've stopped looking over my shoulder to see if I'm being followed or watched. Nothing remarkable has arrived in the mail, either, until today.

"I may have something new about your mother," Rick says, waving the letter he just received. "Check this out."

My heart picks up its pace. This feels like something totally out of left field – we ran out of new ideas almost a year ago in our detective work, or I should say, Rick's detective work.

"I had forgotten I even sent out this inquiry. Look here – one of the Social Security numbers in the range we were looking at was picked up as an error or possible fraud years ago," he says, reading through the cover letter.

"So, what does that really mean?"

"Apparently, a business tried to report earnings with this number, but the name they gave didn't match the official records." He flips to the next page and we both gasp simultaneously.

"It's her!" I squeal, pointing to the name, clearly printed – Katharine Gibb. "That's her maiden name!"

Further down the page is a revelation. The number was originally issued to one Edith Mary Richter.

"Look at her date of birth," I say, bouncing with excitement. "January 10, 1958. That's off by two years, but it's the same month and day."

"So she lied about her age. That's odd. I thought women of her generation usually lied to make people think they're younger, not older. Maybe so she and your dad could get married without her parents' permission?"

I throw my arms around him and he hugs me back, rocking me gently. "It's her. It's got to be her," I say, my eyes growing wet. "Edith Richter. That's my mother's real name."

"This is great. Now I've got something to work with."

I push him toward our home office. "Go! Go! Maybe you can find out something else about her."

As I listen to the faint tapping of his fingers on the keyboard, I sit with the pages laid out in front of me and read every word. Edith Richter. I practice the sound of it on my tongue. This information must have come from someone Rick "reached out to" (as he put it) back when we first met. How they eventually dug up this information, I don't know and I don't really care. I have something new to cling to.

The euphoria drops away as quickly as it began. Why am I pursuing this again? What good will it do? Suppose we actually find my mother – not just learn more about where she's been all these years, but actually locate her? If I could walk up to her, what would I say?

"Hi, Mom. Where the fuck did you go twenty-six years ago? If you didn't want to be our mother anymore, why didn't you say something to someone instead of leaving your kids totally alone?"

I know Rick cares very much for me. He loves me. He does all he can to understand what I went through and how it felt to be abandoned, not just by her but by my father as well, just in a different way. But he can't really know what I feel. The only person with a chance of doing that would be Annie, but she's like a stranger, raised by a different family. No, even Annie can't truly understand.

If Rick is able to discover where my mother is, I'm not sure I want to do anything with that knowledge. Would Edith Richter know what it's like to grow up in a house where she's belittled and terrified of being struck? Would she understand how it feels to be abandoned by someone she loves? To try to make it on her own when she's much too young and all alone?

She and I have nothing in common. Nothing. We'll always be strangers to each other.

# CHAPTER 38 – ROBIN

Claire props her trekking poles against a large boulder and leans against it, untying her right boot. "I've really missed getting out, just the two of us," she says as she pulls the shoe off, turns it upside down, and gives it a good shake.

"Same here," I say, settling onto the rock for a moment. "Not that I don't enjoy having Rick and the others along. But this is like old times – just me and my best bud."

This was always one of our favorite trails. It's not very long – maybe six miles round trip – but it leads to a gorgeous overlook and, for reasons I can't fathom, has never been crowded when we've hiked it. With our early start this morning, Claire and I are the only ones around at the moment.

Her boot cleared of the pebble that was bothering her, Claire gives me a thumbs up and I hop to my feet.

"You know what's really great about today? Not re-hashing all the stuff about researching my mother. I know Rick's heart is in the right place, but he won't let it go." I kick a small stone off the edge of the trail. "I'm tired of thinking about her and the past. There's nothing more to be learned and I just don't care any longer."

Claire turns back toward me and stops in the middle of

the path. "Right. Which is why you just brought it up anyway." She tilts her head and twists her mouth to one side – the epitome of a skeptical look.

"I'm just...never mind. We'll talk about something else."

"Hey, if you want to talk about it, I'm fine with that."

I step off the trail and move past her. "I'm not saying I want to talk about *her*. I'm tired of Rick continuing to pursue it, that's all. He's still sending off emails to god-knows-who to check old newspaper articles and what not and I just caught him last week messing with some sort of facial recognition app. He just won't leave it be."

I've picked up my pace, but Claire is keeping right at my heels. "What does he say when you tell him how you feel about it?" she says, her words coming out in breathy phrases. "Robin, please stop. I can't carry on a conversation like this."

I halt and turn toward her. "I told him I was tired of searching. He said he still has hope that he'll find something new. That was about it."

Pursing her lips, she says, "Have you told him that you want him to quit? Or that you don't want to talk about her anymore?"

"Not in those words, no."

"Is he supposed to be a mind reader? Try telling him exactly how you're feeling and ask him to stop."

"You don't know what Rick's like. He gets ahold of an idea and won't let it go."

"So, you'll say nothing but keep getting more and more annoyed with him. I know how you are."

It takes a conscious effort for me to unclench my hands. "What's that supposed to mean?"

She's poking the tip of one of her poles in the dirt,

pushing harder with each tap. "Look, Robin. You and Rick have a good thing going. I'd hate to see you blow him off with one of your notes instead of sitting down and communicating about what's going on."

"One of my *notes*? What are you talking about?" I'm practically shouting. An inner voice is telling me to start counting to ten, but I ignore it.

She switches to the other pole, pounding a second hole in the ground. "Okay. Like when you broke up with Leonard by writing him a note instead of telling him to his face. And blocking him from calling?"

"That relationship wasn't going anywhere."

"Or Vance. Same thing – you broke things off with him and he never had a chance to give any input, because you just packed up the stuff you had at his place, *wrote him a note*," she says, emphasizing her words, "and disappeared from his life."

"Vance was so needy. He would have literally started crying if I'd told him I was leaving. You remember how jealous he used to get if any of our male friends were along for our hikes. He was smothering me."

She stands there, shaking her head and attacking the ground by her feet with the pole. "*Feygeleh*," she says, her voice softening with her pet name for me, "I'd hate to see you walk out on Rick over something like this. Not without talking things over. Please don't let it come to that."

"Is that what you think? That I'm getting ready to dump him and *write him a note*?" I pour as much sarcasm as possible into those last four words. "Well, screw you!"

My legs churn harder and harder as I race up the trail. How could my best friend say something like that? I push faster, my lungs fighting for enough air, my gasps and the pounding of my boots the only sounds I hear.

So what if I don't like getting into a confrontation that's going to end up in the same way as if I simply walk away?

Rick and I are fine. We haven't been together for over two years without knowing how to work things out for ourselves. Claire's one to talk – when's the last time she had a relationship with a guy that wasn't platonic?

My body refusing to continue, I stumble to a stop and gasp for air, doubled over, hands on my knees. As I start to recover, I remove my pack and let it drop to the ground. A slight breeze chills my back, wet with sweat.

I count to ten. And again. And again.

Recalling our discussions about moving in together, I remember insisting on moving into Rick's place instead of mine, even though my home was in a much more convenient location. Why? So I could gather together my important belongings and leave quickly if things didn't work out. Otherwise, I'd have to leave my own house and not come back, and that would have created legal hassles.

Maybe Claire is right. I've been planning ahead for a break-up all along. But I really care for Rick – he's the best thing that's ever happened to me.

How do I learn to believe in a future with another person?

"Hey." Claire's voice brings me back to here and now. "Are we going to be okay?"

She drops her pack next to mine and opens her arms to me. I fall into her embrace and we hold each other tightly. "I'm so sorry," I whisper.

"Me, too."

"You didn't do anything to be sorry about," I answer. "I've got some thinking to do. Thank you for being so honest."

***

"Let's face it. The woman doesn't use social media, she doesn't show up in searches with anything we don't already know, and you've tried everything imaginable for two years."

Rick's eyebrows are knitted, as if he's contemplating even more approaches to finding information about my mother at this very moment. "Honey, I'm sure one of my leads is going to hit pay dirt at some point. She—"

"Wait! You missed my point. I don't want to think about her anymore. It's making me crazy. I can't focus on today when all these memories and old hurts keep coming up. Every time you bring her up, I feel like I'm being ambushed by my past. We need to stop."

He looks hurt – I knew it. I knew this would turn into a painful argument. My eyes dart around the living room as if I'm already reconnoitering my escape.

"I'm sorry, hon," he says, taking my hands in his and forcing my focus back toward him. "I didn't realize what effect this was having on you. I guess I got carried away with trying to solve an intriguing mystery and lost sight of the real reason behind it. If you don't want me to continue, I won't."

Squirming into his lap, I wrap my arms around his neck and hold him tight. "Really?" I whisper.

"Really, honey. I wish you had told me earlier. I didn't mean to upset you."

God, I'm an idiot. Stupid, stupid, stupid.

# CHAPTER 39 – ROBIN

"Excuse me," I say as I stick my head inside the office door. "I want to change my contribution amount for my 401(k). They said you'd have the form I need."

The payroll temp who's been filling in for Samantha while she's on maternity leave glances up from her computer and, I swear, actually jerks her head back as if she's shocked to have to speak to an actual human being. I feel kind of sorry for her. She strikes me as painfully shy, always ducking her head when I've seen her in the hallway, as if the thought of looking someone in the eye is to be avoided at all costs. Not that I've run into her very often – she keeps to herself most of the time.

"Yes...right," she says quietly, spinning her chair away from me to rummage through a filing cabinet behind her. She locates the form and holds it out to me, her hand trembling slightly.

Poor thing.

I accept the paper and smile broadly, in case she accidentally raises her eyes to see my face. "Thanks. Do I bring this back to you after I fill it out?"

She's already turned back to her computer. "Yes," she mutters, her eyes flicking up for an instant.

"Okay. Well...thanks again."

As I reach the doorway, she speaks in a normal voice for the first time I can remember. "No problem, kiddo."

*Kiddo?*

For someone who can't seem to deal with even the most basic of normal pleasantries, that's about the last thing I'd expect to come out of her mouth. *Kiddo.* I manage four steps back down the hall toward my office when I seem to forget to keep moving forward.

Feeling like I'm moving in slow motion, I turn back toward her office and step to the doorway. The placard by the door still reads Samantha Barnes, but underneath it someone has taped a handwritten note, Edie R.

Isn't Edie short for Edith? Edith R...

I realize she's looking directly at me for the first time since she started working here.

"Edith?" I ask.

She nods, but doesn't speak. I can't read her face, but her expression seems to roll like waves of nervousness, joy, sorrow, fear. Perhaps I'm seeing a mirror of my own emotions.

"Katharine?" I say, so quietly I'm not sure she can hear. As she nods again, almost unperceptively, I can only mouth the next question. "Mom?"

She clears her throat and blinks rapidly before speaking. "I assumed you already knew...but since you wouldn't acknowledge me, I thought of quitting. But with just another month to go, I decided to stick it out until Samantha comes back."

I stagger into the room and sink into a chair across the desk from her. "You knew I worked here?"

"I've tried to keep track of both of you girls. When you moved back to Colorado, I realized I might even be able to see you in person once in a while. With Annie, I never picked up on the slightest interest on her part to ever have any contact with me. But you..."

"I was looking for information about you. How did you know?"

She raises her eyebrows. "You were? No, I had no idea. But when you spotted me and even wrote a story about me—"

"About you? *You're* my mystery woman, Aurora Perkenbristle?

My mother smiles and immediately I can see that smile on a much younger and plumper face. "I love that name. You're a great writer, Robin. I'm so pleased to see how well things have turned out for you."

My eyes narrow and I fight to maintain control. My body is demanding that I leap to my feet and scream at her for acting like everything is just fine and wonderful and aren't we having a lovely little reunion here.

"No thanks to you," I say, rising to my feet, but only so I can close the office door. I remain standing, my arms crossed over my chest. "Why?"

Her eyes shift side to side before she lowers her head, gazing into her lap. "I don't know what you're asking," she says, her voice returning to the shy version I've heard before.

"I've been waiting twenty-six years to ask you that question. Don't pretend you don't know what I'm talking about. Why did you abandon us? Why didn't you at least make sure someone would take care of us after you ran off?"

She takes in a long breath and exhales slowly. "I didn't know I wouldn't be back."

"You packed a fucking suitcase! Don't give me that."

276

Watching her cringe, I realize my hands are clenched like claws in front of me, punctuating every word. I fold my arms close over my body again.

"You don't understand. Please, Robin, let me explain."

I nod, but keep my mouth shut. If I say what I've been holding inside, she'll never answer my questions and I doubt I'll ever have this opportunity again. I hug myself tighter.

"We were only supposed to be gone one night. My friend said he was taking me to a beautiful cabin on a lake. But then it turned out...well, this is pretty ugly, but you're a grown woman, so I guess I can tell you now. Essentially, he kidnapped me. He got me drunk that night and I think he must have slipped me some sort of drugs. By the time I could understand what was going on around me, almost a week had gone by."

An old memory pops into my head. Mom used to say I had a built-in lie detector. Well, it's swinging strongly toward the "false" indicator right now, despite her story resembling my childish fantasies in the early years after she disappeared. She looks directly at me, her face the picture of sincerity. I bite back a retort of *bullshit!* and simply nod. "And then?"

Again, her eyes skim back and forth. "Well, by then he had disappeared. Left me in that cabin without any idea where I was or any way to get home. So, I walked to another cabin and another and another and finally found someone to help me. First thing I did was call home, but nobody answered. I was so worried about you girls." Her eyes grow moist.

Nobody answered? Did she think her little girls would still be sitting around our apartment all alone after an entire week? Plus, she's obviously forgotten that our phone had been turned off for almost a month by then. A week after she took off, Annie and I were still staying with the Barolos. Why didn't she try calling them?

"Go on," I say through clenched jaws.

"I tried calling your father, but that bi...uh, his wife... well, I know she wasn't giving him my messages. Finally I caught him at home between trips. He said you were safe and sound at his parents' house and told me he'd do everything he could to get me sent off to prison if I ever tried to contact either of you."

Either Dad has been hiding this conversation all these years, or this is all a pack of lies. While I can imagine him keeping something like this a secret while I was young, he's been forthcoming in recent years about his guilt over shortchanging his oldest two children. I'm sure his divorce from Glenda seven years ago played a substantial role in his soul-searching.

Again, the urge to pummel her with all my anger for what I endured after she deserted me is almost overwhelming, but I manage to shove it aside without even counting to ten. I feel exhausted, drained. My fantasy of finding my mother and finally getting some answers is washed away by the reality of this moment.

The bizarre thing is that I think she truly believes her own story.

Without another word, I rise and exit the room. I close her office door behind me and return to my own desk. I feel spent, yet there's also a sense of crossing a finish line. My search is over. Turning to my computer, I resume working on the article about the joys and benefits of getting outdoors instead of spending weekends watching TV or updating your online profile. I substitute a phrase, read the sentence again, and hit "undo." After changing and restoring the wording in two more spots, I glance at the clock. Realizing I'm not going to accomplish anything useful in the twenty minutes until my usual quitting time, I shut down my computer, gather up my briefcase and purse, and head out the door to catch an express bus home.

# CHAPTER 40 – ROBIN

Minutes after arriving home, I've changed clothes and I'm loping at an easy pace along our street. Instead of following one of my usual routes, I turn at random, following curving residential roads until I no longer recognize any of the houses. The light seems infused with a special intensity – lawns shimmer in the late afternoon sun, the individual leaves in the trees stand out, each one subtly different from the next, flower gardens burst with color. A middle-aged man kneeling by a flower bed looks up as I pass, raising a hand in greeting. I wave back.

After crossing a busy street, I continue to zig and zag through other neighborhoods, my energy level increasing. I've never felt like this when I've run before. My legs urge me to pick up my pace and I feel light, as if my feet are barely touching the surface before launching me forward another step. Instead of anger and rage fueling my body, there's something foreign. A release of knots of tension not only in my muscles, but in my entire soul.

As the sun disappears behind the mountains, I slow my gait. I've discovered a bike path meandering through an open space park, and again I'm engrossed in the beauty of the terrain as I pass through. Finally, thirst catches up with me and I shift to a walking pace, watching the scattered clouds transform to pink and then orange and purple.

I have no idea where I am nor how far I've run. Fortunately, despite having set out without my usual bottle of water, I did tuck my phone in my zippered pocket.

Rick answers with, "Hey, honey. Where're you at? Is everything okay?"

I left him a note saying I'd gone for a run and not to wait on me for dinner, but I'd normally have been back at least an hour ago. "I'm fine. Can you come pick me up?" I expand the map display on my phone and provide him with an intersection where he can find me.

Once in the car, I keep the conversation light, but he clearly senses that something is going on with me. He doesn't push me to open up, instead glancing my way frequently as he drives. When we pull into the garage, I reach over and caress the back of his neck. "Thanks for fetching me...my love." I tried out different terms of endearment while waiting for him to arrive, finally settling on one I thought I could utter aloud. It came out sounding rehearsed, but perhaps with practice it will start to come naturally to me.

His face lights up and he turns to me with a look of wonder. He reaches for me and leans over to kiss me with such tenderness that my eyes brim with tears of happiness. It has been a day filled with firsts.

I keep my big news to myself until after I've taken a quick shower. Rick keeps me company while I eat the meal he prepared and saved for me, and I deflect his questions about my day back at him. Finally, the table cleared and the dishwasher loaded, I take him by the hand and lead him to the living room.

"I had a remarkable day today," I begin.

He nods. "I figured as much. Tell me, sweetheart."

His face reveals a changing display of worry, fear, and curiosity. I dive into my story.

"I found her. Or, more like she found me. My mother has been working as a temp in our office for several weeks."

"Holy shit, Robin! So, you must have talked to her or...?"

He clings to my hand, stroking the back with his other, as he listens to my story, eyes glowing with fascination.

"The craziest thing is that I never got the impression that she was intentionally lying. I think she truly believed what she was telling me was exactly how it happened."

Rick shakes his head slowly. "I imagine it's hard to think back on something you did that was really horrible. For some people, maybe those memories have to be distorted until your own role changes from abhorrent to poor, even twisting things around so you believe somebody else was the culprit, not you."

"I suppose that could happen. Memory is a tricky thing." How many times have I heard Claire or Rick tell a story about something we did together, but the details they remember are slightly different from what I recall? I'm a storyteller. I tweak a tale one time to make it more entertaining, but after I repeat the enhanced version enough, do I always remember that it once happened a different way?

"Did you ask where she's been all these years?" he asks.

A thousand questions that I could have asked chased through my brain while I ran. But then, like a light being turned on, swallowing up all the dark and secret shadows of a room, I realized that none of them matters. If I'd found the answers I've been seeking all these years, they wouldn't erase any of my history. They wouldn't wipe away a single tear.

"I have all the answers I need. Something clicked for me tonight. I've spent most of my life wallowing in my unhappy memories. Countless nights I've laid awake, rehashing as many of the scenes and conversations that hurt me as I can recall, as if I'm testifying every last detail to a judge and jury who will finally convict my mother or my father or my grandparents and punish them for ruining my life. I could write volumes, detailing every wrong."

Taking both his hands in mine, I continue. "Tonight, while I was running, I realized that none of those thoughts resulted in anything other than to remind me to stay angry and hurt. With every repetition, I inflicted the pain back on myself again." I shake my head. "I've never understood how someone could *forgive* somebody who'd done them wrong – I mean, deeply, horribly wrong. I'm not sure I know how to forgive my mother or any of them. But I can let go of it all. Just let it be and move on with my life. Finally. Am I making any sense?"

He wraps me in his arms and I breath in his familiar, warm and comforting smells. "You're making perfect sense, honey." He strokes my hair and I feel like I am exactly where I belong. I don't need to run away again.

My next words flow easily, despite their newness to my tongue. "I love you, Rick."

I can feel his trembling as he holds me even tighter. His voice catches as he says, "I love you, too, Robin."

I've finally come home.

# Author's Notes

Dear Reader,

If If you enjoyed **The Abandoned Girl**, I'd really appreciate it if you would post a review on sites such as Amazon and Goodreads as well as tell your friends about this book. Even if you didn't care for it, I'd still love to hear your feedback. Reviews are essential these days and can make a significant difference in the success of a book.

Keep in touch with Charlie and me on Facebook (www.facebook.com/WingerBooks), Twitter (@WingerBooks), or Pinterest (WingerBooks).

Want to be kept up to date on the latest news from Winger Books? Sign up for our eNewsletter here:

http://ow.ly/tvY72

or just visit our website and subscribe from there. We send out newsletters several times per year. Not too much, not too little, and we never share your information with anyone!

Thanks for reading!

~ Diane

# About the Author

Diane Winger is a self-described "retired software geek" who loves camping, hiking, rock climbing, and cross-country skiing when she isn't glued in front of her computer playing around with website designs, watching cat videos, and writing. She is an enthusiastic volunteer with the service organization, Altrusa International, with a particular fondness for their many literacy-enhancing projects.

She and her husband, Charlie, are co-authors of several guidebooks on outdoor recreation. They live in a small town in western Colorado. Diane was born and raised in Denver.

**WingerBookstore.com**

# Acknowledgments

My sincere thanks go to Val Burnell for her editing and valuable recommendations. Christine Savoie did another marvelous job on the cover – many thanks.

I'm always grateful for the feedback from my early readers. To Dorothy Causey, Dave Covill, Rene'e Eaton, Susan Eppig, and Eileen Ringwald – thank you for your time and your honesty.

As always, my husband, Charlie, has been a source of inspiration, a relentless and honest critic, and my biggest supporter.

Finally, my sincere thanks to everyone who has taken the time to read my novels. I hope you've found them interesting, entertaining, and perhaps even a bit inspiring. I welcome your feedback on my work, as I learn more about the craft of writing from each comment.

# Novels by Diane Winger

### Faces

*(Faces is the 1st book in the FACES series.)*

What if you could no longer recognize faces?

Following a head injury from a rock climbing accident, Jessica faces a disturbing future where everyone looks like a stranger. When a team of embezzlers stumbles upon her diagnosis of prosopagnosia – face blindness – they seize the opportunity to entangle her in their scheme. As she discovers the scam and alerts the authorities, she becomes a target in a masquerade far more dangerous than the extreme sports she loves.

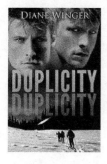

### Duplicity   *(book 2 of the FACES series)*

All Curt wants is a simple, quiet life, and he relishes the solitude of his job as caretaker of a backcountry ski hut. His peaceful world is shattered by the reappearance of his identical twin brother, fresh out of prison, desperate and more dangerous than ever. Conrad has a plan and that plan may destroy Curt's future. Not only is Curt's life at stake, but also the lives of a group of women enjoying a skiing getaway.

Jessie and friends from her Colorado Adventure Women group anticipate a fun-filled weekend of skiing and relaxing in a remote mountain hut. They would never guess that a life-and-death situation is simmering just a few hundred yards away in the caretaker's cabin.

Helpless to act, Curt must try to convince his brother to find a different path. But the mistakes of a lifetime cannot be undone in a weekend.

## *Rockfall*

Two horrified witnesses watch as a mountainside crumbles, crashing down on a party of hikers. Searchers find no signs of life. Three missing, all presumed dead. Three families begin the difficult process of grieving.

But one of the missing is alive. Alone, injured, and terrified, she struggles to survive, hoping against all odds that someone will find her...before time runs out.

Emotionally charged and engrossing, *Rockfall* is a novel that plumbs the depths of tragedy and celebrates the resiliency of the human spirit.

## *Memories & Secrets*

Revealing a secret may be liberating, yet some secrets can never be disclosed.

Ashley is no longer the cheerful, confident tomboy her grandmother, Deborah, remembers. The death of a student at her high school has cut her to the core for reasons she has kept hidden. Deborah has secrets of her own. A year after her husband died, she is still torn over her role in his death.

These two family members, brought together for a summer, learn that even the most painful memories and secrets may be transformed by love.

### *The Daughters' Baggage*

Every piece of baggage carries the tales of the lives it has touched.

Aaliyah Johnson just wants to live a normal life – finish school, have a career, a family, a future. But when her father takes his own life after his return from the war in Afghanistan, she and her mother are plunged into poverty and a homeless struggle to survive.

The unusual circumstances of her mother's acquisition of a small, green suitcase seem to mark a turnaround in their luck as they begin to rebuild their lives. Then, in a heartbeat, a devastating blow rocks her world, and young Aaliyah's baggage may be more than she can bear.

For major news and updates about our books, subscribe to our newsletter:

http://ow.ly/tvY72

CPSIA information can be obtained
at www.ICGtesting.com
Printed in the USA
LVHW081701120919
630869LV00011B/842/P